I0663984

SHAARA OF WESTLA

Book 4 of the Shaarvan Series

Note: *To start at the beginning of this series, please go to:*
Scholar-Ship-Bound.

K. S. Riggin

Table of Contents

Main Characters & Places in the Shaarvan Series

Altar: Original home of the Shapechanger, It is both the name of a planet and the capital city.

Altarian: Those who live or were born on Altar

Baltoff: the Old One on Westla who was manufacturing the drugs that Thenos used to overthrow the government of Altar.

Barquel: The main god worshipped on Freinana

Blair: Owner of the Landoor ranch. Good guy.

Brala: Shaara's friend on Westla

Chaslow: Shapechanger working for Thenos, blew up nursery on Westla & hunted for Shaara

Clofa: one of Altar's two moons. It was where the old Shapechanger liked to retire. Thenos blew it up.

Crimson Black: The horse-like landoor Shaara befriends

Flar: Freinana housemaster that Shaara stays with. Husband of Frieda

Flaorth: A tracker implant which Shapechanger insert under the skin of females for identification purposes.

Frieda: Freinana housemistress that Shaara stays with. Wife of Flar

Goria: Pseudo wife of Pathe. Former lover of Shaarvan. Bad person

Isandor: The commoner who owns Shaara on Freinana. Bad guy

Landoor: An animal that looks like a horse

Mandar: A landoor the Guardians bought Shaara on Westla

Megloztar: Theinian slaver who kidnaps Shaara

Parthrol: An Old One who lived on the former moon. He was thought to have known an antidote for what poisoned Tevor and the other Council members.

Pathe: Son of Tevor & Teea (brother of Shaarvan & Thenos) Doctor, good guy

Saberey: Symbol of the Shapechanger & their origin

Shaara: College student. Wife of Shaarvan and later Stegthal (Thal) Renamed numerous times: Susan, Sletttha, Sleena, Skeva, Thalia, Thenosa

Shaarac: (**Thaarac, Thenon**) Shaara and Shaarvan's son

Shaarvan: Steals his wife, Shaara, from a college campus, Altarian Shapechanger

Skeva: Name given to Shaara on Freinana

Sleena: Name given to Shaara on Freinana

Slettha: Slaver's name for Shaara on Freinana

Spelon: One of Shaara's guardians. Shapechanger Warrior

Starnkor: Teea's Second Husband

Stegthal: (**Thal**) He becomes Shaara's Second Husband. Good & bad

Stubra: The small goat-donkey animal found on Deathstar. They were mostly used to carry loads but were friendly creatures that Shaara and Shaarac treated as pets.

Susan: Shaara's original Earth name

Targone: Shapechanger who arrives on Freinana to verify that Shaara is Shapechanger

Teea: Shaarvan's mother, lives on Altar, wife of Tevor (and later Starnkor)

Tem: Head of Westla, Uncle to Shaarvan, Tevor's brother

Temina: Wife of Tem, mentally unstable

Tenor: One of Shaara's guardians. Shapechanger Warrior

Tessa: High Priestess

Tevor: Shaarvan's father, lives on Altar, husband of Teea

Thal: Stegthal's name on Deathstar

Thalia: Shaara's name on Deathstar

Thandar: Shaara & Thal's son

Thedar: One of Shaara's guardians. Shapechanger Warrior

Theinian: Another species, usually slavers and most often gay

Thenos: Son of Tevor & Teea (brother of Shaarvan & Pathe) Bad guy

Tren: Owner of the casino and of Shaara. Good guy to Shaara

Tura: Westlan Priestess who flies to Altar with Shaara

Westla: Huge artificial satellite. Only Shapechanger may go there or girls and servants

Additional Terminology:

Tide: Approximately one Earth day. Tides are usually grouped, as in a fiveTide, twentyTide, etc.

Pass: Approximately a year. A halfPass and quarterPass are common expressions.

Shapechanger: Never found in the plural. The Shapechanger are an artificially derived species that are capable of shape change, most often as a Saberey (tiger-like cat), This also includes many sensory improvements and abilities.

The Names of Shapechanger: Names beginning with T or S denote Power. Those Shapechanger are deemed Lords. Formal testing on Westla ranks them.

Warrior Shapechanger: Those who meet qualifications of specific battle readiness. Ranking is by formal tests on Westla.

Priestess: Females who have achieved a ranking on Westla denoting their ability to stand up against Shapechanger Power. Always capitalized.

Chapter One
Prelude

I'd been sold as a slave on the planet Freinana. The commoner who bought me, Isandor, brutalized me daily. When he lost me in a poker game, I became the property of the casino owner, Tren. That sounds like a bad thing, but Tren treated me well. I was still his slave, but he allowed me the freedom to ride and care for the landoors at a nearby ranch. One landoor, that I called Crimson Black, became a favorite of mine. So, as long as I wasn't parted with him, I was content.

Except that Tren suspected I was Shapechanger. He notified the wealthy Shapechanger on the planet Altar. Too soon, they found the husband who had supposedly been searching for me.

Happy ending? Not at all. I'd been mindwiped. I had no recollection of my husband or the life I'd formerly lived. Everything I knew was from my Pass in Freinana, and now this stranger not only wanted to take me away from my happiness, but apparently had the right to do so.

Barquel, the main god of Freinana must be up in his imperial skyward realm, laughing up a storm. I was told that he always believed in balance, or at least he did for others. For me, he seemed to counter every brief patch of contentment with a period of change, mostly of the miserable kind. And there was not a thing I could do to stop it.

I was Shaara of Shaarvan, the huge Shapechanger said, and he was about to take me away from all the happiness I had built for myself. Tren, Targone, Frieda, and Flar — all my Freinanan friends — bowed to his ownership of me, so I had nowhere to turn. Obviously, Barquel's wheel had turned in its periodic rotation and had flung me down into an ever-widening abyss.

Chapter Two

Thenos

Finally, it is done. I, Thenos of Altar, from the House of Trendacons, Direct Descendent of the Old Ones, and of the First Mutations of the Saberey, am the Sovereign Ruler of All.

The Council of Elders has been dissolved. The members are dead, except, of course, my father, who lies placidly and powerlessly in his quiet mansion. There was talk of restoring the Council, but I blasted those who spoke of it with the Power of the True Shapechanger, and they departed with aching heads — quietly and passively. I shall mark them down and administer an appropriate reward for their disrespect if they so much as think it again.

But I do not worry. The Lords of Altar will step softly next time. They felt the ripeness of my Power, and they saw for the first time the hordes of followers who fawn to carry out my bidding. I shall not commence my plans for the establishment of the class system until I am well entrenched. Let the unevolved peasants believe that they are mighty. Let them consider themselves to be our equals. They may suppose it for this short period of time I shall call the "Adjustment."

The peons form such a useful shield against the Shapechanger lords. My brethren were too gentle to squash the peasant worms they found writhing at their feet. And so, these dirtwalkers, these simpletons of a stagnating race, have carried me to the Great Hall, where now I reside in great splendor.

I had already designed a stately chair with sparkly jewels, trimmed with copper and gold mountings. It was ordered weeks ago and was delivered today. They placed it in the audience room. The chair was everything that I had envisioned. Its variegated golden-threaded cloth was soft and tastefully elegant. I felt royal as I sat on its comfortably raised cushion.

But I was distressed by something. I twisted about and sought a position that would ease my disquiet. It was impossible. I flung myself out of the chair's arms and, ignoring the peons, who fled before my irritated pacing, I strode back and forth across the wide expanse of the room. The polished black marble floor shone like mirrors. It disturbed me. I stopped and stared at it, wondering if I should have it ripped up and replaced with a quieter finish. Then I threw my head back and laughed.

Shaara has never seen this room. She might like the marble finish. I shall wait to see how her eyes view the grandeur of the room. Will they sparkle with pleasure? Will they be awed by its elegance?

I know, too, where I have erred with the chair. Every king must have a throne for his queen. Of course, I must order a matching chair, not as high as mine, perhaps not quite as grand, but my Shaara must have a suitable place at my side.

Content with my brilliance, I cast a smile at the dirtwalkers who floundered about, hoping to absorb some of my greatness. They bowed most properly. I was pleased.

Pathe

I have found the perpetrators. Three commoners brought about the death of my Goria. I proved it through the semen in her womb. By the time I had gathered up my evidence, several days had gone by, and, except for Goria's Ceremony of Passing, I had been locked in my lab. Even Teea's sweet requests for visitation I denied. Only my father's request/demand would I have heeded, but he, of course, lies like a stone upon his bed.

So I arose, freed from my labors, to petition for justice, and I discovered that the Elders were no more. As a physician, I had known when each had Passed on, but I had assumed, as had everyone else, that others would be installed in their places. But my brother Thenos, had dissolved the council. If we let him have his will, there will be no more Shapechanger justice on Altar. Perhaps even worse than that is the news that Thenos has declared himself Sovereign Ruler.

It was at the house of my parents that I learned of this horrendous situation. Although my mother did not berate me for failing to allow her visits during my research, I know that she is quite irritated with my failure to do so. But what good would it have done us? Father, as ill as he is, can do nothing. Mother, due to her gender, is helpless, and I, as always, am without the Power to influence even a commoner.

Yet, still, I must demand blood-right for my Goria. I have sent a messenger to ask for an audience with the "Sovereign Ruler." We shall see what justice prevails under Thenos' reign.

Shaara

We visited a dining hall for dinner. I had never known there were such places. Seeing people sitting around, being waited on by a living server they did not know seemed very odd to me.

Flar and Isandor had so often told tales of poisonings committed during feasts and festivals. Had their stories only been to frighten Frieda and me?

I had been surprised by the absolute trust of strangers at Tren's casino, but there, it was mostly alcohol that was served, and those drinks came out of a bottle or a keg that was usually poured in front of the buyer. I was about to ask Shaarvan about the veracity of Flar and Isandor's tales when two male Theinians passed us on their way out. For a moment, I thought the taller one was the slaver who had captured me. I gasped and whirled around to flee. Shaarvan's sudden grip on my neck was all that kept me from escaping from the hall of diners.

I froze, afraid of the Theinians but almost equally afraid of Shaarvan. The Theinians continued their departure, unaware of my panic. One would think that the speed of my loudly beating heart would have drawn their eyes, but their conversation never paused, and the door closed behind them. Neither of them had been the slaver who had captured me.

My eyes reluctantly moved up to look at Shaarvan's face. My heart had not slowed its pace. I knew that the Shapechanger would beat me for trying to run away from him. It was the law for slaves. I cowered and waited.

Shaarvan's hand lowered from my neck and slowly encircled my body. Gently, he pulled me towards him. His lips traveled across my trembling head, and he whispered, "It is all right now, Shaara. You are safe with me."

I wanted to look up at him, to study his eyes, to see why he had not hit me, but all courage had fled with the sight of the Theinians.

"My lord," came the courteous voice of one of the servers. The employee's eyes glared at me, but he did not dare reprove Shaarvan for bringing a slave inside. The man led us to a darkened corner and seated us there. I was glad we sat with our backs against the wall. It reassured me to know that the Theinians could not sneak up on us. It was enough for me to deal with the presence of my new owner.

A girl came over to tell us the choices offered that evening. She was a slave and could not raise her eyes to look at us, but she knew me. I knew her, too. I'd seen her often at the market. She had had a black eye once, and I'd wondered if her master was like Isandor.

The girl listened diligently to Shaarvan's order, but when he gave it, she paled. "My lord," she said, cringing down, her head almost touching her chest. "You wish two servings for yourself? I will bring them, my lord, but your slave cannot eat here."

"Bring the food, girl. What I choose to do with it is my business," Shaarvan told her calmly.

"I will wait outside if you will permit it," I offered.

Shaarvan's eyes studied me. "That will not be acceptable."

I offered nothing more, nor did I move. My eyes pretended to be analyzing the wooden table. I felt, more than I saw, Shaarvan's eyes circle back to the employee server.

"Girl," Shaarvan called to her and flashed the sign for obedience. I do not know if she understood Shapechanger signals, but she scurried over.

"Send your master here. Tell him that Shaarvan of Altar demands him to come."

The girl hurried off. I heard her steps as she moved away. There was a hesitance to her stride when she reached the vicinity of her master. I looked up and watched. As I had guessed, the owner listened and then angrily slapped her across her face.

I wanted to say something in her defense, but Shaarvan guessed what I would say. "Not a word, Shaara. It is not your business."

I stared at the pattern in the wood again. The slave girl's service of Shaarvan had been meant as an insult. A slave would never have attended someone as important as a Shapechanger if the owner had not been slighting Shaarvan for bringing a slave into the restaurant.

The owner came rushing over. "My lord," he said, bowing briefly to Shaarvan, "I am the girl's master. I will beat her if she has displeased you in some way." His manner was barely polite. There was scorn in his face as his eyes flicked over me.

"I was told that you would not serve us," Shaarvan said in his quiet, calm manner. His voice was deceptive. There was a feeling of danger thick around our table, the same feeling one gets when a cloud of hungry skitterbugs comes lusting for your flesh.

The owner may have been a fool, but the feeling of menace was so obvious the whole hall had become silent.

"No, that is not true," the man gushed. He glanced at Shaarvan's eyes again and gulped hard. "We . . . will be . . . most honored . . . to serve you . . . my lord," he stuttered.

His words sounded like he was choking, and his face was growing blotchy with huge areas of red. Tiny beads of sweat coated his forehead. He reached up and swabbed at it.

"And my companion?" Shaarvan asked casually. Not a spoon lifted in the hall. Not one person spoke, laughed, or moved.

"It is your wish . . . that . . . that . . . the sl . . . slave . . . ea . . . eat with you . . . my lord? He . . . he . . . can . . . d . . . dine . . . in the . . . kitchen . . . "

Shaarvan rose up. Towering like an angry stone deity, he glared down at the owner. "Bring us the food. Quickly. She will dine with me."

"She?" The eyes of the owner shot back to gape at me. "The . . . the . . . slave is a girl?"

"She is my wife. Be careful. I do not wish to *kill* you in front of her, but I will do so if you persist in your insults."

I thought the man would wet his pants, but instead, his ruddy face paled until he looked like a dead man. I began to feel sorry for him, even though I thought he was probably a bad slave owner. Shaarvan was being intolerably cruel. How was the owner to know that I was supposed to be a wife?

Shaarvan's eyes flashed at me, and I dropped my eyes. I did not look up until the man was gone.

"You interest me, Shaara," he said. "Why do you feel pity for a man who refuses you a seat here?"

I continued to stare at my hands. I could feel the violence in Shaarvan's blood, but I would answer him truthfully. It would be worth the beating. "Because you bullied him, my lord."

The silence that followed was like being in the center of a winter storm. My skin shivered at the cold breath of it.

"You brave much, Shaara," he said at last.

We were both silent then. His anger was fierce, yet he did nothing. I could feel his emotions tossing about with his thoughts. It was like when he had judged Tren. The shifts of his deliberation were the changes in the wind at the beginning of a storm. I felt it the moment he decided to overlook my words. It was as dramatic as when our sun, Ywequi, finally conquered the night.

Our food arrived. The owner brought it himself. I hoped the girl would not be beaten for relaying Shaarvan's words. It had not been her fault that she had obeyed the owner's orders. But, slaves often suffered for the wrongs of their masters.

I ate my meal in silence, letting the abundance of the food chase away my worries over the slave girl. Interspersed with bites, the training of Frieda plagued me. I kept thinking I should rise up and offer to bring Shaarvan more fruit or wine. At one point, I forgot we were dining out, and I stood to refill his glass.

"Shaara, sit down," he said angrily. "I shall do the pouring. It is the Shapechanger male who feeds and cares for his wife."

My knowledge of the world was only of this one planet. It seemed that Shapechanger did things very differently.

The meal was delicious. I had forgotten to worry about poison. I was sure the owner had been tempted, but everyone knew that Shapechanger acted with swift and painful retaliation. Therefore, I ate an enormous amount, stuffing myself in case the next day Shaarvan should choose not to offer me food. When I sat back, unable to eat even a bite more of the grula, Shaarvan began to chuckle.

"Before, I was often forced to order you to eat, Shaara. You used to nibble at your food."

I sat up defensively. "I work at least five landoors a day, and that's after I groom them. I'm always hungry."

Shaarvan nodded. "You will miss the landoors. On the ship, you used to enjoy the riding simulator. It was your favorite exercise, but you used to tell me often, that it was not the same as riding a real animal."

Shaarvan had said the words that unlocked my tongue. I could no longer be still. "I wish you could have seen me ride Crimson Black," I told him. "We flew over the jump course. Crimson is like kind words, music, and trees, all in one."

Shaarvan was sitting back, watching me. His body was totally relaxed, and his face wore one of his perfect smiles. I figured it was safe to continue to talk. "Crimson Black is like the highest of the high. His real name is High Mountain Peak. It really does fit him."

"But . . . ?"

"Blair keeps working him with different grooms, but he's 'off.' I mean, it's not like he's a one-person landoor. Landoors aren't like that. It's just that the grooms can't seem to 'read' him, to sense what he's feeling. They don't treat him like he's special, so he isn't. And he should be."

Shaarvan continued to smile at me in his amused fashion, but I thought it might be a good thing to check that I was not irritating him. "Am I talking too much, Shaarvan? Tren always says that the only time I'm not asking questions is when I'm babbling about landoors."

Unbelievably, the dimples in the sides of Shaarvan's cheeks deepened. Somewhere inside my stomach, I felt a sharp pang. I couldn't tell if it was from Shaarvan's smile or because I'd eaten too much.

"It is a shock to hear you, my wife," Shaarvan admitted. "Shapechanger women are quiet."

I forgot about my stomach and his gorgeous smile. I sat up abruptly. "That's because Shapechanger women are forced to be mute. Targone said you'd beat me if I didn't learn to be silent."

"So you and Targone *did* get along?" Shaarvan asked. His eyes held a contemplative look as if he were trying to understand new information. "I thought that from the way he spoke, you two were not exactly friendly."

I sighed. "Targone was always ordering me around at first, but after he found out about you, he just kept repeating gloom messages."

"Gloom messages?"

"Yes, like when he told me you'd beat me for breaking all the Shapechanger laws he tried to get me to learn." I sipped at my drink. "They're really stupid laws, Shaarvan. How could I saddle a landoor if I'm not allowed to carry anything? And how could I see anything if my eyes are supposed to be lowered when I walk in public? And not to talk with men? Men are the only ones I *can* talk to. The women are all afraid of me because my eyes are gray."

Surprisingly, Shaarvan was not irritated by my opinions. He just kept watching me as if studying a rare new species of animal.

"What did Targone say when you told him all that?" he asked curiously.

Again, I sighed. "He laughed at me and said I'd be black and blue all over. But Targone was wrong about you. I think you're nicer than I thought you'd be."

Shaarvan had been leaning back against the wall, but with my praise of him, he sat forward and leaned towards me. "Shaara, I am not 'nice.' That is an insult the way you use it. 'Tolerant' would be more precise. Targone has given you correct information. I have merely been allowing you certain freedoms, so I could assess the changes in you."

Holding my eyes to his, Shaarvan reached over and pulled off my hat. My hair tumbled down all around my face, forcing me to finger-comb it out of my eyes. When I could see again, I grabbed for the hat, but Shaarvan tossed it up against the wall, and it stuck on the corner of a picture frame. The frame would be above my head if I stood underneath it. I looked at Shaarvan, puzzled by his action.

"Why did you do that? I need . . ."

"You will not wear it again."

I started to braid my curly mess.

"You will leave your hair down," he ordered.

I obeyed, but I raised my chin and frowned at him. How dare he tell me what I could or couldn't do with my hair.

As if it were the cue he awaited, Shaarvan began to lecture me: "Do not believe that I will accept less than your obedience to the laws of the Shapechanger. You have been allowed to run free for a space. That is past. Your retraining only waits until tomorrow."

"I don't need any training," I said, starting to stand up. I don't know why. I already knew that Shaarvan wouldn't let me walk away.

"Sit down, Shaara," he said, with the glint in his eyes that gave warning. I sat down and lowered my eyes.

"Good," he said and reached out for my hands. Taking them into his own, he stared at them. My eyes followed his. He was threading his fingers with mine. What did he see in the clasp of our hands?

The threading of our fingers reminded me of the pale purple flowers that sprang up in the woods. They struggled to exist, even when surrounded by wild grasses. I had often wondered how those delicate flowers could survive with the strong grass blades so overbearing. How long did they last? How long would I?

Shaarvan smiled at me, shaking his head as if he had read my thought. "I shall try to explain, Shaara." He raised one of my hands, still entwined with his, and kissed each of my fingers. "Crimson Black was a fine landoor when you first saw him, right?"

"Oh, yes! He was wild. Nobody could even get near him. They were going to kill Crimson when I offered to train him."

"So. to persist in his untrained behavior would have been dangerous for him?" asked Shaarvan, watching me carefully.

"Yes, with Blair."

"So you began to gentle Crimson and calm him, and you trained him to fulfill his purpose?"

"Yes." I was pretty sure I knew where Shaarvan was going, and I didn't like the comparison.

"Tomorrow, I must gentle you, calm you, and train you to fulfill your purpose," Shaarvan said.

"I am not a landoor," I spat out.

"True, Shaara. I am fully aware of that." Shaarvan's smile was back, although his amusement was very shallow.

"Do you see that man there?" he asked, pointing over to the rear of the hall. I looked and nodded.

"What would happen if that man started urinating in the restaurant?"

I looked again at the strange man, wondering why he would do that. "They'd kick him out of here," I answered.

"But how does he know that he cannot do that in the restaurant?" Shaarvan asked.

"He's been told not to, I suppose."

"You mean, Shaara, he has been trained about appropriate and inappropriate behavior?"

I sighed. "I understand what you mean, Shaarvan, but I like the way I am." I raised my chin and met his eyes. "Tren was happy with me the way I am," I bravely said.

"Smelling like landoors and looking like a wayward waif?" Shaarvan asked, stretching out his legs clear to the other side of the table.

"You think I smell, too?"

"Like a landoor," Shaarvan laughed.

"I'm sorry. I don't smell anything."

"Tomorrow, you will bathe," he told me. "I would take you this evening, but first, in the morning, I shall take you to say goodbye to your beloved landoors and to ride your Crimson Black once more."

"I wish," I sighed. "Blair won't let me. He only lets the grooms ride Crimson now. He says he has to choose the best rider to show High Mountain Peak in the coming trials."

"You will ride Crimson tomorrow, and you will say goodbye to your landoors. And then you will be *Shapechanger* once more."

The look on Shaarvan's face kept me from arguing. I didn't doubt the saying goodbye part. I knew how easy it was for a man to enforce his wishes on a girl. A Shapechanger would find it even easier. But how would he get Blair to allow me to ride Crimson?

We got up then and left. Out in the street, I was suddenly the recipient of a great many searching looks. I wanted my hat back.

With the lustful looks in the eyes that passed us, I began to remember that we were about to return to my room. I knew I could not dispute Shaarvan's rights, but I was not thrilled about being mounted by a Shapechanger. I still didn't know exactly how they went about it.

When we arrived at the house, Flar and Frieda were just finishing their dinner. I introduced them to Shaarvan. The meeting did not go well. Shaarvan's anger flared when he saw the house's owner. He demanded to know why Flar had not notified the Shapechanger of my presence. Then, without allowing him to respond, Shaarvan began to berate Flar about permitting the abuse by Isandor. Shaarvan's words reduced Flar to the point where his blubber was a quivering mass of agitation.

Flar was so intimidated that he wasn't able to say a single word. Of course, I was put into the neck hold the moment that I tried to stick up for my friend. Frieda bravely replied to Shaarvan's accusations by quoting the Shapechanger's own policy of noninterference between a girl and her master.

Shaarvan was so incensed that a female initiated conversation with him that I thought the roof would shake with his recoil. It was even worse than at the restaurant. I was afraid Shaarvan would Shapechange and rend Flar and Frieda with his massive claws. I cried out, "They're my friends!"

Shaarvan's attention left Flar and Frieda and centered on me. I met his eyes, accepting that he would punish me. I offered no further challenge, but I could not stand to see my friends hurt by some Shapechanger code of justice. Flar and Frieda, and the landoors, and Tren and Blair had been all that kept me secure. They had saved my life. They had tried to help me. Couldn't Shaarvan understand that most people would not dare to contact the Shapechanger? And Flar and Frieda had *tried* to help me . . .

I felt Shaarvan's probe the moment he entered my mind. I didn't fight. Shaarvan was quick. He was turning back to Flar and Frieda before I realized that he'd even departed from my thoughts.

"I would have rewarded you abundantly for your 'interference,'" he told them. "You knew that Shaara was Shapechanger, yet you did nothing. That is an offense that I do not hold lightly. It was foolish on your part and merits retribution."

Neck hold or not, I was not been able to stop my gasp or my sudden struggle against his hold. Shaarvan's hand tightened, and the pain increased. I discovered that I could not breathe.

"Shaara, be still. I do not wish to hurt you like this," he told me.

I froze, not because of what he'd said, but because I was scared, and I wanted to breathe. As I stopped fighting him, the air came back in.

Shaarvan shifted me. He freed my neck, and his arm stretched across my chest, locking me against him. I was not able to move with that hold either, but I was able to breathe freely, and my neck was not screaming in agony.

He whispered into my ear, "I am not Isandor, Shaara. I do not hurt you to give myself pleasure. Obey me, and I shall never cause you a moment of pain."

The hold he placed on me did not prevent my speaking, but it didn't matter; I was defeated. *I am sorry, my friends,* I whispered in my mind. *It is my fault, yet I cannot help you.*

With the subjugation, came my tears. How I hated them — the humble display of a firmly trampled slave.

Having conquered, Shaarvan turned back to Flar and Frieda. Flar had stopped quaking, but his skin was still pale and dripping with perspiration. Frieda was comforting him. Her arm was stretched across his body, as far she could reach, and she was kissing his cheek and reassuring him that all would be fine.

Shaarvan called Flar's name softly. They both looked up.

"As I said, your apathy demands retribution, but I must also consider that my wife has been grateful for the meager compassion you *did* offer her. For some reason, she considers you her friends. Because she has found you worthy of mercy, I shall not render punishment."

I didn't dare speak, but I knew Shaarvan could read the relief in my mind. He said nothing more to Flar and Frieda, and they left to celebrate with the cycle of the Wheel.

I was quiet as I prepared for bed that night. I wondered if Shaarvan would require me to disrobe. I was not used to doing so any longer. I slipped under the cover when he was removing his shoes, and I turned to face the window.

Shaarvan's body lay down beside me. He had not disrobed either. For a moment, neither of us moved. Then, an arm slipped out to enfold me. He pulled me close to his body, but still, no words were spoken. His hands did not roam. I closed my eyes, and in minutes, I was asleep.

Tren

Targone has not left my side since I met Shaara's husband. I think he does not trust me, yet he must know that I would not leave my casino just to escape his company. He pays for his drinks, so I have no complaints, but it does grow tedious to see his face constantly, especially since it is rather cheerless to look at. He will not admit it, but I think he misses Shaara almost as much as I do. She does have a way of attaching herself to your heart.

I was glad that I met her husband. I think he will be good for her, better than I would have been. He was right that she was becoming a bit more than I could handle. That Shapechanger Power of hers kept getting stronger. It was only Targone's warning that saved me from her eyes a couple of times. Why do I find that, almost, I do not care? To have known her in my bed would have been the death of me, but I wonder if it would have been worth it.

Shaarvan seemed a reasonable sort. I was pleasantly surprised. Targone keeps talking about what an important Shapechanger he is in their hierarchy, yet Shaarvan didn't seem arrogant, and he wasn't condescending. I know that some Shapechanger view us commoners as beneath them, but Shaarvan didn't appear to feel that way.

I was impressed with the way he handled Shaara. She can be difficult. He was a lot more levelheaded with her than Targone, and I think Shaarvan understands Shaara better than Targone ever could. The lord was firm with her, stricter than I would have been, but not harsh. I think he loves her. I can't dispute that they are bonded securely. That was a thorough demonstration. What would it have been like to kiss Shaara like that? Besides being a death sentence . . .

I liked the way he seemed to understand that Shaara had had a rough time. I know Targone told him about the beatings by Isandor, but unless you saw her body, you couldn't imagine what that poor kid had to live with.

A couple of gamblers have hit it big. Their loudness causes me to glance up. I look for Shaara in the middle of the disturbance, but no waif with smelly clothes advances, battling her way towards me. She is Shaarvan's wife. I say it over and over. My heart slows, and I turn and take another swallow of my drink.

Shaara

Although Shaarvan was already up when I woke, he still did not require my services. He waited for me as I used the hole behind the green wooden door, and then we walked down the stairs.

I asked for and received permission to bake the last loaves of bread that Freida and I had prepared the day before. Shaarvan sat at the table, watching as I placed them in the baker's oven. I gave instructions to the new maid that Flar had hired to replace me. She would see to it that the bread was taken out on schedule.

I was uneasy about our morning meal. Shaarvan had instructed me on Shapechanger etiquette, but curiously when I asked for permission, he allowed me to prepare his meal. I think he was even amused by my cooking for him. The mushrooms I'd sprinkled over the lizard eggs were from the cellar hatchery. There were sweet stussen berries for the bread. I'd jammed them on a rainy day when I couldn't ride. Shaarvan ate it all.

I cleaned up after, not wishing the new maid to have an added burden. It would be enough for her to deal with Flar and Frieda when they finally came in for a meal. The Wheel had moved into a new strait, taking over completely from the Golden Chair, and my good friends, as they had become, had spent the night drunker than a landoor eating chimma weed. I was sure they would not be awake before the zenith of Ywequi. I checked the bread once more. Then, I left the only home I could remember.

Blair was working a brand new colt when we arrived. I wanted to ask him questions, but I knew to stay quiet. The discussion would be between Blair and Shaarvan.

Blair had always been as skittish as a colt around Targone. The best that could be said for their relationship was that they'd learned to ignore each other. With Shaarvan, it was different. Blair took to Shaarvan from the first moment they met. But when Shaarvan told Blair why we'd come, Blair looked so sad I thought he'd cry.

"I'll miss the girl," he told Shaarvan like I wasn't standing there. "She's a sweet kid but awfully stubborn. I had trouble sometimes with her minding me. I had to kick her off the place for a day once, but she settled down after that."

He studied Shaarvan a moment. "Tell you what. I don't want the money you offered me. It would be like taking back the wages that I handed over to Tren. If you won't take offense, you being a Shapechanger and all, I'll make a deal with you. I'll let the girl ride her stallion one last time if you promise me you'll treat her right."

Shaarvan started to speak, but Blair held up his hand, wanting to finish. "I know you could kill me for interfering, Shaarvan, but I've got to say it. Isandor was a bad owner, and that girl of yours never once complained. She's got more grit than I've ever seen in a female — but did Tren tell you he stopped her from cutting her wrists one night?"

That was all I could take. I had to burst in. "Blair, stop it!"

Both males turned angry eyes in my direction. Shaarvan's hand was squeezing my neck before I'd even finished the sentence. I gasped from the shock of it, but I snapped my mouth shut. Shaarvan loosened his grip, but his hand stayed there warningly.

"I agree with you, Shaarvan," Blair said, nodding that he approved of the disciplining. "I think you'll be good for her. Tren was too easy. She had him dancing a pirouette around her."

Blair's foot lifted up to rest on the bottom rail of the fence. He leaned over the top, looking fully into Shaarvan's eyes. "You have to keep this filly under a tight rein," he said, pointing to me. "She's like some of the younger landoors I work. Loosen up even a mite, and they'll be kicking up their heels and trying to strike out for independence."

If I were one of those landoors they kept comparing me to, I'd have kicked both of them. Shaarvan darted me a quick look, but I didn't look up to meet his eyes. I wondered how much he could read of my thoughts. He sure seemed to pick up a lot of them.

Blair had not finished his lecture. He went on. "What I really wanted to talk to you about, Shaarvan, is that time the girl tried to kill herself."

I flinched. Darn Blair! Why couldn't he leave it alone? What did he know about someone who kept hurting you over and over just for the joy of seeing your pain?

Nothing — just like the rest of the males. Maybe they thought women *liked* to wear bruises all over their bodies. Maybe they thought . . .

"Easy, Shaara," Shaarvan whispered. His hand was massaging my neck, attempting to relax me, but I couldn't calm down, not with Blair stirring up all those memories!

Blair hadn't heard Shaarvan. He was staring out into the pasture. He wasn't even aware how painful his words were to me. "You press her too hard," Blair was saying, "and she'll take that exit. I don't want that to happen to her, not to little Skeva or Sleena or whatever you call her now. You understand what I'm getting at, Shaarvan?"

Finally, Blair had run down, but I couldn't look at Shaarvan or meet Blair's eyes, either. I'd never wanted anyone to know about that day, and I certainly didn't want to talk about it or hear about it or even to have to think about it.

Nervously, I drew a circle in the dirt with my foot, completely forgetting about the hand on my neck. Shaarvan didn't try to restrain me. He loosened his grip further. In the heavy silence, I looked up to see their eyes both staring at the shape I'd made. Angrily, I wiped it out, dragging my foot across it.

The silence around me was almost unbearable. I could hardly take in air, and my lungs were burning from my refusal to cry. I took in quick, shallow breaths, fighting against the tears.

"Shaara, go tack up Crimson," Shaarvan said. It was a command, but his voice was surprisingly gentle. I was out of there in an instant and running towards Crimson's stall. The stallion nickered at my arrival and thrust his muzzle into my hand, expecting his lump of grain. I didn't disappoint him.

Crimson Black was always easy to saddle. He never blew his stomach fat like some landoors, and he accepted the bit almost eagerly. I led him out of his stall and swung up on him, wondering when his last workout had been. Several days, I'd guess by the attitude he was giving me. When I urged him into a trot, he kicked out his heels and tossed his head in a neck roll. For the first time, the reins were pulled out of my hands.

"Naughty Crimson," I said and told him sharply, "whoa." Reluctantly, he obeyed, but his hoof pawed the ground.

I gathered up the reins and said, "All right! Go for it," and I let him run, leaning down on his neck, low and close. The warm, sweaty smell of him was like a choice perfume. I breathed it in with delight. Five times, we galloped around, only slowing as we neared the bends. When Crimson began breathing hard, I curbed him down to a walk. He was relaxed now. His head lowered down, stretching almost to the ground. He didn't look like a challenge, then. The wildness was gone from his eyes, but I could still feel the tenseness of his muscles through the thin strip of saddle.

He was resting a moment, probably plotting his next move. I pulled in the reins and collected him, then set him through his paces. Crimson was eager, proud of his ability. He showed off like the summit of a high mountain peak against the blue of a distant sky. He would earn his name. I felt the greatness in him.

I cantered Crimson in collection, the cross counter, and in several perfect flying changes. He performed the pirouette and a circle on the forelegs with one leg as a pivot, perfectly. His passage at a trot had suspension in each stride, and, finally, his most difficult, the piaffe, a standing trot with no forward propulsion. It was all show-perfect! I flung myself off and hugged his mighty head. He lowered it closer and rumbled into my chest, as close to a chuckle as I'd ever heard a landoor come. I walked closer to Shaarvan and Blair, leading Crimson, no — leading High Mountain Peak.

"Isn't he wonderful?" I called to them from a distance sufficient for Crimson not to get upset about a Shapechanger standing close by.

"Wonderful, and the rider is remarkable," Shaarvan called back.

I smiled at him and thanked Blair for letting me ride Crimson this last time.

"Shaara, if he weren't your husband, I'd have offered to buy you. You are the spittin' best rider I've seen. I admit it, but . . . I still wouldn't have let you show him."

"Thank you, Blair. It's a shame you feel like that. I would have won."

"It is time to go, Shaara," Shaarvan said.

"But I was going to jump Crimson!"

The *no argument sign* flashed. I handed the reins to one of the grooms who'd come out to watch. (All their mouths were ajar as they'd discovered the length of my hair and realized for the first time what gender I was.)

"He'll try to rush the jumps, you know. You have to feel his stride, then the second the jump is over, correct his rush towards the next."

The groom I spoke to was still in shock. His hands reached out for the reins, but he didn't respond to my directions.

"Shaara," Shaarvan's voice made it a command.

I sighed and gave Crimson one last hug and kiss. He nickered as I left him. I stopped, but Shaarvan's arms corralled me and urged me forward.

As we walked down the long, graveled driveway, I turned and looked back. The groom was riding Crimson, and Blair was still standing there, watching me. I waved goodbye until Shaarvan gently forced me on.

Teea

I was so relieved that Shaarvan found his wife. How happy he must be. We heard that she was mindwiped. I hoped the sight of him brought her memory back. I prayed that she was all right, otherwise. The two of them needed each other, and poor Shaarac in Westla, in deep sleep, has been a nagging worry on my shoulders. I did not agree that he was as safe there as Shaarvan assured me.

Unfortunately, the discovery of Shaara was all that was good. Altar has gone mad. The commoners have risen up against us. They are deluded and mind locked by my son, Thenos. (Privately, I have cursed him and removed him from the family tree. But even with Tevor lying on his bed, mute and Powerless, I have no such authority.)

Thenos used the Old Powers on the commoners, to the shame of all Shapechanger, who enforced their will on no one (except the females of their house). We will not counter his attack with our own Powers. To fight with the minds of those who cannot defend themselves. . . how could we use the commoners in that way?

I speak of myself as one of them, and in truth, in this battle, I am. I have tested in Westla, to the third level, I can say proudly. I longed to test higher — the excitement of it, and the feeling that it gave me, was extremely pleasurable. Testing spurs the Power, so my sister Temina told me, and I think that she was correct, based on what I felt within my body. I would have continued the testing, but Tevor refused to allow it. Such a struggle it was for me not to challenge him on that issue. The wildness in me had grown strong, and I am sure that Tevor knew that. In fact, I believe that is why he didn't allow me to continue.

But I mentioned my testing only to prove that I am Shapechanger, and my Powers were formally approved by the Lords of Westla. There I was given rank, not with the commoners, but with the Shapechanger, who stand against Thenos.

You see, the commoners have declared Thenos the Sovereign Ruler of Altar. Mind locked or not, can they not see my son for what he is? He is deranged from the drugs of the Old Ones. He should be held in confinement, where he is carefully monitored and can do no damage to himself or to those around him. I will never understand how the commoners were willing to position him in a place of authority.

Sovereign Ruler! We Shapechanger laugh at his false title. But the laughter grows weaker as we see Thenos' plans successfully falling into place.

The Elders have all died, except for my husband. Many of us believe that Thenos was the cause of the deaths. (Oh, Thenos, if you are the source of Tevor's illness, I will never forgive you.) We do not know how it was possible for him to have created the illness without the Elders reading such evilness in his mind, but it is the only answer as to why the Elders all died within the same twentyTide. And, as if their Passing were not enough damage, Thenos declared the government of Elders dissolved within almost the same breath. That also corroborates our theory. The speed of his move was too premeditated for coincidence, as is the fact that out of all of them, it is only Thenos' own father who survives.

Thenos, you always were a scheming child, but I do not remember your being so callous. Never have you come home to visit your father. Nor did you show the least concern when the strongest of the Altarian lords fell ill. Only once did you attend the ceremony of their Passings.

Perhaps your brothers covered for you in those years when you were growing up. Maybe the coldness was always in you. But wouldn't I have known? You spent as much time in my lap as the others. I told as many stories to you as to my other sons. Where did I go wrong? When did you turn evil?

I never heard a rumor of your depravity until after you had experimented with the drugs of Westla. It was only when you returned that you became overbearing and rough with the girls you took. I thought it was only because you were young, but I think that many things were kept from me.

Your father looked worried, now that I think back, for many, many Passes. Then, you began to wage your war against Shaarvan. We never knew why. You began stealing his girls, one by one, yet it was seemingly without cause. And, when you had won against him, the girls were never important to you. Heartlessly, you brushed them aside. It was Shaarvan who always checked up on them and made certain that they were taken care of.

If only Tevor had not sent you boys to Westla for testing and training. If only you and Shaarvan had not been so attracted to the Power of the Old Ones . . .

Pathe grieves for his wife's death. My poor son! Oh, that is dreadful of me. I should say, poor Goria. No one would wish such a fate to befall anyone, but deep inside me, I battle against the thought that it was a blessing. Goria brought no happiness to our house. We of the Shapechanger believe that Death leads one into a different horizon. What that is, is something of which not even the Legends speak. Yet, if that is so, I ask by the branches of the mighty Somber Tree that Goria's path be a better one.

Pathe has been attempting to find justice in the courts of Thenos. He waved his evidence, naming three of Thenos' key followers, but Thenos did not accept the findings. He defended the commoners. It was hard to believe that Thenos might shoulder part of the blame for Goria's death, but I am sure he knows that Pathe's evidence was valid. Yet, still, Thenos did nothing.

I fear that Pathe will never see his blood-rights granted. Thenos only played with him. I pray to the Stars that Pathe does not lose his temper. Thenos might order Pathe imprisoned or worse.

How far Thenos will go, I do not know. Already, he stripped us of our rights. He installed fear where once there was peace. How is it that the mighty Shapechanger allowed this to happen?

But misgivings and finding fault serve no purpose. The past is history. I cannot stand up for our rights from my powerless position.

Certain Shapechanger, whose names I will not mention here, have asked to assemble at our house so they may convene with Tevor. I, of course, tried to tell them of the condition of my husband, but they are Altarian. They would not listen to a woman. So, they will come and use their Power on Tevor. I do not think that it will aid them in communicating with my husband. I have also tried. I shall plead, very humbly, that I be allowed to stay within the room during their attempts. If they think that the bond between Tevor and myself will help their cause, perhaps they will permit it.

It is a modest beginning, but I am beginning to feel as I did each time I took another test in Westla. My heart is racing, and my blood runs thick with the strength my Tevor grafted me with. I feel the Power within me rising to climb the Somber Tree. (A tale that Tevor explained to me, referring to whatever goal or challenge presents itself.)

Tevor would not like my thoughts. He would put the neck hold on me and march me into the bedroom, the place where all Shapechanger males believe a woman calms her soul and learns her master. But he cannot know what I am thinking now, and I will not let the Lords read it either. It is this: if a mind-sick male can machinate a different future for Altar, cannot a woman envision one as well?

Forgive me, Tevor, but I am not cured of my Terran insubordination. Without your touch and the contact of your thoughts, my mind is a rebel.

Shaara

We went to the baths next. The guards, who had been following us everywhere, handed Shaarvan a package. I hoped it held some clothes for me. I had no others than the boyish clothes I was wearing, and I'd have no time to wash them before Shaarvan would demand me to clothe myself.

Our walk to the public bath drew a measure of strange looks. In my dirty landoor clothes, with my breasts wrapped tightly, I did not usually attract attention, but Shaarvan was still refusing to allow me to bind up my hair, and no male had hair the length of mine. At any moment, I expected to be accosted by someone asking for my services, but, surprisingly (or I suppose not surprisingly since he was a Shapechanger), with Shaarvan by my side, the lookers just kept walking.

The public baths had small individual rooms. Isandor had taken me there, never often enough for my satisfaction, but he had allowed me to bathe when he was through with the water. His baths had never lasted long, and the water was still always hot when I was permitted in. While I'd bathed, Isandor had always locked me inside and allowed me to turn "wrinkly," as he'd called it, while he drank a stein or two of brew out in the lounge.

I expected Shaarvan to do the same or perhaps to rent a room for each of us since Targone had said that Shaarvan was wealthy. Instead, there was only the one room, and Shaarvan stood there staring at me as he demanded that I get out of my smelly clothes.

"Can't we each have our own room?" I asked timidly.

"I shall not let you out of my sight again," Shaarvan said, shaking his head. "Pretend I am your shadow, following you wherever you go."

"Do you disappear on a cloudy day?" I joked nervously.

Shaarvan smiled, amused but he repeated, "Strip," and a different light was in his eyes.

My smile disappeared. "Could you please turn around?"

Shaarvan turned to find the stool. He moved it to the corner, sat down, and tipped it back on its two hind legs so he could lean his shoulders against the wall. Then he crossed his arms and looked comfortable enough to stay there the rest of the day. He had definitely not politely showed me his back. Instead, he looked like he was ready for the show to begin.

"I am your husband. I have seen you before," he stated.

No argument was going to change his mind, but I couldn't keep my tongue from replying, "But I don't remember your doing so."

Again, Shaarvan's smile was a flash of dimples and bright white teeth — perfectly aligned. But the smile was accompanied by a narrowing of his eyes into an expression I recognized as "determination with an undertone of threat."

"Shaara," he said in his usual mild-toned voice of steel. "Usually, a Shapechanger does not give his wife choices, but I shall be gentle with you — for a time."

I started to sigh with relief — until I caught the rest of his words.

"You may strip on you own, my wife, or I shall remove your clothing for you. I am not a patient male, Shaara. You might find my method rather uncomfortable."

His eyes were serious. No bit of smile lurked in the corners of his lips.

"That's being gentle with me?" I spouted off before my brain had been given the time to assess the danger. The warm mists of fog emitted by the hot tub of water perhaps had delayed the clarity of my thinking. The possible consequences caused me to begin unbuttoning my shirt.

When I was nude, I held the clothes, all balled up in front of me, as a cover for my nakedness.

"Drop them into the garbage, Shaara," Shaarvan ordered.

"They're all I have." My eyes flew to Shaarvan's, and I did not question further. Then I stood in front of him, bare as a bald man's head, and I remembered the slave market where I'd walked the path in front of all those men. It felt the same.

Only for a moment did Shaarvan's eyes travel me, and then he was ordering me to get into the tub. I was surprised that he allowed me to enter first. Isandor never had. I certainly did not argue about it. I slipped into the water gratefully.

The bath was lovely, just the right temperature. I lay back and shut my eyes. I let my hair get wet. It swirled all around me. I wiggled it about, enjoying the feel.

I knew Shaarvan was disrobing. I figured I'd have only a moment more to enjoy the luxury of the hot water before he'd order me out. I wished I had some soap, but I didn't dare ask.

Shaarvan walked toward the tub. He had a soap bar in his hand.

"Please, may I use it, my lord, before I get out?"

Shaarvan didn't answer me but reached down to grab at my hair. I sat up swiftly to avoid the pain of his pulling me out of the tub by it and bolted up.

"Be still," he growled, a hand on my shoulders, pushing me down. Before I'd analyzed the situation, he began to wash my hair with his own hands. It was strange having a man do such an intimate thing. As the soap ran down my face, I had to clench my eyes shut. It made me even more nervous not to be able to watch Shaarvan's face so I could attempt to predict his actions.

Without a word, he pushed me under and held me there. I thought he had decided to drown me, and I fought him, but he'd only been rinsing the soap out of my hair. When he brought my head back up, through my coughing and sputtering, I heard him laugh.

"You could have warned me," I cried out, but he was still laughing and didn't respond. He toweled off my face, allowing me to rub the soap out of my eyes, and then tossed the towel over onto the stool where he'd sat a moment before.

He stood for an instant, then swung his leg over into the tub. The rest of his enormous body followed. I attempted to flee, but the water was churning, the bottom of the tub was slippery, and two oversized hands were pushing me back down.

"Stay still, Shaara. There is room for both of us."

Swimming with Tren had been an innocent time. I wondered if bathing with Shaarvan would be as safe. The water was still sloshing out of the sides of the tub as Shaarvan slid his body down and pulled me towards him.

"What are you doing?" I cried out.

"Bathing you, my wife. Every inch of you will be clean and smelling of soap instead of landoor."

Shaarvan held up my arm and began to lather it. I attempted to keep it tightly at my side.

"Lift up," he ordered, chuckling. "I promise not to tickle you intentionally."

I gasped at his knowledge. It was a secret I'd never told anyone. "How did you know?"

He just looked at me and continued to chuckle.

Shaarvan thoroughly soaped me. I think he washed half of my skin away as well before he allowed me to get out. I thought the torture was over then, but he toweled me dry. It was not an experience I enjoyed.

The parcel he'd gotten from the guards included a dress for me. When I saw it, I breathed an "Oh!" over its elegance and beauty. Then

I slipped it over my head (having been told that nothing went underneath it). The dress covered me from neck to toe, which sounded chaste and decorous, but there was no modesty in that dress! The material was semi-diaphanous, a word that Freida had taught me, which means almost see-through.

"I cannot wear this, Shaarvan," I begged. "It will cause me trouble."

"You are Shapechanger. Be prideful."

"But you can nearly see through it! I feel naked!"

"No argument, Shaara. The dress suits you well."

I knew the sign he flashed me. I didn't argue, but I wondered if Shaarvan really understood Freinana.

Shaarvan put on his shirt and pants and then got out our shoes. His were reasonable, light, and springy, but mine were slippers, worthless for walking long distances.

Shaarvan opened the door to lead me outside and ordered me to show him the way to Tren's. I stopped and froze. Then I turned and stared up at him. "Tren's casino? I am not allowed there unless I wear my riding clothes. Please, don't make me take you there. Tren would be furious if I showed up dressed like this."

"Tren is not your owner. He will say nothing." Shaarvan's eyes were glowering down at me. I'd made him angry.

I swallowed hard and keeping my eyes on the ground, led the way to the casino.

Chapter Three

Thenos

I am tired of peons. These dirtwalkers are always about me, probing with their miserable questions: How do we do this? What would you like done about this? What should we do next? It infuriates me that they are so incapable of simple analysis and initiative. Why can they not do some of it themselves? How should I know what to tell Despega and Cinda about our trading agreements? Who cares about our trade agreements?

Then there are the rebellious Shapechanger. I am aware of their meetings at Tevor's house. Do they think they can hide that from me? Visiting sick Tevor! Bah! Tevor is out of his skull by now. That drug would not have allowed him to participate in discussions. Is it my mother who meddles with my authority? I have a softness for her; I would hate to see that displaced by her involvement in conspiracy.

Stars! Of course, she cannot be involved. What am I thinking? This is Altar. Shapechanger males would never permit her to join in. I laugh. I shall change that. When my Shaara comes, she will be permitted to speak in the assembly. I shall command everyone to listen to my princess. Perhaps I shall consent to my mother speaking also, if she behaves properly. We shall see.

But my Shaara will speak freely, and they will bow to her and grovel at her feet. She will like that. She will enjoy the freedoms I allow her, but there will be no freedom for her in our bed. She will do everything I tell her. How I shall enjoy that, her soft little body crushed beneath mine . . .

Enough. It is not yet time for me to have a girl fetched for my needs. I must not think of Shaara. I must keep my mind on details. Why have they not brought me her throne? This room is naked without her chair. I shall send a dirtwalker to deal with that.

Where are those reports on the outer districts? Why has no money come in yet? I have demanded that my people pay me taxes. Where is it? Why has it not been collected? Why must I contend with all of this trivia? Do I not have dirtwalkers to handle it?

Shaara

The casino was alive and loud, even though it was daytime. Festive music blared through the heavy metal door. The completion of the change to the Wheel must be in full swing, even inside a casino.

The same guard I'd seen before barred our passage.

"I have come to see Tren," Shaarvan said.

The man nodded. He saw no reason to argue with a Shapechanger. "You want the girl to go in, too? It's pretty rowdy in there. You can leave her here with me if you like. I'll watch over her."

"My wife goes wherever I go," Shaarvan answered.

Their eyes battled only a second. Then, the guard dropped his and said, "I don't blame you, my lord." The man's eyes were resting on the place where my nipples bulged out into the material. My face felt flushed. I lowered my eyes. I was so uncomfortable like this. I desperately wanted my discarded landoor clothes back.

Shaarvan pulled me forward into the casino. As we stepped through the threshold, he whispered, "Do not be concerned if a man ogles you, my wife. It is the nature of the male. Let him enjoy you from a distance. He will never be allowed to touch."

Shaarvan gave me no time to express my opinion about that. He was already leading me into the crowd.

There was loud laughter all around, and a woman was singing on the tiny, circular stage. The same half-naked girl was there, too, assaulting her breasts like they were rubber balls she wished to bounce but could not free.

The floor of the hall was a mass of male bodies, all talking and drinking. Only a few scantily clad girls were dotted here and there. Their small pieces of colored clothing brought cheer to the darkness of the room.

I saw the green woman with the plumed helmet on her head, the one I'd met before. She winked casually at me as if we were fellow conspirators in some secret society. Then she turned hungry, feral eyes at Shaarvan. Suddenly, her eyes shot back to me. They widened as she recognized me. She gave me a thumbs-up sign and moved towards us.

"So, little one," she greeted me. "You have shed your dirty plumage. What a metamorphosis! Introduce me to your luscious lovely."

Shaarvan and I had stopped to listen to her speech. His eyes were amused by her. I wondered if he was interested. She certainly was.

Shaarvan chuckled. His arm swung over my shoulder, and he drew me closer.

"I am Shaarvan," he told her. "The butterfly bird is my wife. You must be from Dergoff to know of such things."

She nodded. "How intelligent! I am exquisite with excitement at meeting you, Shaarvan. Let the butterfly bird flutter. I shall alight with more pronounced vigor. Would you care to see how my wings are decorated?" she drawled droolingly.

Shaarvan's dimples were popping inwards. At the sight of them, the green lady melted with desire.

"Shapechanger do not flit from flower to flower," Shaarvan told her. "Flutter on, girl."

"How very disappointing," she sighed. Her hand reached out to caress Shaarvan's face. "I have heard great tales of you, Shapechanger. I salivate in expectation."

Shaarvan removed her hand and gently pushed me forward. He was still laughing as we walked on.

The crowd ahead of us was a beehive. Swarms buzzed around the counter where alcohol was served and around the machines offering sportive games that teased the senses and the plastic cards of credit that men carried.

We could go no further. Our way was blocked by a mob of bodies. Shaarvan let out a low-pitched snarl. It carried across the room. Men looked up and almost instantly moved away. A pathway in front of us cleared itself miraculously.

"I wish I could do that," I said under my breath.

Shaarvan caught my words. He smiled. "You can, my lovely Shaara." He didn't stop to let me figure out his meaning but strode forward as if he knew the direction of his goal.

Tren was sitting at a table with a large group of men. Malla was attached to the arm of his chair. His hand was resting on the naked skin of her thigh. Her bared breasts jutted out, at eye level, to the other men. Each nipple was a sparkle of purple glitter.

Tren and Malla looked up as we approached, and I saw that Targone sat beside them. He, too, had an extra set of appendages. She sat in his lap, facing him, her arms and legs entwined with his. Her lips at his neck were sucking noisily.

Tren looked at me. His eyes hardened and changed to black balls of coal. He rose up angrily and glared at Shaarvan. "Where have you left Shaara?" he demanded to know.

Shaarvan laughed. "You cannot tell without the smell?"

Tren's eyes slid back to me. His face paled. "Spit on Barquel!" he said and whistled softly.

It was the ultimate profanity. Voices around the table hushed. There were men who would kill for less, but none of them complained about Tren's sacrilege.

Tren sank back into his chair. He pushed Malla away and waved for the others to depart. Then his eyes traveled back to me. "I knew your potential, Shaara, but I never saw you like this," he whispered wonderingly.

His eyes roamed my body quickly. They observed the full display of my breasts, and the other area I wished were not so visible, but his eyes did not linger there. They returned almost immediately to my face.

"Your wife does you honor, Lord Shaarvan," Tren said.

I ignored the praise and blurted out my news. "Shaarvan made Blair allow me to ride Crimson Black. He was wonderful!"

"Shaarvan or Blair?" Tren asked, smiling into my eyes.

I knew that he was kidding me. I laughed. Tren recoiled as if he'd been stung.

"I didn't laugh at you, Tren," I said apologetically. I did not understand his reaction. He'd never been touchy before.

"He knows that," Shaarvan told me. "Sit down, Shaara, and let Tren and me talk. We have business to discuss."

"When you find the girl to be my wife, Shaarvan," Tren said, "bring one with a laugh like Shaara's. I will miss the sound of it and the way her face is alight with joy from such simple things as landoors."

He said it so sadly I understood finally the look of pain in his eyes. I felt guilty for having tried so hard to make him desire me.

A half-empty blue glass of alcohol sat on the table. It drew my interest. I studied the faint blue color inside it as the males talked. I wondered if it was the same drink the bartender had told me about.

"He's downstairs at the back," Tren was telling Shaarvan. "We use that room for storage and sometimes for meetings that should not be overheard. You will find it well sound proofed."

Shaarvan was unexpectedly studying me. I looked up, wondering if he wished me to go with him.

He looked away and met Tren's eyes again. "It is better that Shaara does not see, but I do not like to leave her."

Tren nodded. "That I can understand. I believe you know that I will not betray your trust. Targone can show you how to get to the storage room. He knows the way. When he returns, he and I will watch over Shaara. We will guard her with our lives. Take your time. Savor your revenge. Now that I know you, I wish I had saved Isandor for you as well."

Shaarvan and Targone stood up, and Shaarvan motioned me to stay. I understood enough to know that my Shapechanger husband was going down to kill the Theinian slaver. I was glad I did not have to be present.

I watched Shaarvan leave. It was strange how I felt a stab of pain as he walked away. I hardly knew the male. Why should I care?

"Would you like a drink, Shaara?" Tren asked me. Then, he shook his head and added, "After all this time, I don't even know what it is you like."

I looked up at him. I should have been angry at his words. I should have lashed out, saying, "That's because you never once asked me what I liked," but I couldn't. All I could think of was how much I truly liked Tren. He might not have been my ideal of the perfect male, but he had always treated me kindly.

I nodded to his question, and Tren snapped his fingers. A server came over at once. The server's eyes fastened on me. "Nice boobs this one has, boss. I'd replace Malla with her if I were you."

I wanted to sink down through the floor. I wanted my old clothes back. I watched the bubbles in the blue glass of alcohol slowly zap into the air.

"Tam, she belongs to the Shapechanger you saw a moment ago," Tren told him curtly. "Would you like me to share with you my knowledge of what a Shapechanger does to someone who bothers his wife?"

Tren was so irritated, it was like a towel slapped in my face. I cowered, remembering how he'd told me not to come to the casino without my landoor clothes.

"Shaara, what would you like?" Tren asked. His eyes, despite the anger, were still warm as he looked at me.

I shrugged my shoulders. "Bada juice?"

He nodded, studying me curiously. "You don't drink alcohol?"

"I've never had it," I told him.

Tren turned back to the server. "Bring her the juice, Tam, and remember what I said."

When the server left, I tried to apologize. "I'm sorry, Tren. I know you told me not to come here wearing . . ."

"Stop," he said, shaking his head at me. "Only Shaarvan commands you now. Your husband is from Altar, so of course you are dressed in Altarian clothing. It is as it should be."

Tam returned quickly with my drink. He kept his eyes away from me this time, but no one else in the casino did. Everywhere I looked, eyes were feasting and leering.

Tren observed my embarrassment. "You're very beautiful, Shaara. They cannot help looking."

I drank from the goblet Tam had brought me, but my hand was shaking. I set the drink down and tried to ignore all the stares.

I felt the approach of one of the men whose eyes had been especially intense. His heavy tread brought him within a table's length of me. I looked up, unable to ignore his advance. The man had a nose like a mushroom, except burly and red. I recognized him. He was the one who had grabbed me once when he thought I was a boy.

"Malla's getting very close to Tony," the man told Tren. "Don't you think you should step over there and set her straight?"

The man's eyes were traveling openly and covetously across my body. I could feel his thoughts like rough, dirty hands touching me.

"Malla can take care of herself," Tren snapped. "Why don't you go find the helmet girl? I think she can ease your urges better than taking peeks at a Shapechanger's wife."

The man did not seem to get the idea. He took a step closer. I closed my eyes, wishing I could shut out the loathsomeness of the man's thoughts.

"Move away. You're disturbing us." Tren's voice was the crack of a whip of warning.

The man was not listening. The sight of what my dress revealed mesmerized him. I wondered why, with so many almost-naked women, his eyes couldn't find another to savor.

"I told you, Tren," the man whined. "Malla needs you. I can take care of this sweet little thing while you deal with Malla."

Tren's muscles tensed. Once again, he warned the man. "Last time, I'm going to tell you. Leave or pay the consequences."

The man was a fool. I could hear the threat in Tren's voice. I knew Tren was about to erupt. Why did the man not back away?

Stupidly, the idiot ignored the warnings. He took another step towards us. It was the last step he ever took.

Tren threw one arm over my head, pushing me down, and the next instant, there was a pipe in his hand and a sparkle of fluorescence shooting through the air.

I struggled free, wheeled around, and screamed. The man was lying on the ground. From the corner of my eyes, I saw Tren slide the pipe back under his jacket.

The three guards who had been our shadow each time we walked outside bolted to my side. Their pipes were drawn, and they were pointing them at Tren.

"No!" I cried out. "Tren was protecting me."

They consulted in some other language. Tren joined in. His words to them were sharp. The one with slightly reddish hair appeared to be the leader. He answered angrily, with a stream of fast, choppy statements. Tren replied equally fast and choppy. The guards shrugged and put their pipes away. They sat back down, but they chose a closer table.

Mushroom Nose was lying on the soft, white carpet in a position that didn't look natural for one still breathing. With the guard situation under control, I rose up to go check on him. Tren's hand stopped me with a wrist grip. The guards' eyes glared at Tren. They shifted in their seats.

"Let me see if he's still breathing," I said. "Maybe we can . . . "

"No."

"But, Tren — he might still be alive."

"Sit down, Shaara," Tren ordered, tightening his grip.

I obeyed, but only to keep the guards from joining us again.

"How could you do that?" I whispered.

"Drink your juice and not another word," Tren ordered. His directive had all the force of a Shapechanger command. I picked up my goblet and tried to drink. My hands were shaking too much. I took one sip and put the glass back down.

When I looked up again, Tren was motioning for Tam to remove the body.

Again, I tried to stand up, hoping it wasn't too late to save the man.

"Must I use the Shapechanger's neck grip on you, Shaara?" Tren asked. "Your guards would not like that, would they?" He grabbed both of my wrists and held them so tightly I wondered if the blood could still circulate.

"No, "I said quietly. I dropped my eyes.

When Tam and another had carried the limp body away, I figured I'd been silent long enough. "You didn't have to kill him, Tren."

Tren had still not loosened his grip on my wrists. His eyes were hard as they rested on me. "Extermination of vermin is sometimes necessary, Shaara. I told you it was part of my life."

There was a coldness in Tren's eyes I had never felt before. It frightened me.

"Do not worry over it, Shaara," he ordered when he saw my eyes beginning to tear. His were still stern and watchful as they darted around the room, looking for more trouble. When no one came forward to protest his action, the tension began to leave Tren's shoulders. Gradually, he relaxed.

My tears were dripping down wetly onto my dress, but I could not wipe them away. Tren still had his iron grip on my wrists. It felt like he'd nailed them to the table.

I took a sobbing breath, trying to gain control. Tren's eyes came back to me. "It was not your concern, Shaara. He is better off dead."

Targone walked up then. He'd apparently seen Tam and another carry the body away. His eyes took in my tears and Tren's grip on me.

"Difficulties?" he asked, almost rubbing his hands together in glee. He looked like he'd welcome the chance to shoot someone.

"You will not move, Shaara," Tren ordered.

I nodded, and he released my wrists. Quickly, I wiped at the tears and massaged the marks he'd made with his overly tight grip.

"Get her a rag, Targone," Tren ordered.

The Shapechanger handed one to me. I wiped my eyes and blew my nose.

Tren's eyes were still fastened on me when he spoke to Targone. "We may have to kill more of them if Shaarvan takes too long. I do not mind, but it will be hard on Shaara."

I gasped. "No, Tren!" I said. "Please, you don't have to kill anyone. You could just knock them out and carry them away, or . . ."

The two males were looking at me like I had sprouted horns.

"What do you bet Shaara does not interfere a twoTide from today?" Targone asked, with a gleam in his eyes.

Tren was still watching me, but he said nothing.

I sniffed loudly and used the rag again.

"Come on, Tren," Targone needled. "I will wager that with Shaarvan training her, she learns not to argue in a twoTide. What do you bet?"

Tren stared at me a moment, thinking it over. "A twoTide? Fifty says she will still be arguing."

I picked up a wooden plate lying on the table and tried to decide which one of them to throw it at.

Targone saw my movement. "Do not even think about it, Shaara. Remember what Shaarvan taught you about Shapechanger punishment?"

Tren's eyes were warning me, too. I put the plate down and sighed.

Targone and Tren spit on their deal. Then, thankfully, they lost interest in the subject. Targone's eyes were watching one of the men at the bar who kept looking at me. He glared at the man.

"It should not take too much longer," Targone said. "When I left, Shaarvan had already . . ."

"Targone!" Tren said, cutting him off. Tren nodded at me. "Why don't you order a drink?" he added to smooth away the correction.

Tren snapped his fingers, held up two of them in the air, and Tam brought them drinks. I noticed that the two males were drinking the same thing. They took deep gulps of it, synchronized on the count of three, and swallowed like they were twins. They seemed to relish whatever was in the glass.

I was curious. "What are you drinking?" I asked. "Could I try it?"

Tren looked at Targone. Targone only shrugged. Tren passed the glass to me. "It's Zinka, Shaara," he said.

I took a sip and almost couldn't swallow it. It was nasty stuff! I pushed it back to Tren. "How can you drink that?"

"That is what males drink," Targone said. "You just pretend to be one."

Tren was shaking his head at Targone. I saw it. I knew that Tren was trying to stop him from talking so much.

"Tam," I called out. Tam came right over. "Bring me a Zinka, too," I said, glaring at Targone.

"No, Shaara," Tren said, shaking his head at me.

"Let her have one," Targone laughed. "It will teach her a lesson she will never forget."

I raised my chin and glared at both of them. "Targone says I may. Bring me one, Tam."

"No," Tren said once more, and he waved Tam away.

"But Targone said . . ." I started to defend the request.

"Do I hear you arguing with Tren?" Shaarvan was back and not looking pleased.

I looked down, wishing I'd been contented with my Bada juice. It was just that Targone made me so angry with his superior attitude all the time.

"What did Shaara want?" Shaarvan asked Tren.

"Zinka, I'm afraid." He shot a glance at Targone and pointed at him, saying, "Targone told her it was only for males."

"Shaara and I have a long flight. I am grateful for Tren for remembering that. I would not be pleased to have Shaara throwing up the whole way."

"She would not have drunk it," Targone hedged.

"You do not know Shaara well, do you?" Shaarvan said. He turned back to Tren. "I hope my wife was not a problem otherwise?"

Tren shook his head. He did not mention the dead body, I noticed.

Shaarvan laid down a Kekorian 1000 stoner. It was a large quantity of money, enough to feed a family of five for a year.

"I am sorry for the little problem downstairs," Shaarvan said. "This should take care of the mess."

Tren jerked back in his chair. He lurched to his feet, glaring at Shaarvan. "Remove that note, or I shall be forced to fight a Shapechanger for insulting me, and that would be most inequitable."

Shaarvan studied Tren. I could see a faint twinkle in Shaarvan's eyes, but he wasn't smiling yet. He was waiting to see what Tren would do.

"I would have enjoyed the revenge you took downstairs, Shaarvan," Tren said, "but I had the pleasure of killing Isandor."

Males must live on a more primitive level than women, I decided. Maybe it was because they always carried pipes. Was a pipe like their second male appendage? Did violence give them two erections?

Shaarvan met Tren's eyes. Shaarvan was smiling. He picked up the bill he had laid on the table and stuck it back into his shirt. Then he put out his hand, spit on it, and the two men clapped. "I shall sponsor you when you become Shapechanger," Shaarvan told him. "Ask for me in Altar. I have taken a vow that my brother, Thenos, is to be disowned. I shall see that he is stricken from our family tree, and you will take his place. We shall welcome you to our lineage, Tren."

"You have been given the highest honor," Targone said. His eyes glowed yellow with envy. He reeked of something very near the smell of gasoline, which made gag.

Shaarvan nodded grandly to each of the males, then took my hand and pulled me up. We started to walk away, and I called out, "Goodbye."

Shaarvan stopped and glanced down at me, appalled that I had spoken. He didn't correct me, but he turned me around, and we went back to Targone and Tren.

"Shaara just reminded me of something else that needs to be said. Once we leave your casino, Tren, Shaara will not be allowed to speak to you again . . . until you become her brother. I have given her freedom today with both of you that she will never have again."

I stared at Shaarvan and then glanced over at Targone. He nodded to me. I understood his message. Shapechanger training was about to begin.

Targone

I was delighted to escort Shaarvan of Altar down to the basement of Tren's casino. I was able to thank him for his generous deposit into my account as a reward for my protection of Shaara. (As I thought back over those days she and I had spent together, it hardly seemed fitting that I should have been paid for them. Truthfully, I had come to enjoy our talks. The girl had given me much to ponder, and I would never again regard a female in quite the same manner.)

Shaarvan took up most of our time discussing where to take Tren and what words to use to convince him to join us. The Warlord was emphatic that Tren's adaptation should begin immediately. He wanted to know if I had access to a ship or knew where I could get transport to Westla. I wasn't sure exactly how such was arranged. I had never been off the Freinana. Shaarvan nodded quietly when I told him this and said it would be taken care of.

"I shall give you a fiveTide to convince Tren," Shaarvan said. "If he is not ready by then, I shall see to it that he is seized. You will accompany him and stay by his side throughout the trip. Are you agreeable to this?"

A chance to visit Westla! How could I refuse? I nodded and gave Shaarvan my hand.

"In exchange for this, I shall gift you with a girl or wife, whichever you choose," he told me.

Truly, the day that Shaara was found on Freinana was the day my luck began. My contentment was boundless. With best wishes that he savor the pleasure of his blood-right, I left Shaarvan with the Theinian trader.

Shaara

When we reached the bubble cruiser that would take us back to Shaarvan's ship, the four guards that had been following joined us. (The fourth one I had never seen in all the time the guards were following us. He must have been very skilled at being inconspicuous because he was as ugly as a quagmire's face, and I would not have forgotten the sight of him if I had seen him at all.) The guards did not speak to either of us as they climbed into the seats at the back of the shuttle.

I tried to thank them for their protection, as was suitable. Any service offered in Freinana always received the proper expression of gratefulness, but Shaarvan's temper flared with my first words. He issued the silence command, tossed me up into the front seat, buckled me in roughly, and then glared at me until I looked down at the floor.

I remembered, then, that I was not supposed to have a conversation with a male. I'd forgotten. Shaarvan was still enraged when he shot up into the air and flew us over the town. There was a long period of silence where no one dared to speak except Shaarvan, who didn't seem to have the desire.

I studied the ground beneath us and the clouds just above us. I was not exactly bored, but I was wishing I understood Shaarvan better. Finally, I couldn't keep quiet a minute longer. "I'm sorry, Shaarvan," I said. "I forgot about not speaking to males."

"Initiating, Shaara," Shaarvan corrected me. "You are not allowed to initiate a conversation with a male."

Again, the silence ate into my skin, making me feel itchy and uncomfortable. I kept shooting glances over at Shaarvan. He didn't look like he was still mad, but he wasn't offering a lot of conversation.

I tried again. "You said you would be patient if I made mistakes."

This time, Shaarvan glanced over at me. "I am being patient, Shaara. Had I been otherwise, you would have been punished."

"Oh," I said. Once more, the silence continued.

I noticed the cruiser was picking up altitude. My ears didn't like the feeling. Soon, we were traveling over mountains. I gazed down at the lush greenness and wished we could land and walk in the forest. Something about the trees was calling to me.

"It is a forest of Jarto trees," Shaarvan said.

I looked over at him. He had the first glimmerings of a smile on his face.

"They look like they are upside down, doing headstands," I told Shaarvan.

One of the guards chuckled softly. I turned around to look at him.

"Shaara," Shaarvan reproved me.

I sighed quietly and stared down at the upside down trees. Their dense, feathery leaves flowed out at the bottom of their trunks, and their branches, reaching up as if to wave "hello" to us, looked to me like roots searching for soil.

We flew on and on. My eyes grew weary of looking at the Jarto trees. The more I stared at them, the more the trees appeared to be pointing bony, naked fingers at me. What were they accusing me of?

We soared over an immense lake. It was perfectly rounded and very unlike the lake to which Tren had taken me. From the sky, it looked like a piece of blue glass, so still and deep was the water. Shaarvan smiled over at me when we passed it, but he said nothing.

Then, there was only a stretch of brownish-yellow prairie, floating on and on like a yellow ocean, unvaried in its sameness. I stretched my neck and wiggled in the seat. I was tired of sitting, but there was no place to stand up and walk around. The inside of the bubble cruiser was only seats and controls.

"Shaarvan, you told Tren you'd be on Altar if he decided to come. Is that where we're going?" I asked.

"No, we shall go there later, but first, I shall take you to Westla. I am hoping they will be able to aid you with your memory."

For a moment, I thought about that. What would I remember about Shaarvan? Would I find that I loved him? Would I be more fearful of him or less? Would I remember who I was?

"Westla is where they took you when you were poisoned?" I asked.

"Yes, it is the second home base for the Shapechanger. It is where the Old Ones now reside."

"You mean the elderly ones?" I remembered Targone talking about old ones, but I had forgotten what he'd said about them.

Shaarvan chuckled. "No, Shaara. The Old Ones are Shapechanger who use the old ways, the old magic. Altar is the headquarters of the new Shapechanger, the ones who live like commoners, leaving the teachings of our ancestors behind.

"Our family is of both worlds. Shaarac, our son, will be able to choose his birthright. I shall bring him up with one foot in each path."

"As you were?"

"No, my father does not practice the Old Ways. He believes . . ." Shaarvan glanced back at the guards behind him.

"We shall discuss this at another time, Shaara."

"Was I Altarian before you made me Shapechanger?" I probed curiously.

"You ask too many questions," Shaarvan said, and again, his voice was full of irritation.

"I'm sorry." I was silent then, but I wondered why Shaarvan ran so hot and cold. Would he always be this way?

I fell asleep. The lower pitch of the cruiser's engine coming in for landing woke me up. I was glad I was awake to see the spaceport. It was gigantic. I had not known of anything that big. There were ships everywhere, as far as I could see. All of them had the same dulled metallic gray, but there, the similarities stopped. Some were cones. Others were like spiders with nets webbing them to the ground. A few were mushrooms like what I raised in the cellar. It was to one of those mushrooms that Shaarvan took us.

He landed us without the slightest jarring, even better than Tren. I released my belt, and Shaarvan barked out, "Stay put."

He climbed out, allowed the guards to vacate the back, and then came around to me. He opened up my side of the vehicle and stood looking up at me.

"Shaara," he said, as glum as a drunk during the cycle of the Wheel. "I shall *try* to be patient with you, but it is not in my nature.

Targone has told you the laws of Shapechanger and of Altar. You must obey those laws without argument.

"A man has beaten you, so you know that punishment is painful. On my ship, punishment for disobedience will be immediate and not necessarily private. Do you understand, Shaara?"

Of course, I understood. I wasn't brain dead. I nodded. Shaarvan frightened me, but he didn't cower me. Not much, anyway.

"You will not speak to any man, even me, without permission. That will be the hardest part for you because I know you always have many questions."

I raised my chin and scowled.

"You may not look in the eyes of any male except me."

Shaarvan studied me a moment and then continued. "You will not argue with me, ever."

I sighed loudly. I would not argue generalities. It would depend on what Shaarvan ordered.

"You will obey me at all times."

As long as your orders are fair, I added to myself.

"The most important rule is the Primary. You will please your husband," Shaarvan reminded me.

What about the rule that said husbands must please their wives? Where were all the rules for men?

"Any questions before we enter the ship?"

"Did I used to do all that stuff?"

The question was out before I had time to shape it. Shaarvan's eyes for a moment crinkled as if he thought my question amusing. I was surprised it had not made him angry.

"You were doing well before, Shaara. You did not know how to be Shapechanger, but you tried."

"Did I want to be?"

"You wanted to please me."

"Will everyone onboard know me? Will they stare and make me feel like I'm in the casino?"

"It is a new crew. They do not know you, Shaara, but they know you are my wife. They will not look at you or recognize your presence. No more questions now. You will be silent, Shaara, until I give you permission to speak."

Shaarvan lifted me down from the bubble cruiser. His arms lingered longer than they needed to. For a moment, I thought he would kiss me, but he let me go and drew me forward.

We walked up a long, gray rubber ramp. Patterns and swirls of design were embossed on it. As I looked, the swirls began to make me dizzy. I bumped into Shaarvan.

"Do not stare at the ramp, Shaara," he said, laughing and playing with my hair. "The magic of it is too potent for your level."

I had no idea what a level was, but I raised my eyes and walked upwards without looking down again. We stepped inside, and the guards followed. The ugly one took everyone's pipe weapon and shoved them into a hole in the wall. Shaarvan started pushing buttons. One raised up the ramp. A window next to the door displayed the sight of it, shriveling like a piece of fat in a cooking pan. In a moment, the ramp was gone, and the window glazed over.

Shaarvan made me sit in the strangest chair. It was like a Freinanan willo beast, all shaggy and untrimmed. I sat down, and it began to move. For a moment, I felt sick. It did not move fluidly like the landoor or smoothly like a bubble cruiser, but like a shaking, water-soaked frilla, trying to dry out.

Before the chair had stopped trying to jiggle me off, the ship was shooting up into the sky like a catapulted rock. I hoped its projection would have a different conclusion. It did. The ship halted halfway toward the third moon and hung there. Then, as if it had thought long enough about where it wanted to go, it veered sharply to the right, plowing down towards the second moon, so close I was sure that we were going to crash.

The craters and boulders, small spots from a distance, looked like jagged mountains as we got closer. I closed my eyes. In my mind, I could still see the images of the craters. They told of troubled times. Our crash would soon add one more.

At the last moment, I sensed the ship's sudden change of direction. It lurched like a shying landoor and wrenched us towards the great sun, the child of Barquel. That was even worse. No man could survive the breath of Ywequi. I knew that Shaarvan had made a grave error. Ywequi would melt us like a cube of ice at midday. For our defiance, he would burn us into vapor.

Barquel had been strangely silent with my life until he brought Shaarvan. Perhaps he'd known his son would settle the scales of equity. How strange to die from the vengeance of a god in whom I did not believe.

Ywequi, leering at us with ruby flames, commanded the whole screen. Larger and larger, until I could almost smell the breath of him — hot and putrid as he reached out to embrace us.

Then, Shaarvan, ruler of his own small dominion, defied Ywequi. "Now," he commanded, and Ywequi wrinkled and dissolved like a distant lake mirage in the desert's heated air.

Shaarvan strode forward, calm and sure of his Power. I was very impressed. He had fought the gods themselves, but his battle was not fully waged. The other sons of Barquel attacked, flinging themselves against him. Hundreds of them hurled themselves at the ship.

Shaarvan did not tremble. He stood firm, undaunted by the rock-like-suns that shimmered and glowed. They were overcome as easily as Ywequi.

But Barquel was angry now. His revenge followed. The ship spun sickeningly through space. Gravity, which had made itself known far too often on my rides on the landoors, began to desert us.

I must have turned green. I know I felt sick enough to discharge all my inner parts and soul. Shaarvan came to my side.

"Hold on, Shaara," he said. "It will last only a little while longer — a gallop around your landoor track."

"Arena," I said without thinking. I closed my eyes and tried to think of Crimson Black, but instead, all I could think about was Shaarvan. I was humbled before him. I had heard it said that Shapechanger were gods. I knew now that it was true. Shaarvan *was* the equal of Barquel. Even the attacking suns and the departure of gravity could not bow him to the gods' will.

My stomach knew when gravity returned to normal. It was a heaviness, like guilt, but of an outer sense. I opened my eyes and stared up at Shaarvan.

"Good girl," he said. He raised me up, touched my lips with his, and led me from the control room.

We walked through a series of halls and arrived at a door that opened to Shaarvan's touch. Nothing he did surprised me now. I entered quietly.

It was a room without any bed. I walked around, looking at things, but I knew not to touch them. The wall with the blinking lights drew me. It had patterns going in many directions, similar to the murals of the casino walls, but without the scenes of joining. For a moment, I watched the lines wavering and melding. Spirals and circles intersected and spread apart. The colors changed, blending in hues;

then, they darkened into others. It was pretty at first but monotonous. The same patterns and colors kept swirling like snakes, then off and on in their sequence. I would have varied the pattern into people, trees and landoors had I been the artist. I moved on to explore.

There were buttons on one of the other walls. I wondered what their purpose was. I saw no ovens or tables for the preparation of food. Hadn't Shaarvan pressed one to make the window for the ramp appear and disappear? What other purpose could buttons have? I knew not to touch them.

There was a second door. As I neared it, the door slid open. "May I go in?" I asked.

Shaarvan waved me on. He was sitting on a chair I hadn't noticed, watching the repetition of the flashing snakes. I'd thought he was smarter than that. Didn't he see the pattern repeated? But what did I know of how gods thought? Perhaps that was relaxation for him.

The room I entered was tiny. I realized that it was a bathroom when I saw the hole for waste and urine disposal. I could not believe the luxury of Shaarvan's having a necessary all to himself.

I tested the hole. I was surprised when it sprayed me as I started to rise up. Then, it blew at me. I looked inside it to see why it did these things, but whoever planned it had cleverly hidden the mechanisms.

As I left the room, a mist rained down on me. Instantly, it dried me, like the summer winds, and I felt tingly as if tiny bits of sand had scrubbed me. I walked in and out several times, enjoying the sensation. Shaarvan barked at me and ordered me to stop. I had not meant to disturb him.

I returned to the room where he sat. There were no chairs other than the one he was sitting on. I plopped down on the floor. I presumed Shaarvan would require my services when he finished enjoying the lights.

"Why are you sitting on the floor, Shaara?" he demanded.

"You wish me to stand?" I asked. He was becoming angry again. Could a male object to such a small thing, whether I sat or stood?

He sighed. "Go figure out the buttons like you did before."

The buttons? Did he wish me to cook? Yet he had told me I would not be doing so.

"You will permit me to touch the buttons?" I asked to clarify his wishes.

Shaarvan turned and stared at me. "You may, Shaara."

I was unsure still what I had done to irritate the Shaarvan god, but I moved quickly to the buttons and began to pull at one. My touch caused a chair to rise.

I sat down in it. Obviously that was what Shaarvan had intended me to do. I was glad I had chosen the correct button. Perhaps it would please Shaarvan.

"Come here, Shaara," he ordered me gruffly when I had sat only a moment.

I wondered if I should return the chair first or go directly to Shaarvan. If he wished to join with me, the chair might be in the way, but if he wanted my quick obedience, I should go forward at once. I watched the Shaarvan god, trying to read his thoughts.

"Shaara, why do you disobey?" he barked out angrily.

It was very dangerous to anger a god. I spoke immediately. "I am sorry, my lord. I was thinking of the Primary."

Shaarvan stood up to come to me. I realized that I had erred. I looked down at the floor as he came closer. I tried not to cringe, knowing that he would beat me for my disobedience.

"No, Shaara," he said, lifting up my chin. "I shall not hit you for failing to understand."

I was relieved but even more confused. Shapechanger do not lie. Targone had said that Shaarvan would beat me when I did not please him. Shaarvan was not pleased, but he said he would not beat me. Where was the error in my thinking?

"So it is Targone who has confused you?" Shaarvan asked me.

"You read my mind," I said, awed.

"When you send messages with your emotions, I can."

"I did not know I sent messages."

I wondered if it was like the letters transmitted on Tren's computer. Is that why Shaarvan had watched the colored lights? Were there messages in the patterns?

"Enough." Shaarvan's eyes had hardened in anger.

"I'm sorry," I said. Had I sent a bad message? I did not know what I had done wrong, but I looked down at the ground.

Shaarvan strode over to the buttons and pushed one. A bed came up out of the floor. Did the button tell someone to push up from below? I wanted to ask, but I kept silent.

"Sit," Shaarvan said. I was standing by my chair. I started to go to it, but Shaarvan's voice again snapped at me. "No, on the bed."

I walked over and sat down on the bed. I knew Shaarvan would take me soon. Would he be happier then, or would he beat me for being dry, as Isandor had? Should I warn him?

"Shaara, I am trying to understand you, but it is difficult. Why did you not come to me when I ordered you to?"

"I knew I had to please you," I said, "but I did not know how."

Irritation was rising in a pocket around Shaarvan's head. It was a hazy yellow. I watched its circles in the air above him. It created a smell like pampa fruit. The smell was a nice smell, but I knew that a male's irritation was very bad. It was an odor I was most familiar with since it was Isandor's most common odor, next to moldy socks.

"Coming when I called, you would have pleased me," Shaarvan said.

Should I ignore the yellow cloud gathering above his head, or was it OK to observe it?

"I will do that *first* next time," I said.

Shaarvan's frustration was making waves in the yellow haze. The turbulence made the hair on my arms tickle.

"Do you wish me to disrobe?" I asked, not daring to look at his angry eyes.

"Shaara!" he growled.

I had erred again. Should I have disrobed and not asked? Did he wish to undress me?

Shaarvan took a deep breath. I felt him corral the angry winds inside him. The odor of pampa fruit was rotting. It would soon turn into over-ripe garbage. I knew that stench well, too,

"Did Isandor or the slaver ever hit you on the head?" Shaarvan demanded.

"Not often."

I wished I could read the Shapechanger better. His mind was so different. It was like a desert of shifting sands.

Again, I heard Shaarvan gather in a deep, long breath to quiet the roaring of his anger. The turbulence in the air settled little, but his body was not as rigid. The garbage smell dissipated slightly.

"When you said you would come to me first next time, what was the alternative?"

"Trying to figure out how to put away the chair," I answered, wondering why he analyzed everything so carefully. Isandor had not done so. Isandor had only given into the anger and erupted with it.

"Why would you do that?" he continued.

I drew in a breath. All this recall of Isandor pained me. "Most of the time, I had to put away things and clean up, but sometimes I wasn't supposed to. Sometimes, I was supposed to join with Isandor first," I tried to explain. "I never knew which to do, and Isandor beat me for being wrong."

"I am not Isandor."

The force behind Shaarvan's words alarmed me, but I answered as I had been trained.

"Yes, my lord. I am always to come to you first." I responded as meekly as I could, but I stole a glance to read his eyes.

Shaarvan's eyes looked miserable. I realized that I was not performing in the way he expected. I sighed. I knew then that no matter what I did, I would not make the god happy. I had told him I was not the one he'd known before. I think he was beginning to accept that.

"We are not yet far from my planet," I dared to speak. "You could still take me back. I know I do not please you."

Waves of anger lashed at me. I tried not to cringe as the fury slapped against my body. The odorousness of it nauseated me.

Shaarvan gripped my shoulders fiercely and shook me. "You will never say that again. You are mine forever."

I shut my eyes at the pain of his grip and at the blasts of rage that attacked me. The force of it pelted my face and body. My stomach was fighting against the assault of odors.

This was all only a prelude. The beatings would soon start, and this time, there would be no Tren to save me.

As abruptly as my thought, Shaarvan rose up and raged out of the room. I was amazed. He had not beaten me, yet his anger had seared me with its intensity. What manner of god was this?

I lay down on the bed, knowing Shaarvan would be back. It did no good to worry. When Barquel saw fit, I would be beaten. As with Isandor, there was nothing I could do to prevent it. I concentrated on remaining calm, but I fell asleep, listening for the sound of the door swishing open.

I woke up when I felt Shaarvan's body lie down on the bed. He pulled off my dress and tossed it on the floor. I began to tremble, but I didn't struggle when he pulled me close to him. I had long ago learned the danger of fighting. The pain stick teaches well.

Shaarvan's strong arms scooped my body up into his embrace, and he lay there on his side, watching me. I felt his manhood throbbing hard against my leg, but he made no move to plunge it into me.

For a long time, we lay there like that. Shaarvan did not speak, and I wondered if I was supposed to do something. I waited for directions, but none came. The wait stretched too long. My eyes grew so heavy I had to close them for a moment, and I slept.

Shaarvan

It is obvious that Shaara has been injured much more than I realized. Isandor or the slaver must have hit her head. I do not believe the brainwipe alone would cause this much personality alteration. The quick and intelligent woman I knew has been replaced with a passive, frightened little girl. Shaara seems incapable of reasoning skills. She cannot follow the simplest directions. Her inquisitiveness has been beaten out of her, too. When given the choice to explore, instead of figuring out a way to get herself into difficulties through her curiosity or ingenuity as she did in the past, she now chooses to sit and stare into space. She has not asked a single question since we came onboard the ship. I never thought that the rebellious, troublesome nature of my wife was something that I would miss so intensely.

She puts on a bravado act of daring and then attempts to make me think that she is so used to being beaten that she accepts it will happen again. She is, in fact, so convinced I shall beat her that she almost makes me believe that I might do so. I have a terrible urge to shake her at those moments, and to order her to be Shaara once again. Stars, send me patience. I cannot let her down.

Shaara

In the morning, Shaarvan was not as gruff with me. He was more like he'd been at the stables when he had told me about Shaarac. This puzzled me. Isandor had always been gruffer before the joining and gentler after unless it was one of those times when he rampaged about my being dry and cold in his bed. It was so confusing. Were all males so difficult to figure out?

I was given a new dress, a yellow one. The old one was tossed into what Shaarvan called a recycler. I knew a cycle was a circle, and this recycler was a hole that looked rectangular. It bewildered me, but I did not dare ask Shaarvan about it. He did not like questions.

We left his bedroom to travel in the halls. I wished we could walk where there were trees and grass, but I guess the plastic and metal paths were the best I could hope for on a ship.

We ended up in a large, rounded room. I would have called it the recycler, but Shaarvan called it the cafeteria. We walked up to a wall with buttons that were numbered. I thought at first that it must be a calendar, noting the cycle of the gods because there was a long line of them, but dishes of food came out when you pushed a button.

Shaarvan pushed some buttons and carried what he told me was the food to our table. I was skeptical. It looked more like two plastic drop cloths than food to me. I touched one of them, and it was like the frost on top of the garbage bucket outside our house. I'd never felt anything inside a dwelling with that degree of coldness. The iciness of it stung my hand. I blew at my fingers until they warmed.

"We must heat the food before it is eaten," Shaarvan said.

People used to talk like that to Isandor. Did Shaarvan think I was stupid like Isandor?

"I put it in here," Shaarvan said, pointing to the center of the table, "and this cooks it."

I watched as the food lowered into the oven. It was smart to put an oven in the table. That saved a lot of steps. I wondered if the oven maintained the correct temperature for baking bread.

When the food came out, there was a filmy substance on top. Shaarvan pulled it off. I reached out to touch it, curious about what it felt like.

"No, this is not the food, Shaara. The food is on the plate."

He laid the filmy stuff in the center of the table. It dropped down. I was disappointed that he hadn't let me feel it. The way that it had changed its shape had been intriguing. I wondered if saddles could be fashioned from it that rearranged their shape as the landoor jumped over the hurdles. Perhaps it could cushion the landoor's back.

Shaarvan picked up a two-prong thing. He squeezed it together and showed me how to open and shut it.

"You eat your food with this," he said.

I laughed. How could two sticks scoop up a soupy thing?

Shaarvan demonstrated, and it did seem to work for him. I wished for our simple spoons. I knew how to carve them if he had any wood, but I doubted there'd be wood on this plastic and metal ship.

I tried to use the two stick things — tweezers, he called them. I kept dropping them into the food. Each time I picked them up, I'd grab some food with my fingers. It was a lot faster than using the stupid tweezers!

Shaarvan caught me the third time. "No! You will eat nothing with your fingers. If I catch you doing that again, I shall take your food away."

How an individual ate was a personal matter. Even a slave had that right. Shaarvan had no business interfering. I pushed my plate away.

"Is this temper from the woman who always tries to please?" he teased me.

I refused to rise to his bait. I was not a fish, eager to get caught on his painful barb. I would be the fat old stener Tren had shown me, who sat under the shade of a boulder's overhang. Tren had said that some fish, like the old stener, were too smart to bite at a silly fake worm. Surely, I was as smart as a stener!

Shaarvan brushed the dishes towards the center. They sank into the oven. I refused to tell Shaarvan that if he left dishes in an oven, they would be harder to clean. It was his ship. Let him find it out.

Shaarvan then led me back to the control room, and I sat in the same chair. Again, it wiggled, but it grew tired and became still. I watched the sky through the window.

There were many nights after Isandor had used me that I had sat by the window finding star pictures. Isandor had not cared as long as I didn't talk. I had sat and dreamed of galloping though the stars, jumping over planets and spaceships. Before I was allowed to ride, it had been my "sanity fantasy."

Here in the ship, our movement made the pictures change. It was easier to dream I was on Crimson Black, galloping from star to star. Somewhere, the Wheel slept. We could gallop along its spokes and . . .

"You have been staring at those stars without stop," Shaarvan said.

I gasped. He had startled me so. "Have I displeased you?"

"I cannot figure you out," he responded in irritation. I tried to ignore the scent, holding my breath a minute.

"Why should it interest you to do so?"

"Do you challenge me?"

"No," I said quickly. "But is it necessary for a Shapechanger to figure out a girl?"

"I think you are being difficult."

"I am sorry. I do not mean to be." I dropped my eyes quickly.

"Come," he said. I knew again that I had angered him. It seemed that a god was much harder to please than a man.

I stood and followed Shaarvan. Again, we walked the sterile paths. It was no wonder that no one on the ship smiled. They must all have boredom growing like mildew in their brains. The walls lacked the colors that pleased the eyes and brought peace to one's soul.

Shaarvan took me to what he called the "exercise room."

"Take off your dress," he ordered me.

I thought it was an uncomfortable place for a joining, but Shaarvan was very strange. I disrobed and stood, waiting. Shaarvan turned his back on me and walked to the wall, where the buttons drew his interest. He came back with clothes for me to put on, and I was even more puzzled. Did he prefer me as a boy? I slipped on the pants and shirt and waited for further directions.

"This is the 'horse,' he said, pointing to a metal thing. I looked at Shaarvan blankly. I did not know what a *horse* was.

He started talking to me in a funny language. I had been given no directions, so I stood there and watched his face as he spoke. I understood why his face was so beautiful. Of course, a god would be formed perfectly.

"Amazing," he said, shaking his head. "You do not know your native tongue."

"I know where my tongue is," I protested.

He ignored me and turned to the mechanism, "This is a landoor."

Did space travel cause the brain to corrode? Shaarvan had seemed normal before he got on the ship. It was after we went up into the sky that he got peculiar. I wondered if he were having a relapse from the poison someone had injected into him.

"Shaara, sit here," he ordered.

It was not a landoor, and it was not a chair, but I obeyed him and sat.

"Turn and face the front," he said.

How did he figure there was a front? Of course, he thought it was a landoor.

"That direction wears the tail?" I asked, pointing to what he'd indicated was the back. I did not wait for his answer but turned to face what he must think was the head.

"There is no tail, Shaara. It is a machine."

I stared up at him. "You said it was a landoor. I didn't."

"I did not say . . . Never mind. Just sit there, Shaara."

I don't know what he did, but the seat started moving, rocking back and forth and up and down. A picture window showed a grassy area with jumps. The machine lifted up suddenly, and I fell off.

"Shaara, what is wrong with you?"

Shaarvan's frustration was rolling like a boulder towards me. I knew he was angry and ready to begin hitting. I cowered where I had fallen.

Again, he sighed, gathered in his anger, and picked me up. Then, he carried me out of the room. He wasn't beating me, yet, but negative emotions were tumbling around inside him, like Isandor on a losing night.

I realized that Shaarvan was returning to the bedroom. Isandor hadn't beaten me much outside the bedroom, either. I guess males preferred privacy when they played out their rage.

As we entered, Shaarvan threw me down on the bed.

"Please," I begged. "Could I use the bathroom before you start beating me?"

"Go!" The scent of vinegar's disappointment licked at my heels as I ran.

There was a hiding hole in the bathroom. After I'd used the waste hole, I curled up in the other opening. I knew Shaarvan would find me, but I had to work on finding that spot in my mind where I could tune him out. The tension and the violence of his emotions made it so difficult to find the forest.

I concentrated on breathing in and out slowly. Flar had taught me meditation when the beatings started. It had helped. It was going to have to help me again. In and out, in and out, like water, the gentle waves of a lake splashing softly against the pebbles, rolling them smooth, smooth, round, and comfortingly tranquil.

"What are you doing?" Shaarvan yelled at me.

I wasn't ready. I screamed and kept on screaming. Shaarvan slapped me. I stopped screaming and held my breath.

Once, when I'd held my breath a long, long time, I'd gone unconscious. It had scared Isandor so much he'd run away, thinking that he'd killed me. Shaarvan was probably too smart to be fooled, but sweet oblivion would be such a blessing . . .

He picked me up and carried me into the other room. He lay me back down on the bed. And still, I did not breathe.

"Stop it, Shaara, or I shall slap you again to make you breathe."

That was the hardest part, not breathing when you were hit. It was an instinct to breathe in when the shock of the pain came, but you could stop anything if you really concentrated.

Shaarvan didn't hit me. He reached under my arms and tickled me. I couldn't fight that. I breathed.

"Spit in your face!" I snapped.

It was one of the worst things I knew. I sat up, madder than a landoor with a burr under its saddle. I butted my head in Shaarvan's stomach and high-tailed it to the door. I stopped a moment, trying to figure out the door. Hand touch, that's what it was. I reached up and placed my hand flat against the door's surface.

A shock sent me flying. I howled from the pain. It hurt worse than when Dusta had kicked me in the ribs!

Shaarvan came over to me. Again, he picked me up and carried me back to the bed. I hurled every epithet I'd ever heard at him. I kicked, hit, and pounded at him, screaming the whole time. He seemed immune to it all. He threw his body on top of mine, anchoring me down.

"You're not my husband; you're a torturer. I'd rather be owned by Isandor than you. At least he didn't assault me with barbs of anger all day and talk to me like I was stupid. And when he was gone, I could recuperate from the violence. You never leave me alone!"

I had lots more to say, but I was panting so hard, I had to get my breath. I swallowed and took a deep one.

Shaarvan was staring at me in wonder. "You are the same spitball," he said, and he began to laugh.

Now, he was swearing at me. I struggled to free myself again, winded or not.

"Oh, no, wife. We're going to end this right now."

He grabbed my head and held it while his lips lowered to mine. He had me. There was no escape. His lips burned, but I could not prevent his tongue's entry. It barged in, welcome or not, intrusively, demanding in its possession. I resented its attack and fought. Isandor had almost never tried to kiss me. I'd bitten him once, and he'd never trusted me again.

I tried to bite Shaarvan, but he read the thought, and his hand grabbed my neck. I was frozen in pain. His tongue played freely then, flickering here and there, touching the roof of my mouth, my tongue, my lips.

I tried to resist him once more, and the grip on my neck tightened. His lips moved down to bite at the side of my neck. His tongue stroked me with a pattern.

"Stop it!" I cried. "I don't want to feel!"

"You are going to, my wife. I am going to pattern every inch of your body until there is not an inch of resistance."

"No!" I screamed, and again, a surge of his anger lanced me. I cringed, shutting my eyes, but nothing happened. I opened them and looked to see if a fist was coming my way.

"I shall not beat you, Shaara," he said calmly.

He watched me, silent and still as a landoor tasting the wind. Then, slowly, he bent down and pulled off my dress. His lips kissed me between my breasts. I tried to push him away with my hands, but he held them down at my side while his lips traveled.

"No, please. I don't want to feel it. Please don't do this," I begged.

His lips covered my mouth and probed deeply. His hands began the Shapechanger magic, stroking patterns over and over on my skin.

Once more, I cried out. "Please, please. Take me, but don't torment me like this."

It is too late, Shaara. You already feel me. I am in your blood, in the veins that carry your life's force throughout your body. Do not fight me. Feel your body crying out for my hand on your naked skin, feel your lips melting your resistance away. Feel the restraints you have built, springing free. It is too late now, Shaara. Let it go. Feel me.

I shook my head. Again, the patterns started over and over, driving me away from my center, away from the barriers I'd built to protect myself.

Shaarvan had no right to do this. I had no Power over who owned me, but he had no right to make me feel. It was my right to withhold my mind.

Not with a Shapechanger, Shaara.

I'd heard him, but his lips were busy. I was going mad. The feelings were too powerful. I could not withstand his assault. I moaned.

Shaarvan drove into me then, and the wonder of it, the pleasure of him inside me, made me gasp. The joining that came after frightened me beyond measure. It was the amalgamation of heart and soul and mind — the deep bonding of the Shapechanger.

When it was done, Shaarvan held me in his arms, but I ignored him, crying in rasping sobs of confusion and despair.

"It is all right, Shaara," he said. "It is meant to be this way."

"No," I screamed. "You have stolen my soul."

"And you have stolen mine," came his quiet voice.

I stared at him in disbelief. My tears were forgotten as I saw the sincerity in his eyes.

"Listen, my wife," he said. "I shall tell you a Shapechanger poem. It is how I feel:

All that I am I share with you

One heart, one mind, one soul

A union: like hydrogen to oxygen

Not water, without the other

My heart would shatter and break

Like a tree with no earthly roots

Without the support of your love

I would topple in the first wind

Like a single voice in a cavern

My mind would be an empty echo

Without your enticing thoughts

Soothing, entreating, caressing

My soul would be an unfilled vessel

Devoid of earnest purpose or desire

Seeping away my dreams and visions

Through the crack where life flowed out

Life would be a shallow puddle

Muddied, unpleasant, undrinkable

Without your love within, without

Existence would have no value

I could not speak. Shaarvan had touched me with his words. Again, my tears flowed. His words were so beautiful, but I was not ready. I feared the closeness he spoke of. I feared his need.

Shaarvan's hand brushed back my hair so he could see my eyes. "I shall give you time, Shaara — a lifetime. We were almost there when you were taken. It will come once more. Just do not close off on me again."

He brushed his knuckles down my cheek. I cringed and saw the hurt in his eyes. I was sorry.

"You are wounded, Shaara, wounded inside, but you will heal. I shall be gentle, gentle as I can. I shall learn to be patient. I shall work to curb the flashes of my anger. You are so sensitive to them. But you must learn that I shall not beat you. Even if you see the rage inside my mind, I shall never be Isandor."

Shaarvan frightened me with the storm of his emotions. He confused me with his poetry and his words of softness, but he had not beaten me yet, and I had not been dry in the joining. I began to hope that life would not bring me as low as the night when the knife had craved my touch.

Pathe

So, there will be war between us. Thenos sent me from his chambers like a commoner before a lord. The insult burned. Did he think that because my Power is so humble compared to his, I am toothless? I am a Trendacons. My blood is as noble as the Highest of Westla.

It is written in the ancient Legends that when the blood grows cold and yet boils with rage, Power grows in that body. I do not know if the Legends are true, but I know that Thenos has made an enemy today. I *shall* revenge myself with the right of blood. Those three commoners will feel my claws and teeth. And, if Thenos attempts to interfere, he will rue the day!

In fact, I think it is time for me to join in with what Mother has started. I am not amenable to a government of commoner and Thenos.

Chapter Four

Shaara

The days passed slowly. Shaarvan was disappointed that I did not accept his riding machine — that metal and plastic thing. How could he even breathe its name in the same sentence as landoor? It had no feel of life.

I much preferred to walk the ceilings and dream of swimming nude, where I could feel the water lapping at my skin — its gentle undulations soothing me and caressing my body with its liquid hands. Sometimes, while walking, I remembered the softness of dew-dampened grass, springy and cold on my bare feet, and the feel of its moisture plunging me into the cool freshness of morning.

Shaarvan took me sometimes to the small garden on the ship, but nothing there felt right. The plants did not smell of nature. They smelled of his metal and plastic ship. In the garden, the flowers bloomed in their fake sunshine, and the trees attempted to shed their leaves as if they believed they were participating in the seasons. But their leaves were rubbery, and their whispers did not speak of the winds.

Only the grass felt real — scratchy with the itchy feel of its miniature-bladed tickles. It smelled of spring growth and slightly damp soil. I lay on it often and tried to picture landoors grazing, but the artificial sounds of the ship punctured my daydreams.

Still, the garden was preferable to the time spent on the computer. Its metallic mentality drove me to a frenzy. I threatened it with violence, but Shaarvan warned me not to damage it. I was obedient to his wishes, but my soul seethed at the time spent in its enslavement. Shaarvan kept my periods on it short and cleverly stayed nearby when I was attached to its training lessons.

When I had been onboard the ship for close to a twentyTide, Shaarvan took me to a concert. It was inside a huge, circular chamber. Many of the crew were present, sitting in willo beast chairs like the one I was forced to sit on in the control room.

As we entered, the men's eyes swung around to stare. I thought their reaction was normal, but Shaarvan's face glowered. He tensed up, and his anger poured out. I panicked and attempted to pull away from him. If I'd been rational, I would not have done so — where could I go inside this prison of a ship? Of course, Shaarvan had not allowed me to dart away, and as suddenly as my terror had descended, it was gone. I froze, lowered my eyes, and hoped I had not earned a beating.

"Easy, Shaara," was all Shaarvan said, and although the shaking of my legs told otherwise, we continued on as if none of it had happened.

A moment after we had sat in our own willo beast chairs, four men rose up from their seats and walked towards the center of the chamber. They picked up long arrow-like sticks. The arrow-sticks opened up, swelling out like pregnant landoors.

Then, the men began to pluck and rub inside the instrument's belly. I was enthralled with the sounds. It was marvelous. It spoke to me, calling me back home to my landoors and to the woods all around the pastures. The music carried me away from the cold artificiality of the ship's world. With my eyes closed, I heard the sound of birds calling, twitzits chittering, a woodady pecking at a wooden tree trunk. I heard the rustling of the limbs of a tall Sandia tree bowing to the wind. A brook chuckled to the stones, and the pebbles rolled with laughter.

With my eyes closed, I could even smell the flavors of the wind, the sweet nectars, the tart blobers, the rotten, overly bloated spafin berries plopping down from a tree to be ripped at and torn by animals. (Rotting spafin berries was a smell you never forgot. It was like summer grass calling you back to yesterdays and memories you didn't remember, but the smells reminded you.)

The music quieted my inner turmoil, my questions about my future, and the doubts I had about whether it was wrong to leave the landoors and the only home I'd ever known. For long moments, the melodies patterned the air, and I forgot I lived in a plastic tomb, encapsulated like some giant loma bug, flying on its way to find a single Nadar tree among the hundreds of milars.

The poor loma bugs dedicate their lives to that journey, and most of them die never completing it. It worries me that we on this cold, ugly ships are those loma bugs, flying with the same ridiculous odds. How will we ever make it to a place as small as the Nadar tree compared to the vastness of space?

The music kept me from my thoughts on the loma bug, my despair at leaving Crimson Black, and the loss of Tren (a thought I only whispered. Maybe he hadn't been the true love of my life, but he'd been a friend, and I missed him dreadfully). I was lonely also for my conversations with Blair, Frieda, Flar, and even Targone (sometimes).

Shaarvan must have seen how the music calmed me. From that concert on, he took me almost daily to hear the men practice or give a concert. But the music only quieted me while it played, and in between, I was as restless as a landoor mare in heat. I knew I was driving Shaarvan mad with my restless pacing through the overly long days, but I was bored. I desperately needed a challenge, an activity, something to learn.

"Get a book and read, Shaara," Shaarvan snapped at me one day when my impatience had driven me to pacing back and forth in our small room.

I did not wish to disobey him, but how could I comply when it was something I did not know how to do?

"I can't read, Shaarvan," I told him. "I don't know how."

"How do you know?"

His eyes were not angry yet. I gulped and continued. "Frieda, let me try to read one of her books. I could not do so."

Shaarvan's eyes peered down into my soul. What was he seeing? "Did she try offering you a book written in Altarian?"

He didn't wait for me to answer. He flipped off the computer research he'd been poring over and stood up. He walked over to a cabinet, pushed a button, and pulled out two books — a small brown one and a big red one.

"Come sit down next to me," Shaarvan ordered as he pushed a button for the bed to rise up. "Even if you cannot read a book, Shaara, you can look at the pictures."

I sat down beside him cautiously. I figured that Shaarvan would probably become angry once he saw that I was unable to do what he wanted. Sure, I could look at pictures, but would he expect that to keep me occupied for long?

I felt stupid as Shaarvan opened his heavy, fat book and began to read. He was probably going to learn something interesting while I was supposed to sit there and look at stupid pictures.

"Couldn't you teach me to read?" I asked, surprised that my tongue had had the courage to interrupt Shaarvan's reading.

Shaarvan only laughed, not angry at all. "Yes, Shaara," he said. He was sitting with his back against the wall, his legs flat, totally relaxed. His arms stretched out, and immediately, he was pulling me over against him. When he had fit me into the niche he'd formed with his arm, he said, "The first thing, Shaara, is to open the book."

"I know that!" I snapped with annoyance, but I obeyed quickly before he'd think I was arguing with him.

For a moment, I looked through the pages, and then I shut the book disgustedly. "This is a baby book," I complained. "I've already read it."

"What did you say?" Shaarvan was staring at me with the strangest expression, but he did not seem angry.

"I said, I've already . . ." I stared up at Shaarvan for a moment in shock. "I can read. I know what it says!" I cried out excitedly. I sat up and began to read out loud.

"The hill is green. The green hill is big. The big green hill has grass. The grass is green. The hill has green grass."

I was laughing now. "Do you have other books?" I was so excited. I forgot to worry about Shaarvan's anger, about disobeying him, or about anything but the thrill of being able to read.

Shaarvan laughed. He waved me towards the cupboard. I ran over to it, pushed the button, and began to pull out each book, reading the title looking through the pages to see if I could miraculously read it.

In my happiness at finding that I could read, words came tumbling out of my mouth. "I can find out all the answers to a hundred questions you won't answer!" I babbled.

"Shaara. Come here." Shaarvan's voice chilled my joy. I looked up and saw his face. It was enigmatic, but underneath were waves of something that felt an awful lot like anger.

"I'm sorry," I said quickly. "I didn't mean to say that. I didn't mean to challenge you." I made my apologies as quickly as I could, but Shaarvan's hand flashed the command for obedience.

I did not stop to put down the book. I obeyed Shaarvan immediately. With eyes lowered, I dragged myself towards the bed.

"Sit down, Shaara," he said. The moment I had seated myself, he was jerking me towards him. "What questions do I not answer?" he demanded with an irritated voice.

"None. I don't ask them," I said quietly. I wondered if tears would keep Shaarvan from beating me.

"Why?"

"Why?" I moved slightly so I could look at him. "Because you ordered me not to."

"When did I tell you not to ask me questions?"

What was going on here? Didn't he remember? "On the bubble cruiser," I said.

"Shaara, that was a twentyTide ago!"

I didn't say anything. If someone orders you not to do something, I didn't see what difference the number of Tides made.

"I did not mean you could *never* ask me questions, Shaara, just no more, then."

"Oh." Why could males never decide what they wanted?

Shaarvan took me in his arms and hugged me against his chest. "It is difficult to admit, Shaara, but I have missed your questions. I was afraid Isandor had taken away your curiosity." He kissed me gently and then said, "Ask away, Shaara, ask away."

I wanted to sit up so I could watch Shaarvan's face. I still couldn't read his voice, and his mind was almost always closed to me. But when someone offers you a bonus, you don't argue about being held too closely.

"What is Westla like?" I asked. "Is it just like this ship? Are there women there? Where is Shaarac? You never told me . . ."

"Hold it, Shaara," Shaarvan said, with chuckles bubbling up from his chest like the deep rumbles of a small rock avalanche. "I cannot answer your questions if you never stop asking them," he warned me.

I shut up, and he continued. "Shaarac is on Westla. He is in deep sleep. With no parents present, it was decided that it would be less traumatic for him."

I forgot my questions about Westla with the thought of my son.

"How old is he?"

"Slightly more than a quarterPass."

Just a baby! I thought about that a moment. He was almost the same age as the boy Marla took care of. Marla's master had put her in charge of his son when his wife died giving birth. She had gone to market with all the other slaves, but she had had to carry the vegetables in a sack she'd strung across her back. The baby in her arms had googled and smiled, fascinating all of us. We'd been eager to help her, but Marla hadn't been allowed to let us hold the baby.

Would Shaarac look like baby Teztl? Would he smile at me? Would he be mine to hold and love?"

"Does he look like you?" I asked.

"Yes." I heard the pride in Shaarvan's voice as he went on to describe Shaarac.

His hand was stroking my hair. It was gentle for such a big hand. In the niche of his arm, I felt sheltered.

"What is Westla like?"

Shaarvan smiled. "There are women, males, and children there." His hand was moving down to stroke my neck. A spasm of fear passed through me that Shaarvan would suddenly seize me in the neck grip.

"Westla is enormous, Shaara, more like a planet than a ship," he continued. His hand stilled. It lay on the back of my neck, but there was no threat to it.

I was sitting very still, having decided not to move with the hand so close to my neck. I sighed. "I can't believe I have a son! Is he a good boy? Does he cry all the time or fret?"

"Shapechanger children are happy children. They almost never cry because their parents are near."

"Then we have let him down."

"No, he sleeps, Shaara. When he wakes up, we will be there, and he will not know the difference. He will just have had a long nap."

"He will know that I do not know him."

"We will wait awhile to awaken him, but if your memories are not returned by the medics on Westla, you will just have to pretend. Your nature is loving. I do not think it will take you long to find him in your heart, even if the memories are all new."

Shaarvan took my book and placed it on the floor with his. "Come, taste my lips, and know the father of your son more intimately."

I blushed, but my lips moved to join his, and as usual, our passion flowered.

Thenos

My brother, Pathe, has insidiously usurped my authority. I forbade him to take revenge on my commoners, and he has done so anyway.

In the beginning, I found it impossible to believe that my weakling brother, who could barely transform when commanded to do so at the Bridge of Adulthood would have killed. Goria, curse her soul, had once told me that she had never seen him change. Yet, who else could it be that stalked the night and tore the hearts out of each of those particular men?

I ordered Pathe brought before me. At first, he looked no different than his normal passivity, but then I saw the glint in his eyes, and I knew that the fierceness within him had grown. Perhaps Pathe came late into his Power. Such had occurred before. Yet, the testing had found him shallow. How curious.

Goria did not deserve his defense of her honor. She was never Shapechanger, and so was never legally his wife. What a fool Pathe was. Or, maybe he was not the fool we believed. Perhaps his instincts were better than we all thought since he never did make her one of us. She died a slave — how fitting.

When I gave Goria to the men, I chose the most disgusting, dirty, and degenerate of them. One in particular was known for his brutality. She had earned that justice for her treachery in selling Shaara. I wished that I could have watched as she screamed. Unhappily, I thought it better that I was duly witnessed to be elsewhere. Alas, sadly, I can only imagine her degradation.

Pathe's eyes were on me. For a moment, I worried that he could read my thoughts, but then I remembered his lack. I met his eyes fully and invited him to read me, but he turned away. Even when I offered an unshielded invitation, he was not able. Poor weak-willed Pathe!

My commoners were screaming out, "Punish the murderer, punish the murderer."

How dare they tell me what to do. I snarled, and they backed away quietly. "There is no proof that my brother killed these men," I said. I did not stop for fear that my brother would confess. He was known throughout the city for his honesty, poor fool. "It was true that Pathe believed that those three had done him a grievous wrong, but he spent the night in his house. He did not change into a beast. He is a medic, not one of the Warlords. He is not capable of such a vicious deed."

That calmed the dirtwalkers. They looked at him again and remembered that not all Shapechanger were warriors. I pulled my brother close and hugged him to me. He had the good judgment not to resist, but there was no warmth in him for my friendship. His stiffness warned me not to prolong my statement.

Why did I save his life? It was not from brotherly love. I have a use for Pathe. One day, when I can finally squash these irritating dirtwalkers, I shall need one such as he — one too weak to challenge me and too noble to betray me. Besides, Shaara likes him. I have saved his life for my princess. When she bears my son, she will need his services. What could be a better reason to give someone life?

Pathe

He thinks I am weak, and so I am, but I have done the deed as I vowed. The blood-right was satisfied. I am contented.

Thenos thinks I cannot read his eyes, but I have already done so. Could a nest of maggots be any less repugnant? So, Goria was the cause of Shaara's disappearance? Why had Thenos not told me? I would have revenged our brother's loss. I would have given Goria the swift death she had earned. But not even Shaarvan would have demanded such brutality, not for my wife.

Why did Thenos take it upon himself? He had no love of Shaarvan. Would it not have pleased him to see the two of them severed from their happiness? And, if he took Goria's life as a service to me, why did he prevent me my rights? No commoner may attack a

Shapechanger's woman. It is the law. Or did he overthrow that decree, too? If so, why did he protect me now? He knew I satisfied the blood. How could he lie? Why did he want to?

My brother's manipulations have only lately been called to my attention by the death of Goria. Now that my eyes are opened, I see clearly what Thenos has achieved. The sour taste of his domination offends my mouth. It is far worse than the taste of the blood of the night before.

What madness is this that my brother pursues? It is better for commoners to form no allegiance to Shapechanger. We are too different. Shapechanger goals would never be the goals of man, and our dominion over the commoners would not be healthy for either man or Shapechanger. Thenos knows our history. He cannot have forgotten that intimacy with commoners provoked their jealousy. How long does he believe that he can control their resentment? It is a raging tiger held back by string.

Shaara

Being allowed to ask questions unraveled a lot of confusion. There were so many things I didn't understand, and all the technology on board the ship mystified me. I wanted to know how everything worked. But Shaarvan's answers confused me, and he often launched into them with implied insults on my ignorance.

"Think, Shaara!" he'd snap at me, irritated when I didn't understand, but how could I? His world was so different from mine.

One day, when he again cursed Freinana for its primitive level of science and me for my continued lack of knowledge, something in me flared up. I couldn't help responding, "I know I'm ignorant and stupid, but it's not my fault that I'm not a god like you!"

Shaarvan's face grew thunderous at my tone. This time, he would beat me; I could see it in his face. I was preparing myself when Shaarvan's face abruptly changed, and he began to laugh.

"A god?" he chuckled. "Why in the stars would you think that?"

When I explained, ignoring the eyes that mocked my belief, his laughter stopped, and his eyes became sad.

"Those are not gods, Shaara. Barquel is only the name people give to destiny, and the other gods of Freinana are distant constellations, groups of stars like their sun, Ywequi."

"But you battled them. I saw you."

Shaarvan shook his head. He came towards me, threw his arms around me, and hugged me to him. "My poor Shaara. You are so bright. I forget the gaps in your memory. Of course, you believe what you were taught on Freinana. It is all you know. I shall try harder to be patient, my wife."

Shaarvan thought I was smart? I'd always thought he believed I was a candle with only half a flame. I felt a glow inside me. Praise was rare and needed cherishing. I would hold this tribute close to my heart.

As if unaware that he had touched me so miraculously, Shaarvan continued. "You have taken in a heavy dose of superstition, my wife. I am Shapechanger, but I am not a god. I command a ship that journeys through the stars. There were no battles that day on the control deck, Shaara. You only saw the vast speed of the ship as it passed through several solar systems."

Shaarvan's eyes were almost sad enough to make me want to cry. I looked down at his chest and then leaned my head against it, listening to the strength of his heartbeat.

He was wrong, but I did not argue with him. Many do not believe the names given to the gods. I was not sure I did, but it was safer to leave a door open where gods were concerned.

Perhaps Shaarvan did not know he was a god. Frieda had told me that Shapechanger had once been called the Star Wizards. They were the lords of the galaxy because the stars, the children of Barquel, had fashioned the Shapechanger from their firmament. Looking at Shaarvan, I knew that was true.

What puzzled me about it all was how I came to be Shapechanger, too. I knew I was not a child of the gods. Barquel enjoyed hurling too many problems at me. I was not a favored one.

"Targone said that you captured me and made me your wife. Why am I not a slave, then?"

Shaarvan was patient that day. He was not always, but I think my outburst made him perceive me in a different way. He took the time to answer my question, and in the answering, he gave me no insult. Instead, he told me another of his Shapechanger poems:

I stole her from a planet

Wild with primitive shine

Unknowing of her future

Nor of her home to be

She cried huge tears of woe

Because she had been taken

But anger was her only defense

And fear soon conquered that

Her eyes were round with terror

As I taught her of her destiny

But gentled by my Shaper's touch

Her body obeyed the patterns

She learned to crave the feel

Of lips upon her naked skin

She bowed down her alien eyes

And blossomed from the joining

The seed thus planted in her

Gave new life to the family tree

And earned her the name of wife

And the gray of Shapechanger eyes

I clothed and sheltered her

And guided her along her path

Our blood beat with one cadence

Animate in the bounty of lust

I believed that she was my captive

So, how strange it was to discover

That although I owned the woman

It was she who ruled my heart

Shaarvan did not look away when he finished reciting the poem. His eyes glowed, and he searched mine for something I could not give him.

"Shaarvan," I said, "I do not understand how Shapechanger males can have such cold and cruel laws for women and yet have such poetry in their souls."

Shaarvan laughed. "The laws are not cruel, wife. They are for your protection. And Shapechanger males are far from cold. It is the bonding that makes the male soften enough to speak of what he feels inside. The woman brings the poetry with her love. As the poem says, it is the woman who makes the owner the captive."

I ignored Shaarvan's defense of the laws and asked, "Why do males memorize these poems?"

Shaarvan smiled into my eyes. "It is required in Shapechanger schooling," he told me. "The poems are our heritage and the understanding of our nature and our ways. One day, Shaarac will learn them, too.

"How did having a child turn my eyes gray?"

Shaarvan's dimples were fascinating me. I wondered if there was magic in them. My eyes slid to his full, generous lips. I wanted to reach out and trace them.

Shaarvan's smile changed slightly. I knew he had caught my thought. I buried my head back against his chest.

"There have to be some changes made in a captive's body for impregnation to occur," he said, ignoring his knowledge of my interest. "You would not understand if I told you how, Shaara. It is enough to say that your body was altered."

I sighed. "Did it make me look different?" I looked up, curious.

"Very little. There was only a tiny change made in your blood, nothing more."

"But it made my eyes gray? What color were they before?"

"It is not important, Shaara. After a time, with the birth of Shaarac, your eyes became gray, and it made you full Shapechanger."

Shaarvan's eyes were darker than mine. His were, at times, almost a metallic gray. Right now, they were veiled slightly, with a look I knew that meant there were things he wasn't telling me. It was the same way his eyes had looked when he'd told me he had business in the basement at Tren's casino. I wondered why he hid things from me, but I knew that if I pried in a sensitive area, he would stop answering questions.

I changed the conversation. "Do only Shapechanger form bonds?" I asked.

I received a lopsided grin. Had he read my thoughts again?

"Only Shapechanger have the mind-link you feel between us. With the Old Ones sometimes the bond was so tight that the two did not need speech between them. They could feel the unspoken words."

"You do that," I said, surprised.

"And I feel it in you, Shaara. While you were away, your Power rested, but the level of it is rising now that you are being exposed to Shapechanger magic again. I shall have you tested on Westla."

"Will it hurt?"

Again, the dimples flashed. He waited until I looked up into his eyes, then a faint chuckle broke free, and he said, "A lot less than falling off landoors, my dear wife," and his lips on mine cut off any more questions I had planned to ask.

Thenos

Today, one of my repulsive peons delivered the report I had been waiting for. I was so enraged by its contents I almost seized the dirtwalker by his skinny neck and flung him across the hall. It would have been delicious justice. All that saved the worm was his father standing by his side. Cregor has been useful to me so far. He would not continue to be so if I bloodied his son. I did not kill the peasant or his father, but I sent them both from the hall and reread the odious message.

I had ordered information as to the location of Shaarvan's ship. The dirtwalkers took their time obtaining it, as usual. When does a worm ever achieve what a Shapechanger can do with rapidity? The current heading of my brother's ship indicates that he is not returning my bride to Altar, as I intended him to do. He is taking her to Westla.

How dare he. Shaara belongs in Altar. What is Shaarvan thinking? Her family, her home . . . curse that wolf's lair. I shall have it destroyed at once. I shall declare it full of vermin, a plague dwelling, or something equally demanding of its eradication.

It is unbearable that Shaarvan did not return Shaara to me. She is needed here. Her throne sits beside mine. Her bedchamber has been readied — the softest Shapechanger gray, with touches of blue amid the white pelt of the quagmire. Her room adjoins mine, of course, with a door that is hand-printed to me. And I have provided delicacies to please her, a mirror above her bed — I remembered how she wanted one, and *he* would not allow it — soft pillows for her dainty head, a computer station with suitable viewing materials, and an outer chamber, protectively walled, of course, with trees and flowers so she may walk about whenever she pleases. All this, I have prepared for my little innocent. How dare Shaarvan interfere.

Shaarvan has betrayed Altar by his choice. It is time for his demise. This, I shall tell my worms; I shall make my arguments such: It is well known that Shaarvan is heir to the throne of Westla. He journeys now to speak before the Highest concerning the uprising here in Altar. He will enlist Westla to battle against our new commoner government. They and their army of Shapechanger will wage a vile war — Shapechanger beast against proper man.

We must not let it come to that. It is obvious by this theft of *our* princess that Shaarvan's allegiance is to Westla and not to Altar. Shaarvan is in league with the mighty Westla. We, therefore, must order his death. I shall make it my first official decree. Let it be declared that Shaarvan is a traitor to the Kingdom of Altar.

The commoners will be suitably impressed that I am willing to sacrifice my own brother for their good. They will relish that "proper man" business. I can almost see them puffing up with pride. I shall use it infrequently. I do not wish the peasants to internalize it as a seed for defiance. Ah, but I worry needlessly. They are devoted to me.

And I spit on them. They are worms writhing in the dirt. Although they bathe (I command their daily skin purges, but it does them little good), they reek of soil and its baser elements. Their sweat has the stench of rotten bulbs, and it pours from them in streams of fear. How loathsome they are, and how I hate their constant attendance in the hall.

But how well they serve me. They will be the ones who will seize this Westlan spy, my irritating brother. I shall let them use the Pipe and witness the fall of the mighty prince of the Trendacons, heir to the corrupted and corrupting Westla, the planet where only Shapechanger reside. Yes, the plans are delightful. How perfectly everything fits together.

I shall feel such compassion for the grieving widow. She will need a protector. What would be more natural than that I should feel sympathy and concern? I shall comfort her and wed her. See, it is all so easy. When one is deserving, the stars line up the planets. They have done that for me.

What a comfort when it all clicks into place. I have waited so long for my princess. I have worked devotedly to arrange everything to please her, and soon she will be here. I shall keep her apart from the disgusting worms. I shall keep her innocent and free of their fetid company. I shall keep her isolate. Only my loving hands and smiles will she know. I shall give her soft words. She will learn to know how gentle a Shapechanger can be.

My lips moisten. My rod grows new life. Ah, Shaara, come to me, my princess. Let me feel the contours of your body. Let me touch those places that have previously been forbidden. Let our minds soar in the joining as I take you in the Shapechanger deep bonding. Soon, you will be mine.

Shaara

At last, we approached Westla. It was indeed as big as a planet, but its surface reflected the light from its nearby star almost blindingly. As we came nearer, I could see that, as Shaarvan had told me, Westla was a globe of metal, bulging with layers of air pocket all around it.

We headed for its huge north pole, which, from a distance, appeared to be merely a circle of dull olive-green. As we began our descent, I saw that inside the green area was a giant cat's eye. It stared at us unblinkingly. There was such a feeling of life to the eye that I forgot myself and called out, "It's looking at us!"

Shaarvan turned to give warning. I knew it was forbidden to speak in the control room, and I flashed an apology, left hand a gentle fist, right hand flat across it. Shaarvan acknowledged my gesture with a nod and turned away. He did not have time for me now. I was sorry I had distracted him.

I watched the eye grow bigger as we came closer and closer. When we were almost to the center of the diamond's black pupil, it severed into an opening for us. We continued on into it. I stared at the pieces of eye all around us. From that angle, they looked like individual petals of a black and green flower that we were diving into.

Shaarvan came over to stand by me. His hand rested on my shoulder, but his eyes watched our arrival. I could tell from his attitude that he no longer commanded the vessel. The huge monster eye must be pulling us in. I wondered that Shaarvan was not frightened by the pull of the great beast.

The ship lowered deeper into the eye, downward into the part that in a person would have held its brain, but below that, there was only a great, vast emptiness. Giant metal prongs, like the horns on a corlab beast, came at us from the side. The length of them was endless. I could not see the enormous creature to which they were attached, but a sudden fear flowed through me as I realized that the strength of them was going to spear right through the belly of our ship.

"Shaarvan! The monster is going to kill us!" I cried out, rising from my seat.

"Hush! It is only a robot, Shaara," Shaarvan said with a gentleness that drew my eyes away from the horns of the beast. Shaarvan's eyes were not dark with anger at my crying out but soft with understanding.

I could not doubt his words, but my eyes followed the metallic-looking horns until they swooped down under the belly of the ship. No screech of torn metal came to my ears. Instead, I felt the horns of the robot sweep us into a tender embrace and carry us to one side of the huge chamber.

Moments later, the horns released us, and Shaarvan was urging me down the descended ramp. I did not want to be disobedient, but I was dreadfully afraid to leave the ship. My hands locked onto the doorway, and I pleaded with Shaarvan not to force me outside. He shook his head at me, swept me up into his arms, and carried me out through the ship's portal and down the ramp. The tears were falling from my eyes, but I was looking all about me, searching for the great beast. The monster had evidently hidden from the Shapechanger god who carried me. I did not see it anywhere.

At the bottom of the ramp, Shaarvan put me back on my feet. I clung to his arm. I knew it was not safe to let go of my protector. The sky petals overhead, now covered by the monster's mucus, began to close. I watched them with only a hint of trepidation. They were slow-moving, but I saw that soon I would be trapped within another metal construction. The sky beyond, dark, with only a few spots of light twinkling down on us through that filmy substance, grew smaller and smaller. Sadly, I whispered my goodbye to the faraway children of Barquel.

Shaarvan pulled me forward, but I continued to watch as we walked. The flower was still closing. Its petals drew together as if preparing for night; the flower image faded, and again I saw the enormous eye of the tiger. The shiny black diamond center glared at me. I stopped looking then. It did not welcome me to Westla.

Shaarvan was becoming impatient with my slowness. I wondered as I scurried to keep up with him, if Barquel could still control my life inside this huge globe of metal. Could the great eye of the Shapechanger god protect me? Or could Shaarvan, the god at my side, who had already waged the battle against Barquel and his children? Would the force of the eye and Shaarvan's Power prevent interference from Barquel's will?

As we walked, Shaarvan's hand held mine more tightly than usual. I wondered if he feared I would try to run away. My eyes were darting everywhere, but I was not stupid. I knew there was no place to run. I looked up at Shaarvan to see if he was angry. He was pulling me faster than I could walk — at least, faster than I could walk and still see everything.

Shaarvan smiled down at me and teased, "No, I will not beat you today."

It was his joke, and he'd kept it up for far too long, in my opinion, yet I cringed whenever his eyes grew coldly gray or when he moved too fast towards me. The nightmares of Isandor still woke me up at times in a screaming panic, so I guess Shaarvan had reason. And, in a way, although it irritated me, it did reassure me that Shaarvan had not forgotten his promise.

Doors opened and closed before and behind us, and strange noises made clangs and bangs around us. At one point, my stomach complained at a change in gravity, and my ears hurt. It terrified me, but Shaarvan's manner was relaxed. "Be easy, Shaara. These fluctuations are necessary for the protection of the inhabitants. You will only feel them a while. When we have passed through the next few chambers, your ears will no longer bother you."

Shaarvan was right. The pain and the rushing noises soon stopped. Then came a misting, like in the exit of our bathroom, but this mist was a yellow vapor that permeated the air and clung to my skin. It left behind a film that imparted an odd sensation.

"We must strip and toss our clothes now, Shaara," Shaarvan told me. I obeyed him but with a lethargy that seemed foreign to my nature.

My brain was struggling for understanding through this fog of strangeness. People went naked on Westla? Shaarvan had not mentioned that. I should care. I should protest but to argue with Shaarvan would take too much of my energy. I did not speak. I was merely grateful the guards had not stepped inside with us.

When my dress and shoes were off, Shaarvan took them and his clothing and placed them in the recycler. Then, he drew me forward through another door into a chamber that doused us with a silvery spray. It pricked me and made my body ache. Instantly, my lethargy was dispelled, and I hungered. I knew that if I did not fling myself upon Shaarvan and demand release, I would sicken like a person too long denied sustenance.

I threw my arms around him and pressed against him. My lips attacked his, and my hands pulled his body closer. He laughed low and deep, and it set my body tingling deeper with desire. I reached down for that which would fulfill my need.

"Easy, Shaara. I have heard it affected women sometimes, but . . . "

I flashed the *no talking sign* at him and worked at getting him in me. Shaarvan lifted me up and leaned me against the wall. It was a time of frenzied need. We found our release and drove on, desperately craving each other.

We were both exhausted when another spray, a white one this time, delicately misted our bodies. Whatever had come over me slipped away, and I was embarrassed at my abandon. I could barely look at Shaarvan.

Shaarvan was sparse of wind, but he laughed softly between his heavy breaths. "My little wildcat," he said, "we shall have to come back here. You are a pleasure when you lust."

My face burned. I could not understand why I had urged Shaarvan to take me. That was a thing that only males did.

Shaarvan considered me a moment. His huge chest was no longer breathing rapidly. One last deep breath he drew in, and he was fully recovered. He reached out his hand and rubbed his knuckles down my cheek. His eyes still studied me. I knew he read my thoughts.

"Do not be embarrassed, my wife. It was the chemical in the air that impassioned you . . . but I am not adverse to your wanting me." Again, his hand stroked me. His finger brought up my chin to force my eyes to meet his. "Never feel you cannot initiate our joining, Shaara. Women also harbor desire."

Shaarvan's eyes were earnest. I thought of Frieda and how alive she'd been during the sacrifices of the Sky Demon. She had not acted like the sacrifices were a burden. Without pain, the joining was not unpleasant. Perhaps with Shaarvan . . .

The door opened, and we walked on. My mind continued to try to make sense out of what had occurred. Shaarvan had liked my initiating the act, but didn't that make me the dominant one? Had he really given me permission to control his actions? It was contrary to everything I'd understood about Shapechanger and about males.

As we entered the next room, Shaarvan interrupted my thoughts to order me to press my hand against a button. When I did, a wave of light descended over me. It tingled like the mists but was quickly gone. A package dropped. Shaarvan said that the clothes inside it were for me to wear.

I lifted out a dress of a creamy-white transparency. I slipped it on, but its bodice showed too clearly the dark outline of my breasts.

"Shaarvan, this is worse than what you made me wear on Freinana. Must I be half-naked?

Shaarvan turned to view me. "Sweet stars! There is more in the package, Shaara, look." He was laughing at my mistake, but there was nothing more in the wrappings. I was relieved when I found a second package lying at the bottom of the clothing machine. It contained a soft-green velvet overdress.

"Such a pity, wildcat," Shaarvan teased. "I prefer the other, but Westla is much more conservative than Altar."

I smiled at him. Tren had teased me, too, but Isandor had never done so. Was teasing a form of liking? Was it seeing someone as a person?

Shaarvan's shirt was sleeveless, and his muscled arms bulged. Around the thickest part of each arm, he wore a silver band of metallic elastic engraved with black etching. I touched one of the bands, wondering at its meaning.

"Males wear their rank on Westla," Shaarvan told me.

"Why can't I read the words? What determines your rank?"

"It is more or less the level I have tested at, and you cannot read it because it is in the ancient language of the Old Ones."

"They speak a different language?" I sighed and changed the subject. "Why do we both wear the same colors?"

"It is the color of Altar."

"What color does Freinana have?" I asked, puzzled. I did not know anything about Altar. Shouldn't my allegiance be to Freinana?

"There are few Shapechanger living on Freinana, Shaara. If they have a color, I do not know it." Shaarvan was busy fastening his shoes. He was not looking at me, but I could tell my questions were not yet bothering him.

"Shouldn't I find out so I can wear the correct colors?" I asked, confused. If identity markers were important, shouldn't . . .?

"You are Altarian." Shaarvan's voice sounded gruff. His eyes and scent told me my question had irritated him. He had told me I was no longer a slave, but that didn't seem to matter. I was still the property of a male with mood swings.

The guards rejoined us. Apparently, there were no more doors to travel through. We had entered into Westla. Surrounded by seven large men, none of whom were carrying weapons or acted as if they were on high alert, we continued through a shipboard maze of vast halls going every which way. Shaarvan headed down a slightly wider tunnel. The guards behind us kept time to Shaarvan's pace. I struggled to keep up with the much longer stride of male legs.

"How do you know your way?" I asked Shaarvan, hoping to slow him down as much as to assuage my curiosity.

"I have been here many times, Shaara," he told me. His eyes slid over me. Perhaps he saw that I was panting. I think he slowed somewhat. "But, there is another way, also. Do you see the phosphorous glow at the sides?"

"The lighting?"

"Yes, it glows in different patterns to direct visitors."

"You mean yellow to one place and green or something else to another?"

We had come to a stop, and I was staring fixedly at the strips, but I couldn't see any difference in the patterns.

Shaarvan smiled. "Sort of. A male's vision is slightly different than a female's. You might not be able to perceive the disparities."

"How stupid! Why not make it so both genders can see it?" I blurted out.

"Ah, Shaara. Even without your memories, you are the same," Shaarvan said, smiling at me. His knuckles once again stroked my face. I did not understand how I had pleased him.

"Women are always accompanied by a male, Shaara, even here on Westla. There is no need to make the patterns visible to both genders."

I grabbed Shaarvan's hand to halt it. The patterns he had been stroking on my cheeks were making concentration on the subject difficult.

"But what if . . ." I started to say.

There was warning in Shaarvan's eyes. I shut my mouth, frustrated again by the illogical viewpoints of males.

Shaarvan continued on, and we soon arrived at the entrance to a large chamber. People mingled about, displaying gaiety and lightness. Shaarvan ignored them and walked us past the crowd. We sauntered on into a huge chamber of stone and marble pillars. The columns were decorated with gold and silver embossed stars that shone from inward, lighted panels. It was all elegant and rich.

My eyes flitted everywhere, trying to take it in. On each of the three walls of the chamber, stretching upwards at least fifteen feet, were paintings of Saberey cats, the ancient symbol of the Shapechanger. The cats were in various poses, yet, in each one, mean rows of long teeth snarled ferociously, and their eyes stared down at me.

The wall in front of us was almost naked in comparison. Only an enormous abstract carpet hung against it. In front of the carpet sat a huge heavy copper seat upon a pedestal, with steps leading up to it. Sitting in the heavy chair was a rather large Shapechanger who was staring out into a line of people, all apparently waiting to speak to him.

I was curious about everything, but Shaarvan, as usual, flashed warnings to be quiet and to keep my eyes lowered. It was annoying. There was so much to see!

We did not enter the line of people. Shaarvan pushed us forward, cutting in and out, heading for the front. I expected someone to complain, but no one said anything. The crowd parted for him as if the people recognized his divinity.

Finally, we reached the front, and Shaarvan stood waiting for the Shapechanger in the copper seat to finish speaking to the couple standing before him. When he did, and the couple departed, Shaarvan pushed me forward, bowed his head (ordering me to do the same), and said, "My lord, First of Westla, I have returned."

There was no crown on the leader of Westla, yet it was obvious he ruled. His throne was not the only indicator, nor was his robe of gold. His eyes spoke his sovereignty, as did the noble carriage of his body. He awed me. I wanted to slide to the floor and bow to his feet, but Shaarvan's arm surrounded me, and the Shapechanger hold prevented me doing anything.

"So you have found her. Was she worth it?" The Shapechanger examined me. His eyes scanned me with interest. As much as I wanted to, I didn't look up.

Shaarvan's voice was low. He spoke only for the First of Westla. "She is worth it, my lord. Her soul, her mind, and her heart have a hold on me. Our link is great."

The lord's eyes were burning me. Surely, his eyes had the power of Barquel! The force of them was too concentrated. I fidgeted, no longer wanting to prostrate myself but only to flee. Shaarvan ignored my fear.

A silence spread into the chamber. Was everyone aware of the great Power of the one in front of me? He was not speaking, but his eyes no longer assaulted me. Now, the force of his regard was on Shaarvan. Would the god, who claimed he was my husband, cower?

"I feel a slight hesitation in your answer," the huge male said, breaking the long silence. "Was she damaged?"

Shaarvan shot a glance at me. I looked up to meet his eyes, but his had already returned to the great one. Yet Shaarvan stood as straight and firm as always. He didn't seem intimidated by the god in the huge copper seat.

"My wife was mindwiped," Shaarvan answered. "She remembers nothing, not even our son."

I sighed heavily, wishing Shaarvan would not talk about my problems so openly. There was a whole chamber of ears listening. Yet I said nothing. I couldn't speak with the great one sitting there before me.

As Shaarvan began to tell my story, I let my mind drift to memories of Crimson Black. I wished I were free that very moment to feel the wind in my face and the landoor's strong muscles as they gathered before the spring of a jump.

"Her name is Shaara, is it not?" the god asked.

Crimson Black and the jump dissolved like ice in the sun. The vapors shot upwards, leaving me nothing but an empty wish.

Beside me, Shaarvan nodded.

"Come to me, Shaara." The command echoed in the vastness of the chamber. The voice, heavy and full, laid an urgency to the summons. An incredible feeling of Power amplified the order. My ears rang from the sound of it. Of course, it terrified me. I had no wish to go closer to this mighty god.

But I had no choice. Shaarvan had dropped his arm from my shoulder and flashed the gesture for obedience. Slowly and cautiously, I climbed the first step of the dais.

"You fear me, Shaara." Again, the voice echoed through the enormous chamber and into my mind. "I can feel it. Why do you fear me?"

His observation was not deep. He could probably see my legs quaking. And what a silly question. I drew a calming breath and kept my eyes very lowered. "The Powerful are always to be feared, my lord."

"How do you mean Powerful?" he boomed out.

I shot a glance at his face. He gave me no expression. I felt and smelled no anger in him. But his mind was so heavily guarded I could not read his mood. Nor could I guess what he wanted from me.

"I am no stronger than Shaarvan," the god continued before I had a chance to answer him. Again, I tried to read him, pushing harder against the block. It was like being blind in an unfamiliar room or being with Shaarvan when he shut me out. I knew that Shaarvan would not help me with this. He would stand there and let the stranger embarrass me in front of all the people. Why? What was this all about?

Once more, I took a calming breath, and I spoke guardedly. "There is a force that glows about you, my lord."

"Where did you get this girl, Shaarvan?" the strange lord roared out.

The loudness of his voice made me take a step backwards. Then I quivered worse, fearing he would erupt in anger at my disobedience.

"Terra, like my mother, like your wife," Shaarvan responded calmly.

"Has she ever been measured?"

"No, not yet. I shall have her tested while we are here."

Neither mentioned my retreat — perhaps they hadn't noticed. Had I answered correctly? I wished they would stop talking to each other and tell me what to do.

"Good," said the god in a thunderous voice. His eyes once more pierced me. I could feel their power, strong as the rays of Barquel at half-day.

"Shaara, come here and look up," the god demanded. He reached out for my hand and pulled me close until my knees touched his.

I quivered with fear. Proximity was always a threat, but touching? That was forbidden. Why would Shaarvan allow it?

To look a Shapechanger in the eyes, that perhaps was the worst. And this great god, how could I allow that? Yet, how could I defy him?

I looked back at Shaarvan, asking for guidance. He nodded and said, "Obey him, Shaara. Obey him in all he *says*." Shaarvan stressed "says" like that was the key word.

I inhaled deeply, then raised my eyes. The god was not gentle. He slammed into my soul. It didn't hurt me. It was more like having someone dive in and swallow your mind. I was inside him, and his thoughts were all about me, descending like soft-tipped arrows in all directions, arrows that kneaded my brain and explored me.

I saw flashes of my memories — landoors, Tren, the slaver — a kaleidoscope of recollections, most passing so quickly, they were blurred. There was no sharing in it. I received nothing back from the god. His thoughts did not blend with mine. He only took.

I should have been terrified by the process, but he allowed no fear. And there was never any pain. In fact, other than the invasion of my privacy, the sensation was not unpleasant. Where he touched, a warmth, almost a pleasurable sensation, lingered.

When he withdrew, it was instant, like tiny pebbles swooped up into one's hand. Yet, he did not release me completely. His mind still held the reins.

He spoke to me then. I heard his commands, but his lips didn't move. The words badgered me, urging, demanding. "Come closer, touch my face, lay your lips on mine."

The man was evil. I belonged to Shaarvan. Shaarvan owned me. How could this god ask me to betray Shaarvan? Didn't Shapechanger honor their vows?

"No!" I cried out and flung myself away, retreating down the stairs to hurl my body into Shaarvan's arms.

Shaarvan's arms enclosed me, sheltered. He didn't seem angry. His lips kissed my forehead.

"By all the stars in heaven, she did it!" the god on the throne burst out.

Shaarvan nodded. His arms tightened, but he was not cutting off my air. His arms were safety, not punishment.

"I was sure she would be able to. The Shapechanger Power in her is very strong," Shaarvan said with a rooster's crow of pride.

The high god stood and walked towards us. I could feel his approach, but I didn't look up. I whimpered and attempted to bury my face deeper into Shaarvan's chest.

The god placed his hand on my shoulder. I flinched but didn't move otherwise. Where was there left to go?

"Be easy, Shaara. Not for all the ships on Altar would I take you from Shaarvan. I frightened you badly, and I am sorry for that. But it was only a test. I was measuring your Power, little one. I shall not harm you. You are safe with me."

I looked up at Shaarvan, questioning him with my eyes. He smiled down at me. "Tem is a Trendacons, Shaara. He is my father's brother."

Shaarvan turned me to face the great god. I still felt the male's Power, but the force was dimmed. It did not shine so fiercely.

"She must be trained, Shaarvan," Tem said, staring at me. "She projected her outrage at least three rooms over. She is remarkable. You were correct about her value.

"Westla needs her. She must give us many sons — at least three. We require her strength and yours for the lineage. And, if little Shaarac tests as high as I predict, perhaps we shall force her to twin. There is a blackness that threatens our future, Shaarvan. Many will die. We need the Power of such offspring."

Tem's eyes sought mine. "Look up, Shaara. I promise I shall not harm you."

I was not eager to meet the male's eyes again, but Shaarvan's hand on my chin gave me no choice.

"Welcome to Westla, Shaara. I greet you as the Highest and as your kin." He leaned forward and touched his lips to my brow. I was shocked by it, but I felt no tenseness in Shaarvan. As they continued to talk, I finally relaxed.

The gods are strong. I had felt their power. What did it mean to have two of them interacting with me? Was it good luck, or was I in great danger?

I studied the new god. There was the look of Shaarvan in him. He did not have Shaarvan's dimples, but his smile was familiar, and his Power had the flavor of Shaarvan's.

The great god caught me studying him, and he smiled. His lips were full like Shaarvan's and probably just as capable of giving pleasure, but I felt no urge to verify such a thought. His teeth were straight, white, and perfect, with only the hint of the Saberey, which I was fairly sure he would Shapechange into at any time I crossed him.

He was probably almost twice Shaarvan's age, but he was a handsome man. I blushed as his eyes acknowledged the compliment. I looked away.

The two males had much to discuss. I let their words flow around me as my eyes traveled about the huge hall. The crowd behind us were babbling on — laughing and socializing as if it were a party they were attending. Here and there, a louder voice than the others broke through the background noise. Once, a woman's high-pitched cackle pierced the air. I let the voices drift about me.

My eyes focused on the tapestry behind the throne. At first, I had believed it to be only blotches of color — a woven mixture of lovely greens, browns, and blue — but as I stared, a forest of trees came alive, and the trees began to call to me. One tree, more centered than the others and lusciously bowered in variegated greens, told me of the agony of dreams unfilled and of impossibilities. Its branches stretched towards the heavens where the stars sang their songs, and it yearned. I could see the awful straining of its roots as it strove to leave behind what was necessary for its life.

"Shaara and I have hopes," Shaarvan was saying. I looked up at his face. His eyes smiled down at me.

"I hope also, Shaarvan, that the medics will be able to help. I shall go with you. Perhaps my presence will assist," the great god said.

Shaarvan's use of my newest name called me from the forest. I listened as Shaarvan told Tem that he would return soon to talk more. I looked up at him, wondering what it was that he would not discuss in front of me.

We left, then. Shaarvan took me to visit his aunt. She was the twin sister of Shaarvan's mother, I was told. I did not remember Shaarvan's mother, but I knew that Teea and I were supposed to be friends.

We left the god's huge chamber, passing through great wooden doors that glowed with a wondrous luster. Shaarvan had to physically open them. No buttons to push, no automatic withdrawal to the sides. I admired the doors even more for their obstinacy.

The chamber we had entered was lined with the same rich dark wood, but engravings had been carved on it. I could almost feel the wood's outrage. I wished I were tall enough to touch it. I was sure it would tell me of its forest and its life before the Shapechanger had marred its beauty.

Shaarvan was talking to the guards. I turned and walked back to the great doors. I placed my hand on its surface and closed my eyes.

"Shaara, what are you doing? Do you think you can leave? These doors may not shock you, but that does not mean you are free."

Free? When had I ever been free? I started to explain, but what could I say? Wood did not speak. What I had done made no sense.

Shaarvan didn't wait for me to say anything. He lectured on about the guards being watchful and how I was not to attempt to leave while he was gone.

His voice continued, stern and forceful, warning me of consequences, but it was only the part about 'his being gone' that caught my attention. I glanced back at the guards. Only three of them had followed us into the chamber. The others must be on the other side. The men's eyes were as cold as a winter morning. Not unseeing as on the ship, but. . . Shapechanger. How could that be? Shapechanger were all at least minor gods, yet these were Shaarvan's men, treated almost like servants.

Shaarvan saw my glance, although he wasn't reading my thoughts. His knuckles caressed me. "I shall not take chances with you again, my wife. Even on Westla, guards will be a constant. These are Tem's most loyal aides. The men who accompanied us to the Great Hall returned to the ship."

Shaarvan gave me a quick kiss, urged me to relax while I became acquainted with my aunt, then bade me goodbye.

Temina, as she was called, had not come out to greet us. As Shaarvan closed the wooden doors behind me, I went forward into the strange hall ahead in search of her. The guards silently followed.

Teea

The meetings have continued at my house. As I suspected, the Shapechanger were willing to allow me to stay in the room, assisting them in their endeavors to touch Tevor's mind. Whether they were able or not to meet his mind, they did not share with me. But, there must have been some element of productivity because they increased the number of consultations.

It satisfies me greatly that I am able to attend. I sit, each time, in my seat beside Tevor and keep my eyes lowered, my lips stilled. The males find no fault in me, but I am grateful they do not read my mind. It is alive with curiosity, excitement, and the knowledge that I am privileged to hear their plans.

Only Starnkor, my Second, looks suspiciously at me. He is attuned to me, bonded as he is. He, alone, protests my involvement. For him, I curl my hair, pinch my cheeks and distract him with shy smiles and eyes widened with innocence.

I dare do nothing more. Starnkor is a big problem in other ways. Shapechanger believe that a woman unfrequented by her husband's prowess is a woman who goes mad with unruly behaviors. Starnkor, as Tevor's Second, has already moved into the house to guard me. I had no say in that nor in the way his eyes follow me about.

I know he watches for signs I am on the edge, but who would not be, with all that is going on about us? Still, I monitor my calmness and practice the deep-breathing exercises that Tevor long ago drilled into me. I will do nothing to warrant Starnkor's taking me or what Tevor used to call with a twinkle in his eye, 'sexual management.'

Shaara

Tem's wife was sitting in a large room with dark wood, wood exactly like the double doors I'd admired. But in this room, no carvings marred the surface of the deep, rich grains. The natural patterns in it were intensely inviting. I could not help stretching out my hand to touch, even if my doing so broke with another of the strange Shapechanger traditions that I had yet to learn or, more possibly, forgotten.

Too long, I stood before the wood, my hand attached in wonder, but curiosity began to tickle my senses. Why was Temina still silent? Why had she not greeted me, criticized me, or even asked who I was and what I was doing in her rooms?

Recessed lighting gave the wood a shine that held my eyes, but, unfortunately, it also left the center of the room dark. I shut my eyes a moment to improve their sight, then walked closer to the presence I felt. She sat on a low-backed chair exactly in the middle of the room. As I approached, I saw her eyes peer up at me, but she still said nothing.

I was struck by her beauty. Her hair was healthy and thick, full of waves, and very shiny. It was fading into soft grays and lay in wisps about her face as if she often ran her fingers though its strands, disheveling it.

I stopped, stood in front of her, and waited for her to welcome me. Her brow wrinkled up, but not in a friendly way. The lines across it spoke of sadness and something I couldn't yet identify.

At last, she spoke, but not to me, but to the guards who had followed me in. "Get out of here," she screamed. "No males allowed."

I gasped, which drew her eyes for a moment. Then she glared at the guards, who had not only ignored her wishes but taken a step closer.

The woman cackled rudely, then threw a pillow at them. It was a small brown one. It fell short, landing on the floor about a foot away. The guards didn't react.

I had no clue as to proper etiquette. Was I supposed to pick up the pillow? Should I ignore her temper tantrum? Should I retreat, taking myself and the guards away?

I inhaled deeply to calm myself, then stared down at the floor. Silence. The silence of a forest unpopulated by bird song, a windless forest, a place of perfect stillness. Temina's chamber must be sound-proofed. No noise from beyond the wooden doors permeated from outside. I took another deep breath, and ignoring the protocol I'd been drilled with, I said, "I am told you are called Temina. Shaarvan, your nephew, calls me Shaara. I am sorry to disturb you if you are not well. Please, tell me if you would like me to leave."

"xxxxx xxxxx xxx," she said, but I couldn't understand.

For a long moment, Temina glared. I began to think she would not answer. Then, she waved her hand in the direction of a chair and said, "Sit down, wife of Shaarvan."

I did, then waited. Again, the silence stretched. I'd just decided that perhaps she was waiting for me to speak when she ordered me to get up and serve drinks.

A side table over against one of the walls held glasses, and what I assumed was fruit juice, filled a tall, slender pitcher. I poured a glass for each of us, served Temina, and sat down, glass in hand. I did not think Westla would treat a Shapechanger's wife as a slave, but I knew so little of the world, as Shaarvan had told me frequently. And I didn't mind. It was Shaarvan who I feared might have objected.

Temina drank her juice but said nothing else. Her silence should have been well-received, for I was tired from our travels and the newness of everything around me, but there were undercurrents that were pricking at me. The woman's silence discomforted.

At last, I sought answers. "Temina, have I done something that you hold against me?"

Her mouth twisted into ugliness, and she spat out words in Altarian. "You don't even speak our language, you little slave whore! You're not from Terra. You have lied."

That was the worst insult you could give a Shapechanger — not the slave part, but the lying.

I put down my drink and sat in silence. I didn't understand Temina's accusation. I hadn't told her I was Terran. If she'd asked, I would have said I was Freinanan, even though Shaarvan kept telling me that wasn't true.

Again, the silence stretched. Temina spent her time staring up at the ceiling. I lifted my eyes and found what drew hers.

Stars were etched into the ceiling — like a small piece of the heavens. There were patterns, constellations I had never seen, yet I knew them all as the sons of Barquel.

Temina rose. I was surprised; I'd thought she couldn't walk, but she was as agile as a young girl. She turned off all the lights and sat back down. Together, she and I remained like that in a great silence, staring up at her artificial sky.

The patterns shifted so slowly it took a while before I realized that I was wrong. The stars were actually real. Like in my room on Freinana, where I'd sat watching their slow-moving dance through the night, the two of us drank in the nourishment of tranquility. Our silence ebbed into peacefulness, and I saw that the anger of Temina's eyes slowly faded.

Shaarvan and Tem entered the chamber later. I rose and walked to Shaarvan. At his urging, I said goodbye to Temina, but she chose not to answer. As we passed through the doorway, I tried once more to use the formality of Freinana.

"I thank you for your hospitality," I said. It was the sentence I'd heard guests use so many times with Frieda. I hoped it was appropriate on Westla.

Unfortunately, the thanks was too close to a lie. Two steps further, the sickness came. I could not retract my thanks. It would insult Tem. Such a tiny bit of a falsehood, surely I could get by with it. But pain ripped my stomach. I doubled over, knowing an eruption was coming.

"Shaara, did you lie? Do not harbor it,' Shaarvan said. "Tell the truth."

"I cannot, Shaarvan. It would not be . . ."

"Polite? You are with Shapechanger. Obey."

My eyes dropped in embarrassment. "There was no hospitality," I muttered.

"Good girl! Tem knows it. He told me I should not have left you there, but I did not realize Temina had worsened. I am sorry, Shaara."

"Thank you. Thank you for caring."

The great god had walked up behind us. He cleared his throat. "If you two are finished being affectionate . . ."

"Sorry, Uncle," Shaarvan said, but his hand still held mine, and his eyes were warm.

"I would like to apologize to your charming wife for the rudeness of my Temina," Tem said. "You see, like you, Shaara, Temina was difficult. She fought everything Shapechanger. I thought it meant she was strong, but when I placed her in the Solitary, her mind could not endure the punishment. We know now that young girls do not tolerate

Transition well, but we knew little of Earth then. Temina was only sixteen. Neither Shapechanger magic nor our biological research has been able to help her."

He'd said the words almost effortlessly, but I could read the sorrow in his soul. His words were costly, and his pain was great.

"We Shapechanger are not as heartless as is often said. I could not give Temina away, as many urged me. She was unable to carry a child. Because of that, she can never be fully Shapechanger, but I continue to care for her, and I shall feel a connection with her always."

This great god, ruler of a whole artificial planet, Shapechanger, and male — all that, I held against him. But he cared about his wife. In that moment, I forgave him for his offenses. I stretched out my hand and touched his arm.

"I am sorry," I said. His eyes held vast Power, but he did not hurt me when he stared into mine. A voice inside my mind said only, "Thank you, child."

In Freinana, I had known of those who suffered from mental disorders. They were shunned and spoken of in whispers. In Freinana, madness traveled in families. Did it here as well? Tem had said that Temina was unbalanced only because she'd been too young, but if Teea had survived, why had Temina not done so?

Were there other reasons for madness? Hadn't Shaarvan called Thenos mad? Could this madness crop up in the sons, the nephews . . . in Shaarac? I kept my eyes lowered so neither could read my thoughts, but it did no good.

"She is quick," Tem said to Shaarvan, and I realized he had read my thoughts despite my precautions. "No, Shaara, there are no genes of madness in your lineage. The Trendacons have all been tested. Only Temina — because I held her in isolation at too young an age, and Thenos — because of his drug use, have had any problems."

I sighed from relief. I had lived through Isandor's madness. I did not believe I could tolerate another's.

It is wise that Barquel never allows us to know the future. One learns to tolerate more when it is served only a day at a time.

Thenos

Do not say that I am an unsympathetic Shapechanger. Yesterday, I journeyed to the house of my parents. I visited my father, a lump of clay atop his bed. I feigned an interest in his illness and took the opportunity to test his mind Power. The rumors of his activities seem to be falsely optimistic. My father seems quite unlikely to rise up from his deathbed and strike me down.

My mother seems worried overly much. Of course, she loves Tevor in her womanly way, and that is the cause of most of her distress, but I think the Shapechanger Warlord, Starnkor also keeps her on edge. It is easy to see that he waits for her as eagerly as a tiger awaits the first leap on his fear-frozen prey. It will not be long before Starnkor takes his due. Father planned well.

Starnkor pleases me. He is stern and levelheaded. He will not allow my mother to "wear the pants," my father's expression, which I find quite suitable for Mother's frequent uprisings. Starnkor will soon teach Teea the proper role of a Shapechanger's wife, of that I have little doubt. Knowing what good friends my mother and my little Shaara are, I heartily approve. I would not want my princess contaminated by the unruliness of my mother.

I shall have a talk with Starnkor today and let him know that I approve of a strong hand with Teea. I shall also inform him that it is time for him to claim a Second's rights. By the stars — what is he waiting for?

Shaara

We walked from Temina's house through corridors of blank, white walls. There were also some tunnels, hallways, and passages that moved underneath us as we stood. Through it all, the two males kept up their conversation, discussing Westlan politics and other things I didn't understand.

We entered through a small portal, and as my eyes scanned the chamber, I saw that people were sitting on white-rimmed chairs that looked stiff and uncomfortable. As we stepped forward, the eyes of many turned towards us but then quickly looked away as if acknowledging that it was rude to stare.

Tem didn't seem to be aware of them. He strode over to a computer built into the wall without a glance around him. Shaarvan pulled me along until all three of us stood peering down at the screen. Tem's fingers flew across the keyboard.

The furtive eyes of the crowd drew my attention. I found it interesting that nobody had overtly shown interest in Tem's entrance. No one had stood up to bow or greet him as I would have thought the honor of his position demanded. They had not even given him the respectful nod Tren would have received on Freinana. (Of course, if Tren had walked into the room, half of the people would have fled.)

Shaarvan suddenly jerked me about as if I had been a child's cloth doll. I had done nothing wrong, but the fierceness of his gaze made me drop my eyes to the ground. It was not a minute later, a door slid open, and a male in a pale blue-hooded robe was waving us in.

Shaarvan pulled me forward. Stupidly, I halted to ask about the others who had been there first. I should have kept silent. Shaarvan's hand rose and cupped my neck.

The blue-robed one led us deep into the inward regions of the medic's offices. After a series of tunnel turns and a string of closed doors, we entered into a large chamber, where a panel of doctors in the same summer-sky wardrobe were sitting. The eyes of the medics surveyed us as if we were specimens of interest. We stood in silence.

We were standing on a stage, and a light was focused blindingly at us. I attempted to gaze down at the doctors, wondering at their thoughts and what they would do, but the hand on my neck squeezed a warning. I lowered my eyes.

The male who had led us into the chamber greeted us. He carried a chair over to Tem and then disappeared. Shaarvan and I remained standing.

One by one, the doctors stood up, gave a brief nod to Tem, greeted Shaarvan, and introduced themselves. It was quite obvious I was not included in the formalities, nor was one of the medics in the back row. He, alone, did not stand and introduce himself or greet Tem and Shaarvan. I wondered why, and as I pretended to study the gray-speckled carpeting, my eyes secretly studied the silent one.

There was a force about him that plagued me. His eyes glowed strangely, although I suspected it was merely the reflection of the light that beamed so blindingly in our direction. Yet, there was some hidden danger in his regard. I had no understanding of how I knew it to be true, but it was a truth that my body recognized as a threat, as clearly as an orange-red flame of fire warned me not to touch it.

I dared the pain of the neck grip to look fully into the eyes of the silent one, but doing so caused a strange spasm in my stomach. I cried out from the pain.

"Behave!" Shaarvan hissed at me.

Obediently, my eyes fell. I didn't want to provoke Shaarvan further. I'd learned something that almost took my breath away or at least gave me much to ponder. The silent one, whose force had almost equaled Tem's or Shaarvan's, was *female*!

One of the doctors, an old, gray-haired, cold-eyed Shapechanger, rose and came towards us. As he neared, his eyes peered at me like I was a medical curiosity he'd like to dissect. He told Shaarvan that in order to help me, they must first analyze my problem. He showed Shaarvan a hand instrument and said it was a brain scanner, which would give the medics a picture of what had gone wrong in my brain.

The metal instrument was shiny as a new water gauge and no longer than a double hand span. At the top of it, the part away from the doctor's hand, lay a clear bubble of glass. Maybe it wouldn't hurt. However, I knew from my own history that pain rarely came from the instrument but from the hand that held it.

The doctor lifted the brain scanner high over my head. I cowered backward, not trusting it or the man. Shaarvan's grip on my neck was all that kept me from fleeing.

The medic attempted to force his way into my mind. I fought that, too, in spite of Shaarvan's grip. "You will be still. Obey me," he ordered brusquely.

Again, the doctor brought the instrument close. A whirring noise, like the faint rumble of faraway thunder, growled out of the tool. I ignored both Shapechanger command and Shaarvan's grip. No one had given me cause to trust them.

As the scanner rumbled louder, my heart beat faster. No words of comfort came from the one who called himself my husband. Anger strengthened me. I remembered how often Tren had reassured me when the world seemed strange and threatening. Tren would not have been so cold.

Anger buoyed me. I raised my chin and glared. The neck grip was agony, but I had lived through worse.

But the instrument's rumbling grew no more ominous. Other than Shaarvan's rough treatment, I felt no pain. A screen on the wall to our right lit up. Blue lines ran up and down like ground worms exposed to the light. The brusque doctor told the watchers the worms were my thoughts (of course, he called them "treznos," not worms). I hoped no one could tell what the blue worms were thinking or that their writhing was from anger.

Next, a second screen flared into life. The doctor said it showed which areas processed, stored, and assessed information. A second medic remarked on how little movement there was in my information storage. Most of it was dark.

I thought the show was really rather stupid. If the little blue worms weren't crawling around in my storage area, it still didn't tell me how to get my memories back.

A sudden burst of laughter broke through the medical babble. All eyes turned to view the female, although she'd become strangely quiet again. The medics ignored her outburst. The discussions continued.

A different doctor stood up and strode forward. This one told Shaarvan that a chemical analysis machine was required. He joined the first doctor with a second scanner. Once more, I felt Shaarvan's neck grip tighten, although this time, I had not fought.

This machine was placed on my forehead. I flinched at contact, but again, there was no pain, only an icy coldness as if the instrument had been stored in snow. It displayed its results on the wall, but showed no wiggling blue worms, only symbols and strings of numbers. I couldn't read it, but I doubted its results helped either. It certainly didn't expand my memory.

Shaarvan loosened his grip, and I breathed a sigh. I risked a glance. He was watching the doctors with the same look he got when I wasted his time with too many questions. How much longer would he allow the medical babble to continue before he exploded with impatience?

"You say she remembers the Altarian language but not her native one? That is interesting," said one of the doctors, still sitting on a stool staring at the blue squiggles.

"Yes, most interesting," agreed another.

"Why would the drug have erased her native language?" another blue robe asked.

"The primary utilization theory seems to . . ."

"Primary utilization theory! It obviously proves the Displacement Analogy Symbiosis Theory. She . . ."

A doctor, who had not spoken yet, began to sputter and make disparaging noises. He burst up like a rearing colt. "What is obvious is the sophistication her abductors implemented in this usage of language. Had they desired the girl speechless or ignorant of the Universal, they would have done so."

"But it proves . . ."

"It proves nothing. She speaks Altarian because she was allowed to retain Altarian," said the medic abruptly.

"I can read Altarian, too!" I blurted out, forgetting how close Shaarvan stood.

"Shaara!" Shaarvan's voice was a lash. I lowered my eyes even before I felt the resumption of the neck grip.

"No, allow her to speak when she wants," one doctor said. "Perhaps her chatter will prove useful."

Shaarvan growled. He turned me slightly, then shook his head. "You know better than that, wife. I shall allow you to speak because they ask it, but you will be punished later."

He dropped his hand. Cautiously, I rubbed at the back of my neck.

"Girl child," came the croak of an ancient voice. The silent one, the female, stood up then and flung the hood off her cloak.

I gasped, amazed she'd spoken.

"Girl child," she said again. "Have you Shapechanged?"

I looked at Shaarvan, then answered when he flashed consent. "I don't think so."

A million questions boiled within me. Why was a woman here? Where was her husband? Why did all the males look at her, waiting for her words? Why was she allowed to speak? Why did she have the feeling of Power?

The old crone met my eyes. Hers were laughing.

I could see her clearly now. She was a wrinkly older woman, but the wrinkles were the good kind — laugh lines, character lines, lines that spoke of a life fully-lived. She was bowed only slightly by age, yet she held herself with pride and a firm strength of will. She was the first woman I'd ever seen with hair cropped short as a man's.

The ancient laughed, smiled at me, then stared at Shaarvan. "And you, Stealer of Women, what do you say?" she demanded.

Shaarvan stiffened. His jaw tightened, his eyes darkened, but he answered. "No, she has not been ready."

The old crone laughed. Her high-pitched cackle echoed around the chamber. No one moved. The echo died slowly. "In the lore of the families," she said, "there was once a case of a brainwipe. Shapechange purged its wipe."

Shaarvan looked at me. "If she no longer remembers how to walk the dreams, how then can she Shapechange?"

Once more, the air was torn by a strident cackle. "A Shapechanger male in his prime asking *me* how to train a young female?"

Her laugh, this time, was even more bold and raucous. She stripped off the blue robe of the doctors and flung it at the nearest chair. Clothed in a gown of gold that writhed with the movement of her slender limbs, she strode closer.

She mounted the steps of the stage, then approached to stare fully into my face. Again, I felt the Power within her. I could scarcely breathe. She held my eyes a moment, probing deeply. "All right, I shall answer you, Woman Bully. You must *force* her. It is the only way."

She was still watching me. Her eyes laughed at my shock. She opened her mouth wide in a grin that showed a mouthful of perfect teeth. Then she turned to the doctors with distain.

"After all you medics take your pretty pictures and discuss and analyze them, you will still have no answers for Tem's nephew. That is why I chose to come. I do not want you prying further into the girl's mind with your worthless toys. This one will be mine."

Shaarvan grew rigid as she spoke. With her final words, his arm swung about me, and he pulled me close.

"No!" he growled. "She is my *wife,* Tessa. She will never be yours."

What were they talking about? Who was this Tessa? What did she mean that I had to Shapechange? She thought I could change into a cat like the males? How?

I was exhausted. First the landing, then the scene with Tem, and later all the strangeness with his wife, and then this? All I wanted to do was crawl into Crimson's stall and sleep in the hay. I needed my quiet corner with Crimson's warm breath blowing down my neck.

The medics began to talk among themselves. I do not think they listened to each other. Shaarvan clutched me against him. I lay my head on his chest and listened to the strong beat of the life that flowed within him. I felt his lips on my neck. His warm breath, so much like Crimson's, began to calm my thoughts.

I closed my eyes and let the sound of the arguments slip away.

At last, one of the doctors stood. "We would like to tell you the Priestess is wrong, but she never is. There is no medical antidote for brainwipe. Do what Tessa says. Make the girl Shapechange. It is your best hope."

I could feel the tenseness of Shaarvan's muscles and the too rapid rise and fall of his heavy chest. It was as if, with each breath, he fought for calm. He reached out to grip my arm above the elbow. I lowered my eyes and gave him no excuse for roughness.

Without a word to the doctors, Tem, or the old crone, Shaarvan, still gripping my arm as if he feared I would attempt to pull free, led me out of the chamber.

We walked no further than the place where the corridor turned before a strident voice yelled out, "Wait!"

The Priestess came running. "Shaara *must* train with me," she demanded.

The grip on my arm tightened. I let out a whimper. Shaarvan's eyes flashed, and I stared at the floor.

"What a waste," said the scratchy voice. "You do not even feel what is in her."

I could not help looking up then, straight into her eyes. Like the depths of the ocean, I sank deeper and deeper. I was looking into a window that could show me my future. It was stretched out before me, picture after picture. If I could only look deeper, just a little further, I would read that . . .

Something prevented it, like a board strung across the way. If only I could move it aside, just a little way, I would see . . .

"Let her be," ordered Shaarvan. It was he who pulled me back. I knew the feel of his Power.

"Tessa, she is married," Tem told her. He had come up from behind and was attempting to squeeze in between Tessa and Shaarvan. "The girl cannot train with you."

I was aware of everything, but inside, I was still focused on what I'd almost seen. Silently, I fought Shaarvan's will. I couldn't have done so had he been fully aware, but he was concentrating on Tessa and on the words of Tem.

I moved the board, inch by inch, to the side. There, beyond it, was my future. I peered in. . .

"Stop it, Shaara!" Shaarvan ordered.

The board shattered. I was falling into the water. It was cold as an ice-laced stream. I couldn't breathe. Water filled my mouth. My shivers were all that were . . .

A hand reached out, an old hand — wrinkled, pillaged by time. Should I trust it?

"Tessa, release her," I heard Shaarvan say.

But I could breathe again, then. There was no water, but Shapechanger magic danced all about me, a fog of Power, pushing. I swayed in Shaarvan's arms.

"It is all right, Shaara. I have broken you free," he whispered into my ear, and his lips touched my skin.

I was safe. I drew Shaarvan's arms even tighter around me and leaned back against him. I stared at the woman. Her gray-black eyes still peered into me. I remembered the water and shivered. "Why did you do that?" I asked.

I was as surprised as Shaarvan and Tem when the question slipped out and even more astonished when Shaarvan did not flash his signs or yell at me. Both he and Tem remained strangely silent.

"Altarian Princess," Tessa said. "You are a pawn of possibilities. Yet, you hold no understanding. You *must* train with me."

She was right. I didn't understand any of this — especially what was happening in the mist and in Shaarvan's silence.

Tessa's eyes were growing bigger than her face — and darkening. She threw back her head and laughed. "The future is a prism in you, little Shaara. In every direction lies a different road." Her hand lifted and waved an eerily lighted path before my eyes.

"You need protection. You are splintered into compartments. There is no Shaara."

That was exactly how I felt! Splintered into compartments and lost inside them!

"Who are you?" I cried. "Why do you know me? What have you done to Shaarvan?"

"I am the memories and the Power of Shapechanger women. I know you because you are one of us. I know the possibilities of what you *may* become."

"What have you done to the one who calls himself my husband? Do you hold Power over him?"

"Sadly, not for long, child. We, the women, the Priestesses of Westla, we can pool our Power to overcome a male, but this male of yours is strong."

Her eyes probed me deeper. I was terrified she would consume me with her strength, but she laughed at my fear. "We shall do no harm to you, child. As Shaarvan follows Tem, so must you follow me. It is written. You *will* train. Remember that."

Shaarvan reached out and pulled me against his chest. He seemed not to know he'd been frozen. "Do not interfere with my training of Shaara. That is forbidden, Tessa. She is mine."

"Temper, temper, male," said the crone. "This one is special. Train her as you like, but permit her to train with me. She *must* start Priestess training."

The circle of Power was swirling angrily about us. I clung to Shaarvan's arms in confusion. I was beginning to believe the circling wind cloud was a sand demon. I'd heard of such things when I'd lived on Freinana.

Tem stepped sideways to stand in front of me protectively. "You brave much for this girl,"he said. "Why?"

I was glad the two gods were there to fight for me, but was the woman a friend or a foe? Was she responsible for the sand demon?

"In the girl lies our future. It is written in her paths. You know it, Tem. Why do you keep it from your nephew?"

Was she fighting for me? The sand demon was lessening, its winds calming. But how had a sand demon entered Westla?

"Enough, Tessa. You have exceeded your limit. Do not take us both on. You would fail," Tem warned her.

A burst of laughter — swirling sands stilled.

"Silly males. I have no wish to take this child from you. She is not ready for that. I merely wish to test her. She is yours, Shaarvan, for as long as you can keep her. But she must begin training *now*. Tell him that, Tem. Insist on it, or there will be trouble. And it has been a long time since the Priestesses warred with the Highest. Let us not bring strife to Westla."

"Do not threaten, Priestess," Shaarvan roared. "There is only one goal for Shaara. You have stated that yourself."

"And if all roads lead to the city?" Tessa cackled.

"Tessa, you are Chief Priestess, but you are still a woman. You cannot teach her to Shapechange. Only her mate can do that," Tem reminded her.

I'd been quiet, listening to them argue, understanding little, but I understood one thing: Tessa, a female, had Power here on Westla, and she'd killed a sand demon. A male could not do that. Frieda had told me so. The woman had other knowledge, too, knowledge that males listened to. If she could help me understand who I was and who I could be, I knew I wanted to learn from her.

"Please, Shaarvan, please let me," I cried, turning in his arms to look up. Even when I saw the rage there, I didn't stop. "Please, Shaarvan, please, permit it."

The flash of his anger simmered down as he saw my tears. But, even though his eyes softened, his manner didn't. "You are my wife and the mother of my son. You have no time for such foolish . . ."

I do not know whether Shaarvan saw something in Tem's eyes or Tessa's, but he stopped speaking and looked down at me again. Everyone was silent as Shaarvan searched my eyes.

"Perhaps . . ." "he said. "Perhaps there is reason. I shall think on it, Shaara."

Tessa didn't seem bothered by Shaarvan's doubt. She continued to talk. "Do you not find it interesting that her name has begun so often with an 'S': Shaara, Sleka, Sleena, Sletha, Susan."

How did the Priestess know? I'd never heard the last name, but she was right about the others. "How did you know that?" I asked.

"I know much that you and your fine Shapechanger warrior do not. I wonder if he knows what 'S' is the sign of?"

Shaarvan was watching Tessa intently, but he said nothing.

"For thousands of years, the 'S' has been the sound of Power. Only the 'T' rivals its strength. How interesting: Shaarvan, Shaara, Shaarac . . . In all your life, girl, it is written in your path that you will be with Shapechanger, whose names begin with 'S' or 'T.' There will be Power around and in you. That, I see in your future. No matter, Shaarvan, what you choose for her, that will be the constant. Do not fight what comes, young lord. It will be."

She was still cackling as we walked away.

"Shaarvan . . ." I said, wanting to ask question after question.

"Silence, woman. Do not speak without permission," he said, and his hand slid up into the neck position.

Tem left us at the door to our new residence. Was he going back to his cold house? I was sorry for him but too worried about what would happen to me to dwell on his life.

Shaarvan dropped the grip on my neck. I was determined to be quiet and submissive for a while, but as we stepped inside, I couldn't help my reaction. "Spit in the Wind, look at this!" I blurted out, twirling around to take it in.

"You will not use Freinanan swear words."

"I'm sorry," I said, without really listening. I was too busy examining our new quarters.

For starters, the bed was big enough for two families, and there were no buttons to make it disappear. There was a computer, (unfortunately) a most elegant wooden table with chairs that shared the same delicately carved legs, a rug with blue-and-gold-flowered patterns — as soft as a Landoor's coat, and a window which viewed a small garden attached to the room. The garden contained flowers and ferns and three small trees with green leaves and tiny pink blossoms. I opened the window door and breathed in the smell of spring and sweetness.

Shaarvan came up behind me. Gently, he pulled me back into the room and closed the garden door. He steered me away, but it was then that I saw the huge tapestry of a snow-capped mountain and forest of trees.

"Oh, Shaarvan! This room is beautiful!" I sighed.

"Do not get used to it. It is only temporary," he snapped.

He led me to the bed. With a soft sigh, I sat down, ready for a lecture. The sooner the punishment was over, the sooner tranquility would be restored.

"Remove your dress," Shaarvan ordered.

It wasn't hard to guess that the lecture and punishment had been postponed.

Teea

I cannot help my tears. All my resolutions to act submissive — and then I actually opened my mouth and spoke during a meeting! It was their fault, in a way. They reminded me of a bunch of old women sitting around discussing the way things used to be. How could I help it if my temper got the better of me, and I asked them when and what they were going to do about it.

Starnkor didn't say a word. He simply led me out of Tevor's room and shut me in a vacant room down the hall. Then, he left me there. Will the Shapechanger bar me now from attending their meetings? Will Starnkor forbid me to sit beside my beloved Tevor, holding his hand while they try their mind links? Will Starnkor punish me?

Really, he cannot do much. I have borne three sons. I have earned the rights of a free woman in Altar, but will he see it that way? Will Starnkor demand fresh training? I wish I understood my rights more clearly. Tevor always refused my questions concerning the bonding. What exactly does Starnkor's being Second entail?

Shaara

After our joining, Shaarvan no longer seemed angry. In fact, he was quite the opposite. He lay there playing with my hair, touching me in places that usually indicated his interest, but he did so this time so lightly he was almost playful.

"Ah, Shaara," he said as his lips teased my neck. "It was a miracle men did not see your beauty even disguised in smelly men's clothing. I would have seen it. I would have stolen you away to some back alley and filled you when your owner left you alone. The Freinanans must have been blind."

His words were not the most romantic. The thought of his taking me in an alley did not thrill me, but males thought differently. When they praised a woman's beauty, they were usually seeking what Shaarvan had just had. It was puzzling.

"Shaarvan, I am yours already," I said. "Why do you woo me?"

He laughed. His fingers once again began their tormenting travel over my body. "Because you are mine."

Once more, his lips found the pulse at my throat. The maddening feel of his kisses, and the lips that nibbled made me squirm. Shaarvan swung his leg and anchored me still. Then he began to recite another of his poems:

I saw countless pleasing girls

With eyes bewitchingly pure

Many with long, flowing hair

And bodies designed for play

But no one's curves tantalized

Not one of them seemed to fit

Where was the one to capture

And fly with to the stars

Where was she I needed

To take with to the stars

There, beyond the others

Was one with many curls

Her eyes flared with anger

Her tongue was saucy and sharp

Her palm held a magic sweetness

And desire was in her lips

She was the one I captured

And flew with to the stars

She was the one I chose

To carry to the stars

I thought only of her training

And bending her rebellious will

I demanded that she obey me

I drilled the laws into her brain

Harshly I commanded her

Never bothered by her thoughts

For she was the one I'd captured

And flown with to the stars

She was the one I owned

And had taken to the stars

It was on the ship I learned

What I had never known before

As we walked amid our dreams

And shared words and visions

She became the mate of my soul

Bound to me and I to her

My wife was the one I captured

And flew with to the stars

She has brought me honor

In my journeys to the stars

Shaarvan's soft gray eyes peered into mine. I felt the flare of his Power pulling me. I could not fight him, but I could not accept the call. He was demanding a response. How did one address such oddities of thoughts?

"Your words mean that the girl was special because she belonged to him?" I said. "So any girl would have been OK?"

"No, Shaara." His eyes looked distressed by my analysis, but his mouth sprinkled kisses across my face until I thought I'd die if he didn't find my lips.

He laughed deep in his chest at my effort. "There is a calling deep inside a Shapechanger male. Something draws us to the right girl, and we know the one to choose if we listen carefully."

"So when you saw me, something clicked?"

"No, for you, my little wildcat, it was when I heard your saucy tongue, as in the words of the poem."

"So, it was not my body?"

"That was not what made me turn around and look at you, no."

"But now it does?" My hand stroked Shaarvan's broad, hairless chest. The muscles beneath my fingers rippled.

"Saucy enchantress!" he laughed.

We walked through the cleaner spray and then stopped at the clothes machine. When we were dressed, he ordered me to sit down on one of the chairs at the table, and his eyes grew serious.

"Be still and listen," he said. "I am going to Shapechange. I do not wish to frighten you, but you must become reacquainted with what I am. Do not run from me. I shall not hurt you."

I watched with interest as Shaarvan melded into a cat. He was bigger and fiercer than Targone, but I was not afraid. I knew his Change would not hurt me. His huge mouth opened wide in a yawn bigger than my head. His teeth glowed like tusk knives, sharpened to the finest point. I observed it all, wondering why he had decided to display his altered shape.

Shaarvan's mouth came closer and seized my hand. His fierce eyes stared into mine. What did he want?

My wrist was being pulled. Was I supposed to go with him somewhere? As I stood up, he backed away, pulling my arm gently towards the rug in the center of the room. When I reached the spot he desired, he let go of my wrist.

I stood there, baffled. It was strange how the Shapechange of Targone and Shaarvan were so different. Targone had been a large cat, as he had been a large Shapechanger, but he had been rather thin and bony with little muscling. Shaarvan was only slightly larger than Targone, but his mass was considerably more. His muscles rippled underneath his hide, and he was massively big with bulk, and even in his cat image, he conveyed a feeling of Power. Shaarvan's eyes were greener than Targone's, or maybe they just seemed to glow more fiercely. His coat was shinier and thicker, too, like a landoor in the wintertime.

Shaarvan was sitting on the carpet, staring into my eyes. He did not look pleased. I wondered if he could read my mind in his cat shape as clearly as in his man shape. Suddenly, his mouth opened wide, and he let out a roar so loud the table rattled against a chair. Spit in the wind, he scared me. I jumped worse than the table.

The cat began to change. In a minute, he was once more Shaarvan.

"Do you compare me with Targone?" he demanded.

"Is that bad? I decided your cat is much more handsome than Targone's," I said, trying to appease him, although there was no lie in the telling of it.

Shaarvan ignored the compliment. "I did not feel fear in you. Why?" He sat down on the chair and pulled me into his lap. His gray eyes stared down at me. I had a sudden fear then that I would say something wrong. Nervously, I attempted to explain. "Targone introduced me to the . . . Shapechanger. He slept like that every night . . . at my door . . . to make sure Tren or somebody else didn't come."

"I see. Good," Shaarvan said, kissing my forehead. "Tonight, then, you will be ready to walk the forest with me."

"In my dreams?" I'd heard Shaarvan mention it to Tessa, but how could I choose a dream?

He nodded. His eyes were cat eyes, watchful.

"Shaarvan, I don't understand how to dream with you, but if you will explain how to do so, I will try."

"You will do more than try, my wife."

His eyes dared me to argue. I kept silent.

For a moment more, he held me in his arms, and then he more or less dumped me off and was soon dragging me out the door. Did Shaarvan never go anywhere slowly?

We walked towards the medical lab but took a different path than where we'd gone with Tem. It was only a brief time later that Shaarvan was introducing me to my son.

Shaarac was brought to us from the nursery ward. He'd just been given the drug to start the awakening process, and when the medic handed him to me, the child was sleeping a natural sleep.

Both Shaarvan and I unwrapped him from the blanket to peer down at his body. One tiny hand curled around Shaarvan's finger, and, for a moment, as if we'd disturbed his rest, Shaarac sucked hard on the finger he kept inside his mouth. I couldn't help reaching out to stroke his little cheek. I felt his breath — warm and rhythmical.

Shaarvan let me carry Shaarac back to our residence. It felt natural to feel Shaarac's warm little body close to mine. Shaarvan at my side

139

peeked beneath the blankets as often as I did. He wore a look of pride and wonder on his face each time his eyes fell on his son.

I was gazing at Shaarvan in fascination, but I must admit that I, too, smiled a great deal at baby Shaarac. I didn't understand how I could have lost the memory of such a beautiful little boy, nor of this man who claimed to be my husband.

Shaarac's laugh when he finally awakened in our chamber tore at my heart. I vowed I would never let my son know that I'd forgotten him. He would always be mine. From that first smile, I loved him.

Shaarac wanted to nurse me, but I had no milk to offer him. I'd been given a bottle, and although Shaarac seemed surprised by it, he was content to suckle from it as long as he lay in my arms. I placed a kiss on his sweet baby face, and he stopped for a moment and smiled up at me. My heart lurched. I felt contented. I wanted to cry. How sweet the love of a child is!

I looked up, although it was not easy to part from Shaarac's gaze. Shaarvan was watching us. He, too, was smiling. I did not understand his rages or what his expectations of me were, but for a male, he seemed mostly to be a good person. I wondered if I could ever feel love for him.

Shaarac was staring at me again. His little hand reached for my hair. A curl had fallen close enough for him to grasp. His hand closed on it, and again, he smiled, studying his captured prize.

"Shaarac, what will you do with that, you silly little boy?" I said.

"He shows good taste. Your hair is pleasing." Shaarvan bent over and kissed his son. Shaarac reached out to grab at his father's hair, too, but Shaarvan was much too quick. The little face began to pucker as if his smile was Shapechanging.

"Your father has the reflexes of a cat, Shaarac. You cannot catch him."

I turned Shaarac over my shoulder and patted his back. The belch that followed was loud, but I hardly heard it. I was watching Shaarvan Shapechange.

"You will frighten Shaarac," I said in a whisper, but I was ignored. A whiskery tiger's face pushed into my lap.

"Shaarvan!" I cried out in dismay, but I knew he intended the child to see. I put Shaarac down on my lap. His eyes went at once to the cat. They were saucer eyes, fascinated. One of Shaarac's fingers went to his mouth for deliberation. Then, the tiny hand stretched out to grab at the hairy thing in front of him.

Shaarac caught the whiskers and patted them, bouncing them up and down. Then he moved on to softer stuff, patting and touching. His eyes moved to mine. He sat and thought, and then once more, he stared at the cat.

I put Shaarac down on the floor on his stomach. Immediately, his arms pushed himself up, and he lay there with his head erect, regarding the tiger. He lasted for a minute before plopping back down. He was almost rolling over, rocking himself from side to side in his eagerness at seeing this strange creature on the floor with him.

Shaarvan, in his tiger form, lay down beside Shaarac. His big paws were what drew his son's eyes, then. The paws were at Shaarac's level. Shaarac's eyes studied their giant fuzziness. His stare went on and on.

I watched the scene with fascination. So this was how a Shapechanger raised his young? I wondered how old Shaarac would need to be before he could frolic as a tiger in the forests with his father. Shaarac fell asleep between his father's great furry paws.

"May I put him in his little bed?" I asked.

The tiger-eyes stared solemnly at me. They didn't blink. I stepped closer and bent down to pick up our son. As my hands lowered, one giant paw reached out and settled on my wrist, anchoring me to the floor.

"Shaarvan, please, let me go."

I hadn't touched Shaarac yet. I wondered if Shaarvan was forbidding me to do so.

"If you do not wish me to remove Shaarac, could you make a noise?"

The tiger-eyes continued to stare at me. I dropped to my knees.

"I don't understand what you want, Shaarvan."

A large pale, pink tongue shot out and licked my arm.

"What are you doing?"

I tried to pull away, but I couldn't get free. The huge, rough tongue continued bathing my arm.

"Your tongue is harsh, Shaarvan," I complained. I tried again to push his head away. He nipped me.

"Ow!" The teeth didn't sever my skin, but the bite was a painful pinch. I knew then that I must endure Shaarvan's will, no matter what the strangeness. I grew perfectly still. For a moment more, Shaarvan continued licking, then he stopped and watched my eyes.

In one smooth movement, Shaarvan rose and strolled away from Shaarac and me. I scooped up our son and held him close. I was shaking. Shaarvan had frightened me.

I took a long breath and studied my son. He was so beautiful. His eyelashes twitched in his dreams. His tiny mouth made little sucking sounds. I watched the rise and fall of his chest and wondered at the miracle of babies, so tiny yet so perfectly formed.

"You may put him to bed now, Shaara,"

I looked up and saw that Shaarvan was once again in his man shape. I was relieved that he didn't look angry.

I placed a blanket over Shaarac, then kissed his cheek, and stood a moment, watching him sleep.

"Come here," my husband ordered.

The chamber was big. I was at least thirty feet from Shaarvan. Each step forward, I worried. There was something in Shaarvan's look and manner that boded ill.

When I was a foot away, I halted.

"When I Shapechange, am I still your master?" Shaarvan asked me.

"Yes, my lord."

"You are my wife. I have told you before not to call me that."

"I'm sorry, my . . . "I sighed. It looked like a long lecture.

"You will obey all my wishes, no matter my shape?"

"I will try, but I did not understand what you wanted in your tiger shape."

"Did you understand that I wished to lick you?"

"But you hurt me with your tongue."

"Did it hurt worse than when I bit you?"

"No, that hurt more."

"Remember that, Shaara. Tomorrow, it is my pleasure to join with you in my cat shape. Do you understand?"

I backed away. "No, please don't do that," I begged. "Not as an animal!" I searched his eyes for mercy.

"I am Shapechanger. You are my wife. You will obey," Shaarvan warned me.

I took a deep breath. I'd heard whispers of such a thing, but I'd hoped the tales were wrong. I took a deeper breath and tried to steel my nerves.

"Shaarvan . . . "

"Yes?"

His eyes were watching me, exactly as he had in his cat image. I shuddered. "I don't know how a cat joins, but . . . won't it injure me?"

"It will do no damage to your body, but there may be some pain."

I began to cry. I was confused. I didn't understand all Shaarvan's stories and poems about loving me, if he would want to cause me pain. I would rather be beaten than endure that.

Shaarvan continued. "Because of the pain, most wives don't enjoy mating in their first form. Most of them choose to change their shape as well. That is, of course, an option."

I couldn't believe his coldness. "But I can't. I don't know how!"

"The fact that you *have not* does not mean that you *cannot*. Past transition, Shapechange is always an option for a woman."

He walked over to the computer, and just like that, the subject was over. I begin to pace. I kept remembering the size of his cat, the tongue like sandpaper sliding back and forth against my skin. Why must I do this? Why did he demand it? Couldn't Shaarvan be content with the joining of human bodies?

"Shaarvan, please, . . . how do you Shapechange?"

He turned around to look at me. "The cat shape is the easiest. It is our alternate self, but any shape simply needs a picture in your mind, and the decision to change. Of course, you have to believe you can do it."

"Shaarvan." I went to him and fell to my knees. "Shaarvan, please, if you care for me, why will you cause me pain?"

"Because taking you in the cat shape completes the Shapechanger bonding."

"Even if it hurts me?"

"You will learn."

"What will I learn? I *already* obey you!"

"You will learn to adapt."

I sprang up and began to pace again. Shaarvan returned to his reading. My mind was whirling. It couldn't be possible. Surely, he wouldn't . . . but I knew Shaarvan enough to know that if he said he would do something, it would occur.

"Shaarvan." Once more, I disturbed him. Twice, I had interrupted him, and he had not barked at me. He was being very patient.

"Shaarvan, I want to Shapechange. Please, couldn't you show me how?"

He blanked his screen and turned to give me his full attention. "Shaara, if you want to Change badly enough, you will Change. You do not need me to show you anything."

"But I do!" I took Shaarvan's hands in mine and held them. "Please, Shaarvan." A lone tear rolled down my cheek. Shaarvan reached out to stop it.

"All right, Shaara."

He stood up and pulled me to a standing position. "We will move over there first," he said, pointing to the rug.

He led me to the carpet and ordered me to lie down. At once, his body followed, and his lips merged with mine. I was disappointed he had changed his mind about helping me, but men were flighty. The thought of sex often drove away their other intentions. Shaarvan's lips soon erased my worries about Shapechanging. In the back of my head, I heard his words, "Come walk with me, walk the forests."

I opened my eyes to stare into Shaarvan's. How could I walk the forests? We were in space.

"Come with me." I heard the words echoing over and over. "Close your eyes, and we shall prowl beneath the shade of the soft-padded pine needles. Come."

I shut my eyes, and I was there. The forest was above me, cool, comforting, soft . . . contentment. Beside me, Shaarvan padded along, sniffing the winds for the scent of deer and wilsby. I breathed it in and held it, sorting through the smells. Oh, lovely scents: grass, dead and dying leaves turning to acid peat, mushrooms in damp, moldy places, and there a touch, yes, wilsby.

Beside me, my mate smelled it, too. He turned to me, his tongue lapping out, cleaning and smoothing the fur around my eyes. He butted my neck and playfully rolled me over. I batted at him in light sport. We played a moment more. Then his tongue darted out. This time my whiskers drew him. It tickled as he cleaned me.

He yawned full, and then his long, pointed teeth gathered around my neck. I grew still, acknowledging his dominance, but he bit harder. My coat of fur was thick, but his teeth were sharp and bearing down fiercely. I let out a whimper. At once, the death grip released, and he moved back to bathing my face.

The roughened tongue felt good. I purred softly.

"Good," Shaarvan said. I opened my eyes in shock. The forest was gone. We were still lying on the carpet.

"Did we Shapechange?"

Shaarvan smiled. His smile pulled at me, like when I had gazed at Shaarac.

"You were half-way there."

"But, that isn't enough. I have to be fully changed." My voice was panicked. I remembered the sharpness of the tiger's teeth on my neck. I wouldn't survive such contact if I were a person.

For a moment, Shaarvan studied me. His eyes turned silver in the light. "So be it," he said, and he began to meld into the cat.

I was frozen, unprepared, frightened. If the tiger decided to play with me, my skin would have ridges like a freshly plowed field. If he bit me, as he'd done in the forest, my blood would spurt like red gushers across the flowered rug.

"Shaarvan," I protested. "This doesn't help me." I backed from him. "I asked you to help me learn to Change!"

The cat butted me with its head. Its eyes, green-yellow cat eyes, peered intensely into mine. I started to rise, but it leaped on me and pushed me down. Teeth ripped at my dress, tearing it to shreds.

"No, Shaarvan," I cried out in horror, "You said I had until tomorrow."

Again, I tried to rise, but I fell, trapped in the mangled dress. Lying on the rug as I was, I saw it. The cat's penis was erect, and as large as the heavy muscles of its flank. I screamed. Again, it butted me, then cuffed me with a sheathed paw.

The cat could have hurt me, and it chose not to, but I knew there was no way my human shape could survive being taken by a lance the size of that.

"Shaarvan, I'm frightened. Please, don't punish me. Not like this."

The tiger growled. My words angered it. I attempted to crawl away. Too quickly, I realized I'd gotten into the wrong position.

Once more, its tongue licked me. Raspy as sand, it licked at my buttocks.

"No!" I screamed. I tried to move. Teeth bit into my exposed bottom. The pain drove me into anger.

I was Shaarvan's wife. How dare he bite my flank! I turned and yowled at him. One of my paws lifted to slash at him. My claws extended.

He backed away and roared softly. I saw that he was laughing. I crept forward and pounced. We tussled, growling, playfully snapping at the air. Once, I bit his shoulder, but too quickly his teeth found the flap of skin around my neck. He held me still.

"Change," he ordered.

I tried to fight him, but his hold was too secure. I growled low in my throat, full of displeasure. He shifted his grip and sank his teeth in deeper. I growled again, but it turned quickly into the whimper of submission as his teeth ground deeper.

"Change," he commanded once more.

"Change to what?" I wondered.

His teeth let go, but I didn't move. I knew how lightning swift his reclaiming of me would be. I would not challenge my mate.

"Change." The word brought all the force of a blow to my head. I watched as his body melded back to a human's. Against my wishes, I followed his lead.

"You did it, my wife. You Shapechanged," Shaarvan said. His smile could have replaced a light bulb.

My hands flew to my head. It hurt. I began to sob. "Shaarvan," I cried.

"What is it, Shaara? What is wrong?"

I stared at him — my mind was a whirl of images. They were coming too fast. I shut my eyes and tried to slow them down.

"Easy, Shaara. Do not fight it. Relax, my love."

I opened my eyes and took in the sight of him.

"Shaarvan!" I threw my arms around him and planted kisses across his face. "I remember! I remember everything. I love you! And Shaarac! And Teea and Tevor! I remember it all!"

I hugged him harder and decorated him with kisses. Then, I attacked his mouth. I couldn't get enough of him.

"Take me, Shaarvan. Take me now. Take me so I'm yours forever. Take me until I can't remember anyone else ever touching me!"

Like water released from a dam, pressured by a false containment, lust burst free, and Shaarvan flowed into me fiercely. I craved his violence and his being, and all the maelstrom of currents that swept through us in the mingling of two bonded souls. And when we'd calmed, spent and sated, there were words of sharing.

"Shaarvan, how could I forget you?" I cried. "You're my soul, my life. How could I breathe without you there to breathe life into me?"

"It is over, Shaara," he whispered into my ear. His hands, caressing my face, calmed me. "We are one. We have healed the wall between us. Our future will be the freshness of a budding bloom. We shall savor its awakening."

Shaarvan's lips soothed me with kisses. I moaned, not in need for him, but in contentment, like the purring of my cat.

"I have waited for you," he told me, "severed like a tree with an uncertain graft, but we are whole, and more closely joined now. No one can part our bond. It stretches to the root of us. It is the life force we share."

"But how can you accept me, Shaarvan? I have been with another . . ."

"Hush! It was not of your doing. You are as innocent as you were when I captured you. It is in the past. That I order."

"I may not speak of it?"

"You will talk of it whenever you have need, but you will not nurture any guilt."

"And you, will you still hold the guilt within you?"

For a long moment, Shaarvan's eyes searched mine. I knew what he was thinking, but I would not allow it.

"If there is guilt, we will share it," I said. My eyes glowed as defiant as they'd ever been with him.

"I see it will be difficult to keep you in check," he said, but his lips softened the words. "I shall have to be twice as stern to make up for it."

"I fear you will need to take me daily to keep me tame," I teased him, feeling as cocky as a threeTide colt.

My words amused him. He laughed and rubbed his knuckles on my cheek.

I knew Shaarvan was right. Where we walked, there were no footprints. I was Shaara, but I was different. There now memories from Sleena and Sleka, as well as Shaara. It made me a stronger woman.

I loved Shaarvan, I respected him, and I knew he was my owner, but he was not a god, and I didn't think he would ever frighten me in the same way.

"Change is the only constant," he said, nodding. His eyes were soft, but thoughtful. He was reading me, yet he didn't seem alarmed. Could something have shifted in Shaarvan, too?

Tessa

So he has forced her to Change already, has he? And she has remembered! The girl's words still rang in my ears. "Take me, Shaarvan. Take me now. Take me so I'm yours forever, and I can't remember anyone else ever touching me!"

How did such a small child get such a loud voice? Four quads away, and it felt like she was in the room beside me, screaming out those ridiculous words. How far had the girl projected? How many had heard it? The Old Ones must be chuckling. They would be calling for me to come and explain.

Such promise this one has. There have been no others this strong for ages. She *must* be trained. Tem must order it. The young Warlord is Tem's nephew. Family obedience demands that he heed his uncle.

Shaarvan, the young Warlord, he is called, and his name is also written in the stars, Shaarvan of Altar, Highest of Westla. Such a strong young buck. "Lucky Shaara," I thought, closing my eyes to listen for the call of the Old Ones.

Teea

I curse Starnkor. No sooner had the others left than he was removing me from the room where I'd been held prisoner.

"I am sorry," I signaled.

He didn't answer. His hand first gripped my arm and then my neck before I had a chance to pull away.

"Tevor did not use the neck grip on me very often," I told Starnkor, but his hold on me did not loosen, and he dragged me forward into Tevor's room.

"I am your Second," he told me.

My eyes flew to Tevor. Could he hear? Did he know we were there? Did he see what Starnkor was doing to me? Surely my husband would not lie there so still and silent if he had a choice.

"Tevor," I mind-talked. *"Please, come back to me. I need you."*

"He cannot, Teea. But I am here. You must recognize me."

Starnkor's hand had only loosened slightly. I turned slowly to look at him. "I do acknowledge you. I have obeyed you, as I did Tevor. I do not understand."

His eyes held mine. I didn't fight him. He was puzzling me, but I did not fear him.

"Tevor did not explain my role, did he?"

"Yes, he said that you would watch over me when he died."

"Or was incapacitated or absent for a long period," Starnkor added.

I looked over at Tevor again, and mind-spoke with renewed vigor. *"Please get up, Tevor. Please, tell Starnkor that you are well. Do not let him do this. Please, Tevor . . ."*

"Enough. You plague your husband, and he cannot respond. This is his will, Teea, and you will accept it."

I had no time to answer him. Starnkor lifted me up and carried me to the room where he had been sleeping. I remembered the Primary. I knew, even at that moment, that I must obey the will of Tevor *and* of

Starnkor, but I could not. I could not go willingly or easily into the arms of my Second.

Starnkor did not discuss it. He webbed me and covered me with three layers of patterns, yet still I resisted. Shaara would have understood.

But in the end, it was like all the battles of a female against a Shapechanger. My opposition caused him little difficulty. Starnkor pleasured us both and deep-bonded me so I could not fight him again.

Since then, he has taken me each day, and I have not been left alone for a moment. Even when I visit the necessary, Starnkor has ordered that the door be kept open, and he waits nearby. I am appalled by his mistrust, but I know there is reason. I would seek the Path of Death, if I knew how. I cannot live without my Tevor.

Shaara

To wake up beside the one I loved was an ecstasy of Heaven. His smile, tender with love, the knowledge of all we had shared, and our soul bond — newly awakened, so familiar and so comfortable — it was a wonderful way to greet the day. And, as a special bonus, there was our son, so sweet and full of smiles.

Shaarvan was right. The new day was an awakening. It was a fresh new bloom of what our lives would be together. Yet, although there was a wholeness, a unity between us, a shiver of unease troubled me. All was not well. Shaarvan was hiding something. He laughed at my disquiet, but he left my questions dangling without answers. My probes found no access. His mind was tighter than the cork on a bottle as it floats out to sea.

Shaarvan took me to see the Hall of Wives that day. He left me there, telling me that I was to mingle and choose friends. I entered into the white marbled room and saw alabaster benches all about, and cushions softly colored in blues and purples, yellows, and pinks. The cushions and the dresses of the women were the only color in the room. No tapestries hung from the walls, and no paintings or sketches formed decorations.

Several women came towards me and gathered around me to see Shaarac. He was asleep in my arms and did not wake as they peeked.

"I am Grena," one told me. She had a warm, gentle smile, but very little Shapechanger force. I smiled back at her and gave her my name.

"We know your name," said another, laughing softly. "It was a cry in the middle of the day that came to everyone."

"Shaara, we will never forget your name! You made every Shapechanger male on this side of Westla horny as gleezles," said a tall, dark woman.

"I don't understand," I said, looking at the laughing faces around me. They were all friendly, not mocking, but I had no idea what joke they were sharing.

"She's not complaining, you know, Shaara!" said a laughing blonde, with hair the color of melted butter.

"What they mean is that you projected your love and lust for Shaarvan and with words, too!"

What were they talking about? They couldn't have heard what I said to Shaarvan.

"Take me, take me," giggled one of them. "Take me until I'm yours forever until . . ."

"Enough." The woman who spoke and then stepped forward had all the force of Teea. She was lanky tall, but she moved with the grace of a panther. Her long, brown hair had patches of red orange in it, reminding me of a calico cat I'd once owned. I wondered at her origins. She seemed exotic and as close to nonhuman as I'd ever seen.

Her eyes assessed me. "Grena, get Shaara a fruit drink. Thella, take the child. Shaara can talk more comfortably then."

For a moment, I thought about disputing her orders. Although she was forceful, I knew she would not fight my wishes. She waited, watching me make my decision. I handed Shaarac to Thella but first kissed his sweet, little cheek.

"He will grow up to steal women, you know," Thella said as she took him.

I shrugged. It was true, but there would be many years before that time.

Grena brought me the drink. I thanked her and sipped it politely.

"Tell us why you cried out last night," the blonde demanded.

Was this an inquisition?

"Why did another take you?" asked one of the women.

"Fresa, enough. I told you."

"Brala, you know we are all dying of curiosity!"

"It is Shaara's to tell or not to tell." Brala turned her eyes back to me, and again, I felt the force of her Power. Like the spray of a shower, the strength of it pounded me. There was no pain, just the steady flow of her demand.

"I will tell you if you turn off the Shapechanger magic," I said to all of them, but it was Brala I meant, and she knew it.

"You are different," Brala told me. "One who projects cannot usually impress."

"What does impress mean?"

"One who feels the Power and knows it for what it is," she answered me.

I was vaguely surprised. I'd thought everyone could do that. I changed the subject away from me.

"Shaarvan said that Westla is the home of the Old Ones. Are any of you Old Ones?"

The women laughed.

"None of us. You would know instantly if we were. Our husbands and sons are here to study with them," said the one Brala had called Fresa.

"Are we allowed to meet the Old Ones?" I asked.

"Us? Not likely. We are too new. They won't even let Brala go to them, and she's strong!" said the blonde.

"They will let you." Brala made the statement like it was fact, not opinion.

"Why do you think that, Brala?" Thella asked.

"Shall I list the reasons?"

She had our attention.

"One, we all know the volume of Shaara's projection," Brala said. "Two, Shaara is also an impressor. Three, she's the wife of the Highest's nephew. Four, she's the wife of the Shapechanger, who will probably be our next Highest."

I hadn't thought about Shaarvan being the Highest. Was it hereditary? The uncle with no issue . . . Would that mean we could never return to Altar? Would we be forced to live on an artificial metal globe forever?

"Fifth," Brala continued. "She's a curiosity. She was bonded in the Old Way."

How did Brala get all her information? She knew more about me than I'd known a day ago!

"In the Old Way?" Grena's eyes grew round as ping-pong balls. "He took you in the Old Way?"

"Sixth, she's more Shapechanger than all the rest of us. She has gotten a great deal of information from us without answering the one question we asked her. Who does that remind you of?" Brala asked.

They all turned and glared at me.

Shaarac chose that moment to waken. He began to cry when he found other arms holding him.

"It's all right, Shaarac. I am here," I said, holding out my hands to Thella to take him back.

I had brought a bottle for Shaarac, and I began feeding him. He smiled up at me for a second and then greedily sucked away at his bottle.

"Why is he on a bottle? I thought all Shapechanger women had to breast feed," Fresa said.

I looked down at Shaarac, and for a moment, I was sad. "I did breast feed him at the beginning, but then I was stolen in a raid and sold. Shaarvan put Shaarac in deep sleep and hunted for me. When he found me, I had no memories of him or of being Shapechanger."

"How could that be? How could you forget?" Fresa wanted to know.

"Hush, let her speak!" said Brala.

"I was mindwiped. Shaarvan taught me to Shapechange. When I Changed, it purged the mindwipe. That's why I disturbed you all, I guess. My emotions were pretty wild there when I suddenly remembered who I was."

Shaarac had caught a lock of my hair and was twirling it around his finger. He laughed and started to choke on his milk. I removed the bottle and lifted him up, patting his back. He burped and then began to wail in anger at being deprived of the bottle. I returned it to him.

The others watched with open mouths.

"What a temper! He must be strong with the Power."

"He's a baby!"

I looked up and tried to sort the names of the faces.

"Forget Shaarac . . . What a story! Do you still remember being sold and who your owner was?" Grena asked.

"Yes," I said, but the word came forth grudgingly, and it made my eyes water with its memories.

"Did Shaarvan kill him?" Thella demanded.

"No, Isandor was already dead when Shaarvan found me."

"Who killed him?" Fresa asked.

"My second owner, the one who won me in a casino."

"What! You had another owner?" said the woman whose name I didn't know.

"Kind of. He did not want me. He notified the Shapechanger."

"He sounds nice. Was he handsome?" Grena wanted to know.

"I would not even think about that. Grenazen would decorate your thighs with a knotted whip for asking that question," Brala warned.

"What about your first owner? What was he like?" Fresa asked.

"Horrible," I said, shuddering.

"I cannot believe you had all that excitement while I've been stuck here day after day!" Sana, a short, slightly plump, redheaded woman, said. She had been so quiet I'd barely noticed her.

"Sana, there is plenty to do. You just never do it," argued Grena.

The door whooshed open, and three Shapechanger males walked in. I stood up, but no one else did. I felt like a fool.

"Ah, an Altarian," said the tallest one. My eyes were focused on the ground, so it was hard to be sure.

"Grena, come." The other two flashed signs, and Thella and Sana walked to their husbands.

They started to leave, but the tall male lingered. "What is your name, woman?"

"Shaara," I answered quietly.

"Shooting stars! She is the one who broke into our quiet yesterday."

"I thought so," one of the others said. "Shaarvan has good taste."

"Good taste? Do you know how much work a woman with that kind of Power would be? Too argumentative for me!"

I felt like I was back with the buyers on Altar.

"What is your origin, woman?"

"Terra."

Sana's husband was urging them on. "Come on, we shall be late for the concert."

I watched the door whoosh closed behind them.

"You handled that well," Brala said. "But on Westla, it is not necessary to stand up for Shapechanger males. We would be standing all the time if we did. The lords are constantly in and out."

The blonde's owner came in almost immediately after that. His eyes scanned me, but he didn't ask any questions. He spoke to his wife by name, so I discovered that she was Catha. She smiled her goodbye to us. Her long blonde hair bounced saucily as she walked away.

Then, Fresa's husband came. I did not like his attitude. He stared at Brala and me for the longest time with the kind of look that makes every female cringe. He questioned us about our owners and then left, leading Fresa away before we had the chance to smile a goodbye.

Brala and I were alone then. We moved closer.

"My husband is Braltar," she told me. "He is not one of the Old Family, like your husband. Our son is in training, which is why we have come. We live on Prega. Have you ever been there?"

I shook my head and wiped Shaarac's mouth.

"It's an interesting planet, with geological marvels found nowhere else. Braltar is a geologist. He studies the rocks and minerals of the planet. I like to help him, but I prefer flowers and trees to rocks."

I smiled at her. I agreed that flowers and trees were always better than rocks.

I had thawed to Brala. At first, I'd felt leery of her authoritative manner, but a woman who loved flowers and trees could only be a friend.

The door whooshed open all too soon, and it was Shaarvan. I did not stand up as he entered. It felt strange. Shaarvan didn't mention my disrespect, so I knew Brala was correct about Westlan etiquette.

In fact, Shaarvan paid almost no attention to me after his eyes had scanned Shaarac and me. He seemed fascinated by Brala.

"Stand up, woman," he ordered her. "What is your origin?"

"Treheman," Brala told him in a toneless voice.

"Who is your owner?" Shaarvan demanded.

"Braltar."

She answered Shaarvan adequately, but I could feel the anger burning inside her. She was so hot I felt like backing up.

"Shaara, come," Shaarvan ordered abruptly.

I wanted to tell Brala "goodbye," but the others had not spoken when they left. I didn't know the protocol. I walked to Shaarvan, smiling at Brala as I passed her. She smiled back at me, but it didn't reach her eyes. She was still angered by Shaarvan's questions.

My husband took Shaarac from me and led me through the door, stopping in the hall to look down at me. He raised up my chin and studied my eyes. "You are well. Was it pleasurable?"

"Kind of," I answered him.

"Brala is rebellious. I would prefer you to choose another to be your friend."

I gasped and pulled away from his hand. "Shaarvan, she is the one I liked the best!"

I didn't need to read him to know he disliked my tone. I lowered my eyes and held my breath until I'd regained full control over my temper.

"I am sorry. Please do not forbid me her friendship, Shaarvan."

I could read nothing from Shaarvan's body posture, and he barred his thoughts from me, but I knew his sharp burst of anger had died with my change of tone.

"Why was Brala your favorite?"

"She was the smartest; she is from someplace I've never heard of, and she likes flowers and trees."

"I see," Shaarvan said, and I heard the smile in his words. I dared to look up.

"Flowers and trees?" He chuckled and shook his head at me. "She will lead you to trouble if you are with her much, Shaara, but the choice is yours. I shall not forbid you."

I was surprised. I smiled and threw my arms around his neck, giving him a kiss that landed on his chin because he was laughing too hard to bend over and let me kiss him properly.

The rest of the day was spent with Shaarvan showing me Westla. It was a marvel. There was a place for summer-like swimming, a snow zone for skiing and sledding, a lake for fishing and water sports, and mountains for hiking, with a forest of trees. I was overwhelmed by it all. Each dome was even enclosed with its own sky and had a cycle of nights and days!

There were night spots for dancing, concerts, restaurants for sitting and talking, history plays, comedies, and animal shows with live creatures from many galaxies, and classes too numerous to name. We toured the outer windows of it all, and Shaarvan offered me my choice of entertainment.

We sat at an "outdoor" cafe, watching the sun set over the hills in the east, which seemed backward to me until Shaarvan explained that many planets rotated differently than Earth and Freinana. While Shaarvan was speaking, I'd been attempting to feed Shaarac some strained barca fruit, but he seemed more interested in grabbing at the spoon. He was making a dreadful mess, and I was becoming frustrated.

"Shaara, I shall take him," Shaarvan told me.

I laughed, not believing he would have more success than I, but, of course, when Shaarvan moved Shaarac onto his lap, the baby behaved perfectly. The barca fruit actually made it into Shaarac's mouth instead of down his front.

I sighed loudly and drew Shaarvan's smile. He looked down again, concentrating on the birdlike mouth open for its next mouthful.

I watched them in silence, but my mind was churning. Shaarvan had offered me many choices for activities, but he had not mentioned training with the Priestess. I wondered if I dared bring it up. I took in a deep breath for courage.

"Shaarvan," I said. "You say that you will permit me to take classes and learn something new. I would love to learn to ski or study a language, but what I really want most is . . . to train with Tessa."

He placed the spoon down on the table and wiped up his son's mouth with a cloth. "You do not let anything go, do you?"

I tried to read him, but he was still blocking me. His words sounded more tired than angry.

"Do you wish me *not* to train with her?" I asked, confused.

Shaarvan put Shaarac's blanket down on the ground and set the baby on it. Our son made no protest. There was too much for him to see there.

Then, Shaarvan turned to me. His eyes were so unhappy I wanted to tell him it wasn't important if I ever trained with Tessa, but I knew better than to tell a lie.

He read my thought, picked up my hands, and kissed them. "Shaara, my little Shaara." he said. "You have been through so much. I would protect you from more harshness if I could. I do not know why our lives seem to be entwined with so many difficulties."

"There will not be any more now, Shaarvan. You said it was all over. You said . . ."

"Hush."

His arms held me to him tighter than I would have liked, but I didn't mention it. The lips that usually seared my skin with their touch,

I hardly felt. Shaarvan was keeping something from me, something horrible. Why wouldn't he tell me?

Shaarvan released his bear hug and looked deep into my eyes. "If times were different, I would *never* let you near that woman, Shaara."

His eyes studied mine. What was he searching for?

"I would rather you had let it rest awhile, but if Tessa draws you that strongly, Shaara, it must be where you need to go."

I'd won, yet I felt as if I'd lost something. Even with all my memories returned, there were many things I still didn't understand.

We gathered up Shaarac and his blanket, and Shaarvan led me directly to Tessa's quarters. It was late, and we were tired, but neither of us spoke of putting off the visit.

Tessa opened the door before Shaarvan even had time to lay his handprint on it. She waved us in and told us to sit.

The inside of Tessa's was strange. She had been without her Shapechanger husband for nineteen Passes and had reverted to some of the ways of her origin. All around the chamber were skins of hunted beasts, and woven tapestries displaying scenes of animals hung from the walls. Across her couch lay a large cat, similar to the Shapechanger tiger, but smaller. Its eyes were fierce and yellow green, but I could tell from looking at it that it had only the intelligence of a beast and not that of a man.

"I wasted the entire day waiting for you," Tessa complained after she'd seated us. "Why were you so slow to come?"

My eyes were watching the cat. It was stretching now. Its rear peaked upwards as if bowing to us, but there was no sign it attended to us at all.

"Klagor is its name," she said, seeing my stare. "It is a relative of ours. Our genes are mixed with its a thousand kinships back."

"You mean Shapechanger were made, like in the poem."

"What an innocent child. A babe with a babe in arms," Tessa cackled. "Could you not have given her a brief growing time before seeding your future, Shaarvan?"

That did it. I was so tired of everyone calling me a child. "I am much older than I look," I said, and the words flowed with my anger. "And, although my age is not as great as yours, Shaarvan says that wisdom is not measured by Passes but by thoughts and knowledge."

"So the doe has claws, does she, and a mind beneath the outer beauty?"

Tessa stared through me and into me, and I felt the beginning of her probe into my mind.

I shivered in memory of what she'd done before. "No, I will not allow . . ." I blurted out, standing up and backing away.

Tessa cut me off. "You child! You seedling springing out of the damp soil of birth! You tell *me* you will not allow! Have you told her nothing, Shaarvan?"

"Sit down, Shaara," he said, shaking his head at me. When I obeyed, his arm wrapped around my shoulder. I expected to feel his neck grip, but he didn't seem angry.

"She is all promise, Tessa," Shaarvan said. "It is for you to decide to refine it or leave it. I do not welcome your invasion, but my uncle has demanded it for the good of Westla, my wife has requested it, and I have my own reasons for thinking that some training might be useful."

I was staring at Shaarvan, desperately trying to read through his block. He turned to me and smiled. "Ah, Shaara," he said, laughing at my efforts.

Then he turned back to Tessa. "I shall stand aside and watch your progress with her. Should you do harm in any way, even in the discussion of such matters that could lead to her disobedience, Shaara will be kept forever from your reach."

Tessa laughed shrilly. "You are indeed the son of Tevor. He stopped Teea from testing. She could have been much more. And, now, you stand in Shaara's way . . . That is your right, Warlord, but know this. It is *your* pride that will harm Shaara, not my training."

Tessa turned her attention away from Shaarvan. For minutes, she studied me, but I did not feel the force of her Power. I held my chin up, and my eyes locked into hers. I vowed to myself that she would not intimidate me. It was perhaps a minute later I felt her probe. It nibbled at the edges of my mind, darting her and there. It was very different from Tem's, but I knew I didn't have the skills to block her, either. Still, I tried.

Again, she cackled. "You offer up a tasty morsel, Shaarvan. She is emotionally too young to work with, but her time is now. I feel her Power, raw and pubescent. What a shame that already the time grows too short for what I must teach her."

Tessa filled a goblet and drank from it. Then, she turned to face Shaarvan. "You will allow her to be untouched for the period I need?"

"What!" I cried out. "Untouched? You mean . . ."

Shaarvan smiled and shook his head. "There will be no abstinence, Priestess."

Tessa's fury was like a single puff of smoke. I was amazed how quickly she suppressed its force. "You expect me to work to harness a girl's Power while she services you?"

She was angry, but so was I. "Tessa, I asked Shaarvan to bring me here. I didn't know what you required. I was wrong. Even if Shaarvan permitted it, I would not want to be severed from our joining." I looked fully into Shaarvan's eyes. "It is to us as breathing. Without his touch, I would die."

Shaarvan reached out his hand to touch my cheek. His caress was like mountain air, clear and clean. I felt renewed. He took Shaarac from me, and we stood, ready to go.

"Aye," Tessa screamed out. "Save me from young love! Get out, you two. There's naught that I can do. You have chosen poorly."

Shaarvan's arm stretched out and embraced me. I rested my head on his shoulder. "It's strange what she asked," I said as we walked towards the outer door, "Our joining makes me stronger."

"What!" Tessa shrieked. "Come back here. Say that again, girl."

I stared up at my husband in bewilderment. What had I said that had caused her to get so excited? "Our joining makes me stronger," I repeated.

"Stars! I'm an idiot! No wonder she's so strong. You bonded her in the Old Way, not in the chemical way. I'm right, aren't I?"

"Actually, she received both bondings," Shaarvan said.

"Show me your arms, girl."

I should have resented her calling me "girl," but both of them were urging me. I rolled up my sleeves.

And so it was that I began my tutelage with Tessa.

Chapter Five

Shaarvan

She is everything to me, she and my son. Altar asks too great a sacrifice. Yet, how can I turn my back on what is happening there?

Tem and the Old Ones have discussed it with me. We have met for long periods and have arrived at no other conclusion. Westla must not interfere, yet I am not bound by such vows. I still hold my foot in each path. Usually, that means I feel the pull of each, but both are united this time. I must . . .

It is more than allegiance to Altar that calls me. My fathers' illness, my mother's safety, the death of Goria — does Pathe need me by his side, or would I only stir resentments better left alone? All these thoughts dwell on my mind, but none of them is as great as Thenos' wrongs to the government. My duty to the Trendacons does not allow his continued reign. He brings dishonor to the family.

There is a personal matter still between Thenos and myself as well that I must resolve. I claim blood-right for the seizing of my wife, the poisoning of myself, and the tortures Shaara was forced to live through. But blood-right means Thenos' death. How can I kill the brother I helped raise? How can I stop seeing a young boy's eyes lifted up in hero worship, asking my opinion, begging me to teach him, entreating me to save him from Tevor's wrath for some silly prank he had done?

I keep reminding myself that Thenos is no longer my brother. Long ago, that brother died. My little brother is not the malevolent one who sits on Altar's throne. Tren will soon take Thenos' place in the Trendacons family.

Tevor should have been the one to disown Thenos. I know he would have done so if he were able.

My father would have liked Tren. He would have been proud to name him son. Yet, what am I saying? Trevor has not Passed on like the others. There is hope where life continues.

But that thought leads me to the next. I must ask myself why my father lies on his bed, an empty husk. Is that not also by the hand of Thenos? I must take revenge for Shaara, Goria, *and* my father. I must put an end to the shame of the Trendacons.

But am I free of the bondage of love I felt for Thenos? Shall I be able to pierce his heart and end his falseness? I ask myself this question day after day. It burns my soul, as does the thought of leaving Shaara.

Shaara

My lessons with Tessa began, and as the Tides passed, sometimes I wished that I'd never asked to go to her. For if I'd thought that Shaarvan was a stern task maker, it was only because I'd been given no comparison. Tessa drove me with her words and her mind until late at night. I could scarcely eat, and often, Shaarvan's needs were unmet because I dived too quickly into the depths of sleep.

Shaarvan was never angered by my exhaustion. As when I had carried Shaarac, he became more patient with me. And, when I begged him to take me before I ate when I knew my hunger would prod my wakefulness, he would not, knowing I'd been allowed no food throughout the long day of training.

This continued for a sevenTide, draining me of all my strength until the day Shaarvan called a halt. He said nothing to me that morning, but at noon, he stole within Tessa's chambers, swept me up in his arms, and took me away amid the screams and curses of Tessa.

"Shaara is mine, and I claim her," Shaarvan said. "You, old woman, must find another to torment. Shaara will not return until tomorrow."

Shaarvan carried me through the halls despite the whispering and giggling of the Shapechanger females we passed. I was well-content. My arms were wrapped around his neck, touching the soft pelt of his hair. And as he walked, I stole kisses from lips, eager to savor mine.

When we entered our chamber and Shaarvan placed me on the bed, I told him he should not have carried me all that way because he would be too tired to take advantage of my presence.

"Too tired! You mock me, wife," he feigned anger. "You were so light, I had to continually look down to see if you were still there!"

Those were the only words we shared before we flew at each other. No Shapechanger magic fanned our need. The flames burned brightly.

It was only when we had reached our conclusion that we remembered Shaarac was still sleeping at Tessa's. Shaarvan fed me my lunch in bed, refusing to allow me to get up, and then made the trip back to her house to pick up our little son.

For the rest of the day, I was forced to stay in bed, and Shaarac and Shaarvan entertained me. I wanted to protest my enforced confinement, but it was too much of a luxury to object.

Shaarac was such a little person now. He was rolling over and edging his body in any direction he wanted to go. His crawling was incredibly skillful. As quickly as he was able to move around the room, would he ever desire to walk?

I wanted to halt time, to freeze this period of happiness. I wanted to stay forever as we were. I wished, once again, that Shapechanger had cameras. Why could I not have this memory always before me in a small five by six?

The next morning, when I returned to Tessa, she sulked, but I knew I performed better on her tests. By the time Shaarvan picked Shaarac and me up in the evening, Tessa had lost all her anger. Even when Shaarvan told her that he had decided that every other day would be noon dismissal, Tessa no longer glowered.

It was only a short time after that when Tessa told my husband that I was ready for the first of my tests. I thought Shaarvan would argue. I expected him to refuse, but strangely, he agreed and then demanded that I should not only take the first but the first *four*.

Even Tessa was amazed. She sputtered and tried to argue with him.

But Shaarvan just kept asking, "Is she ready?"

The two of them bickered for several minutes. They were both so strong of will it fascinated me to watch them lock horns. Abruptly, Shaarvan ordered me out of the room and told me to go feed Shaarac.

Of course, Shaarvan won the argument. I'd had no doubts. It wasn't only that Shaarvan owned me, and so had the final say; it was Shaarvan. My husband always accomplished what he set out to achieve.

I worried over the tests from then on, but they told me that there was nothing I could do to prepare for them. Yet, Tessa continued to stretch my Power, and the lessons increased and became even more difficult.

Shaarvan arranged for Shaarac to spend time at a nearby nursery, and my lessons for the sevenTide that followed had few interruptions.

I missed my afternoons off with Shaarvan and Shaarac, and I missed enormously not having my son at my side through the long days.

I knew that sometimes Shaarvan visited Shaarac in the nursery, but the fact that he would allow our son out of our sight was very un-Shapechanger like. And, although that was strange enough, there was more to it. Something was wrong and getting worse. And it was driving Shaarvan away from me. It felt it like a splinter, wedging in deeper as the days passed. I began to think of my life as being a beautiful ship with a crack in the side. The splinter was widening the crack, sinking us. Why?

More and more, Shaarvan spent his days with Tem, and when we were together, he was sharp with me and refused to discuss my questions.

Tessa, driving me frantically though the days, Shaarvan in the evenings — brittle as cracked glass, and Shaarac, fretting from all the tension, made me feel like a rubber band pulled to its utmost length.

All that kept me sane were the nights when Shaarvan made me walk the forest with him. The scent of pine needles and the springy softness of the dirt trails of Altar sang their rightness. The breeze ruffled my coat, and the raspy tongue of my mate at my side forced me to purr. And, under the green spires of pine trees with the blue of the sky beyond, our pairing was a wildness that set me free.

Far too soon, the day arrived. Testing day began like any other: we rose, we ate, and we fed Shaarac. Shaarvan dressed me carefully in Altarian clothing. The forest-green velvet reminded me of the woods surrounding Shaarvan's lair. I missed it so.

Shaarvan turned to stare at me. "It is always with you, Shaara. I told you that in Altar. We walked in that forest just last night."

"We dreamed we walked it, Shaarvan," I said bitterly. "We were not there."

"You are Shapechanger, my wife," he said, and his eyes flashed green. His arms reached out, and he pulled me to him. "There is no difference. Our dreams are real. I thought you would understand that by now."

His hands were messing up my hair, but I didn't mention it. His eyes held me in his Shapechanger magic, and I was frozen. Only his lips finding mine released me from his Power, yet I was still so spellbound I couldn't look away. When he let me breathe again, moments passed before I could speak. The glimmer in his eyes, not of mockery exactly, more of gloating, was the amused look of a male who knows his Power over his mate.

Perhaps it was the look in his eyes that gave me the courage to speak. "You are right, Shaarvan," I said. "There is so much I do not understand." I knew my chin had risen dangerously, but I plunged on. "I do not understand our dreams or the Shapechanger or why you are so distant with me now."

My tone was too aggressive, but Shaarvan was not angered. He seemed surprised that I was aware that things were not as they should be. I think he would have spoken then, but Shaarac began to cry. Shaarvan went over to him, picked him up, and we set off for the nursery to drop off Shaarac. After that would be my testing.

I was nervous as we entered the vast chamber where Tem sat upon his throne, but Shaarvan seemed totally relaxed. Did he not care if I passed, or did he have that much confidence I would succeed?

Four older Shapechanger males entered the huge throne room after us. Shaarvan introduced me to them. I, of course, kept my eyes down. I was not given their names. They left right after.

"Shaara," my husband said. "Look at me." I knew the test had begun by the tenseness of his voice. I listened as if each word were a precious drop of water, and I was dying of thirst.

"You must not move from this spot," Shaarvan ordered. "No matter what other Shapechanger males tell you. This, I command you as your husband."

Everyone was so serious. You'd have thought someone died. I looked over at Tessa, sitting next to Tem. She didn't meet my eyes. She stared straight ahead, as did the eight males who were witnesses to the tests.

The first Shapechanger stepped forward. Abruptly, I lowered my eyes.

"Shaara," he said. "Your husband has told me of you. He said you were strong-willed and stubborn. Perhaps he is not man enough for you. Step forward to me, and I shall take you into my arms and show you my strength. My Power at love will take away your stubbornness. Come to me, Shaara. Come to me, Shapechanger woman."

I felt his force. His words called to me. I had not understood Teea when she'd told me of the strength of the Shapechanger male — it was a leash pulling at my body, yanking and jerking at me. I feared that Power, but I would not give in; Shaarvan had commanded me. I didn't move.

"Good girl," the Shapechanger said to me. "Shaarvan, she does you honor."

I didn't wince at his unintended insult. I was frightened that there were three more Shapechanger to endure.

The second male stepped forward. "Stefar, you gave up too easily. I was watching her. She did not even struggle at your web. You have lost your touch."

The male turned to me. I felt the vigor of his regard. "Has Shaarvan told you how pleasing to the eye you are, little one? I would have called you Sleena, the diamond-eyed."

Almost, my eyes lifted to read him. It had startled me to hear him call me by my former name. I caught myself in time. Shapechanger knew everything. But it was an evil trick. My memories of Isandor were far from kind.

"Ah, you wonder how I know," he said. "I have seen your eyes flashing at Shaarvan or shadowed in your fear of him. I have noticed the color of your eyes, and I have learned your history. I agree with Isandor. Your eyes are like the facets of a diamond when pure light hits and shatters them into a myriad of rainbow colors.

"Show me your eyes, my lovely one. Raise them and let me see the lights shimmering in their depths. I am Shapechanger, and I command it!"

I trembled at his command, but I felt no temptation. I was gaining strength.

A moment's silence, and then he, too, turned. "I must pass her. She has an inner Power I cannot reach. I salute your choice, Shaarvan."

A third male stepped forward. I felt his force. He was not as strong as the other two, but there was a cunning look about him that put me on alert.

"I think she bluffs, good friends. Her chin is too delicate to hold the steel you speak of."

He took a step closer to me. "My friends are truthful, though. You are lovely. But where such beauty has grown, a weakness will lie. I have merely to probe to find where your shallowness is.

"I would guess you keep your eyes lowered, not to please your husband, but to hide a lack of intelligence. As most attractive women, you have probably not had to use your brains to get ahead. I suspect that you fluttered your eyelashes and wiggled your hips. No man needed to look further.

"I am right. Your eyes still lie folded, hidden behind Altarian laws. What a shame to find you as stupid as the rest!"

The male was getting on my nerves! I was angry. I knew it was a trick to make me look up, but his words, amplified with Power, made it difficult not to glare at him.

For a moment, he was silent. My anger boiled, but I refused to give into his taunts.

"I pass her to Level Two," the Shapechanger said.

I started to look over at Shaarvan, but the last of the testing males stepped forward.

"It stops here. There are already too many Level One women, and her young owner wants to take her all the way to Level Four? Are you Shapechanger males or *girls* to allow this? I say it stops."

He turned to me, and I was taken aback with his rage. His was no act to test me by. He meant every word.

"Shaara, a suitable name for the property of the man who owns you. You are property, woman, nothing but property. That is why I do not understand your master's willingness to allow you to test.

"I would just as soon ask my shoe to do a dance. I own it, just like Shaarvan owns you.

"Look at me, woman, when I talk to you."

He sprang it on me so quickly that my chin lifted halfway before I realized the trap. With all the will I possessed, I brought my chin back down, and my eyes studied the carpet beneath me.

The Shapechanger stared at me for a moment. "So you do have a brain beneath that mass of curls. Too bad because your husband would be far happier if you would spend more time with your legs spread and leave Tessa and the levels alone."

He sighed long and hard. "Big mistake, Shaarvan, but it is your mistake, not mine. I have better things to do with my time than watch fools."

He wheeled around and began to walk out.

"Do you pass her?" came a voice from the panel.

"Yes, she passes. Such a pity. She really does please the eyes. Sad to think she will wind up looking like Tessa."

I'd passed, but it felt like an uncertain triumph. Why did Shaarvan pledge me to Level Four? I didn't think I could endure this.

Shaarvan ordered me to sit and drink a restorative.

"You did well, my wife. Do not accept their words. Shapechanger cannot lie, but they can disguise the truth in twists and turns that confuse the ear. Erase their words and smooth your brow."

He drew me up, holding me tightly against his hard, muscular body. "What is the Primary?" he asked.

He surprised me, but I recited it: "To please my husband."

"Good, Shaara. Passing to Level Four will please me, do you understand?"

I nodded, but I did not understand. *Why? My mind cried out. Why do you want me to take these tests?*

Shaarvan stared into my eyes. I knew he read my question, but he chose not to answer it. Instead, his lips closed mine with a warm mouth. Even with all the eyes around us, I was his, and he knew it.

"I must leave you now, Shaara. This next level will be easy for you. Our hearts, our souls, and our minds are one. We cannot be parted."

I watched Shaarvan walk away. His desertion hurt me. Why did he have to leave?

It was Tessa who ordered me to stand. She came down from her seat where the judges sat, tied my hands behind my back, and then put a hood down over my head.

I knew it was preparation for the test, but I needed reassurance. "Tessa, did Shaarvan know you would bind me like this?"

"He knew, Shaara," the Priestess said. "It is necessary."

I was silent then, waiting for directions.

Tessa led me away from the chair where I'd sat. I presumed I was led back to the center of the chamber.

"Stay here," she ordered, and the sound of her feet walking away told me I was alone.

A moment, I stood there, trembling. Then I heard the sound of feet coming towards me. They were masculine feet with big, heavy bodies. I could feel that they were Shapechanger. They surrounded me. My hands were tied, and I was blind. My fear tasted of blackness.

Tem's voice rang out into the chamber. I recognized it, but the echoes of the chamber distorted his position. I could only tell that he was far away.

"Shaara, wife of Shaarvan of Altar. Your husband has ordered you to be tested for Level Two. There is no penalty for failure, but you may test only once. Your lord is not at your side, so I must ask you, do you wish the test to begin?"

"My husband believes I am ready to test," I said. "I will test." Such were the words I had been told by Tessa to say.

"The test is as follows," Tem continued. "You must locate your husband. He is in this room, but he may not speak or reach out to you. You may not see him or touch him. When you think you have located him, stand in front of him and say, 'I have found Shaarvan.' Do you understand?"

I nodded. Shaarvan had said this test would be easy. I was afraid to move. I took a step to the right and felt bombarded by voices speaking into my mind.

I shut my eyes and concentrated. Shaarvan's lips had just touched mine. I could still feel their warmth. In my mind, I called out to Shaarvan, and I heard him. He gave me directions: go to my right, turn left, forward, stop. I walked directly to him, following each command. When I stood perfectly in place and he gave me permission, I called out, "I have found Shaarvan."

"You have passed Level 2, Shaara, beating the shortest period of time in our records." I could tell from Tem's voice he was smiling.

Shaarvan removed my hood then and the binding that fastened my hands. His lips rewarded me.

Once more, Shaarvan led me to a chair and forced me to drink a restorative.

"Shaarvan, must I continue today?"

"It will please me if you do."

"But if I am tired, will I not do poorly?"

"You will do fine, Shaara."

"Do you wish me to pass Level 3?"

"Very much."

"Then I will do so."

"Rather cocky, are you not? " he laughed, but his kiss took away the sting.

I looked up into the handsome face of my adored one. I lifted my hand and traced the planes of his face. "No," I said. "I am not cocky, but if my husband says I will pass, I know I can."

"Are you ready?" the voice of the Highest rang out.

"She is prepared," Shaarvan replied, his eyes still fastened to mine.

Four Shapechanger came forward into the center of the chamber. I glanced away from Shaarvan's eyes to scan them, wondering what would now be demanded of me.

"Shaara," Shaarvan said. With both his hands on my face, he gently guided my attention back to him. "This time, you must meet their eyes, Shaara, but you will obey *only me*."

I was shocked. Shaarvan had told me to avoid the eyes of Shapechanger males. And these were young, vigorous Shapechanger. I could not do it!

"Shaarvan, I cannot . . ."

"Obey me, Shaara," he said, with a tone that brooked no argument. "Meet their eyes, but do not move from the place where you stand."

There was no indecision in his eyes. Test or not, I knew I could not ignore his command. I dropped my eyes and said, "I will obey."

The first Shapechanger moved forward. My knees were shaking already. I knew I could not do this. Why had Shaarvan ordered me to?

"Look up, Shaara. Look into my eyes," the Shapechanger ordered.

I obeyed and met the male's eyes. They were gray, as I had known they would be, but it was a dark gray like the metal of a ship, gray as a cleaner robot, not the gray of Shaarvan's eyes. I was relieved, as if a color difference could ease a magnetic pull.

The Shapechanger did not speak further. His eyes were focusing on me. I felt them. I felt the Power within him, but he was not Shaarvan. He did not draw me forward.

He realized he could not make me move from my spot at the same moment that I did. His eyes flared cat eyes, and his force doubled. Still, I denied him. I watched in fascination as the yellow-green eyes grew their diamond centers and the fur began to lengthen about his face.

"Enough," said Tem. "It is not necessary to Shapechange. She has passed your attempt.

"Kestler, step forward."

I'd gained a measure of confidence in the first one's failure, but I soon saw that his force had been trivial compared to the one who stood before me next.

This one's eyes were a deeper gray, with just a hint of blue. His force challenged me. I felt his pull deep in my mind.

"Come to me, Shaara. Feel my Power," he said.

I could not pull away from his force. I could not move my head to prevent his dominion. In an instant, I knew he was too strong for me. I didn't have the strength to deny him.

"Step forward. Come to me, little one."

I would have done so willingly, but Shaarvan had ordered me to stay. I could not disobey my lord. Did this Shapechanger not understand that?

"A third time, I command you. Come to me," the male ordered firmly, and his voice almost drove my feet forward.

I wanted to go to him. I wanted to please him more than breathe. Tears rolled down my face, but I didn't move. Shaarvan had commanded me, and I must obey.

Suddenly, the pull was gone. His eyes no longer held me, sucking me up like a vacuum of will.

I sighed, exhausted from my struggle. When would it end?

Tessa spoke up. "The girl needs a rest. Give her a drink and a short period to sit down."

"No," Tem said. "She must endure through the test, or she does not pass Level 3."

The third Shapechanger stepped forward. His eyes were silver, like the shine of aluminum foil. It no longer mattered. I knew that I would not give in. The third Shapechanger brought no challenge at all. He lacked the skill of the second. I relaxed during his struggle.

The fourth was also not as great in Power as the second. He kept telling me I was under his Power and that I could not resist him. I wondered why the lie did not sicken him. He had so little Power over me that I almost laughed in his face.

And so the testing ended. Shaarvan came to me and lifted me up into his arms. He carried me back to my seat and forced me to eat and drink. I did not want the sustenance, only his lips on mine and his arms about me.

"You have made me proud, Shaara. I would end this now if it were not for the fact that I need you to pass the next test. It is the most important. If you are too tired to continue, I will ask them to reschedule it. Can you endure one more, my little one?"

"Is the last test as hard as the one I just went through?"

"It is a level more difficult."

"Will you be here?"

"Yes."

"Do you believe I can pass it, Shaarvan?"

He studied me. "Shaara, you have reached a level that only a small percentage of women reach. If you pass this test, Tessa says that none of the tests that follow would cause you difficultly when your mind and body are matured into your Power.

"But this is the last test I shall permit you. There will be no more, Shaara. Understand?"

I nodded. I had not asked to take *any* of the tests. Why would I want to continue?

Shaarvan caught my thought. A tweak of a smile rewarded my thinking. It puzzled me that he was glad I did not wish more. Why did he wish me to pass the first four?

"Shaara," Shaarvan said sharply, bringing my attention back to his words. "Test Four will be the most difficult for you *whenever* you take it. Complete it now or on another day. It will not change the difficulty or ease the strain. You have the strength to pass Level Four, but I am unsure if you will have the *obedience*."

"It was only your command that brought me though the last test, Shaarvan. I will obey you," I protested.

"I know, you try." Shaarvan chuckled softly. It was a joke between us. "Try" was my middle ground. Shaarvan always said it was not enough.

He lifted my hand and kissed it. "You will not pass, my sweet Shaara, if 'try' is all you can do. You *must* obey, no matter how challenging the command may seem. It is Level Four that I require from you."

"Then I shall pass it."

"Good. Then you will please me.

"Each time a new lord enters, Tem will ask you if you wish to continue. You will not want to, Shaara, but you must. It is by *my command* that you take this test and pass. You will answer Tem and say, 'It is the will of my husband that I continue.' Obey me in this, my wife. I have my reasons."

"I obey."

"Remember the Primary, Shaara."

He turned my hand over, and I felt his warm breath on my palm.

"Memorize the feel of me, Shaara," he said. "My tongue spreads fire on your palm. Feel it. My lips torture you with ecstasy. My touch is of ownership and possession. You are mine, Shaara. Remember."

"I am branded by you, Shaarvan. I love you. Why do you seek to awaken me? How can I concentrate on tests when I hunger for you?"

"Remember and obey!" was Shaarvan's only answer. His eyes flared green. I whimpered and lowered my eyes.

"She is ready," Shaarvan called out. His voice rang out in the hall, strong and calm.

"Do you wish this test to commence, Shaara of Shaarvan?"

"It is the will of my husband that I continue."

Tem smiled. "You may stop this test, Shaara, at any point. You need only say, 'I yield.' Do you understand, Shaara? You may halt the test, and it will be over, and you will *not* need to continue."

"It is the will of my husband that I continue."

"Level Four commences."

Shaarvan dropped my hand and moved aside. A huge Shapechanger walked up to me. He was one of the ones who'd been introduced to me earlier. The Warlord held out his hand and said, "You will come with me."

I looked over at Shaarvan. He had given me no directions. What was I to do? Shaarvan signaled for me to go.

I walked towards the Shapechanger, but I ignored his outstretched hand.

"You will take my hand, Shaara." His voice demanded. There was Power in it, but my eyes went back to Shaarvan. Once more, he nodded.

To touch a Shapechanger male was to give him Power over you. No wonder Shaarvan feared this test. I feared it, too.

I obeyed my husband and lay my palm on the outstretched hand. The touch of it burned as much as holding a heated pan against my skin. The pain seared me. Then, my hand grew cold as a frostbite warning.

The sting and the shock of it were an inward thing that preyed on my mind. I was amazed to find that I had been led back to the center of the chamber. My hand was numb by then, but the Shapechanger still held it. He lifted up his other hand and touched my hair.

"It pleasures me to test you," he said. "I shall enjoy you greatly."

I knew his look. I knew what he was about to do.

"No!" I cried out.

He grabbed big hunks of hair on each side of my face and held me as his lips drew near my mouth. His eyes were using Shapechanger magic, but it couldn't hold me. I kicked his shin and reared back from him.

"Hold," he ordered, but I would not obey him.

His hand whipped out and grabbed my neck. At once, I was deadly still.

"Silly child, did you think you could fight a Shapechanger lord?"

I said nothing. The neck grip was too painful. I did not dare provoke him.

Again, the Shapechanger's lips lowered to mine, and he whispered, "Give into me. I am your master."

"No!" I wailed. I knew he would punish me, but I couldn't remain silent. I was Shaarvan's. Nothing would change that.

The male didn't punish me for my refusal, but his lips claimed mine. There was no pleasure in it. His tongue in my mouth neither hurt nor drove me to a frenzy. I felt his Power strengthen for a last assault, but I was dead to him. He held me still. I couldn't refuse his tongue and lips, but I gave him nothing, and I took nothing from him.

He stared into my eyes. There was a measure of respect in his.

"You are far beyond a Level Four, Shaara, and your husband has bonded you well."

He released my neck, and I quickly stepped away. If he had been a rattlesnake, I could not have been more repelled.

He watched me and smiled. "She is yours completely, Shaarvan. She passes with honors."

I had forgotten it was only a test, but I had no time to ponder that. The next tester was already stepping forward. I was angry now. If they thought I would allow three more Shapechanger to kiss me, they would see a whirlwind of violence.

"There are three more Warlords," Tem told me with his deep, baritone voice. "They will not treat you with the respect you deserve as the wife of Shaarvan. The test will not be gentle. It is simple to halt it now. You must only say, 'I yield.' Do you still wish to continue, Shaara of Shaarvan?"

I would have loved to stop. This test was madness. Why did Shaarvan want me to pass it? Why hadn't he forbidden me to take it? Tem waited for my response. How silly for me to even think about it. I had no choice. I must do Shaarvan's bidding. It was the Primary.

"It is the will of my husband that I continue," I said out loud.

"Take my hand," said the male.

I glared up at him, and then I turned my back to him, the gravest of insults in Shapechanger. Tessa so loudly sucked in her breath I turned to look at her. From the corner of my eyes, I saw Shaarvan shake his head at me. I knew then that I had not followed the Primary. Insulting this Shapechanger did not please Shaarvan.

I turned back around and bowed to the male, saying, "Please forgive me, my lord." My eyes dropped meekly. He reached out and took my hand. Again, I felt the heat, the cold, and the pain. The male said nothing for a moment, but he raised up my chin and stared into my eyes.

"I understand, Shaara," he said. "You are confused and frightened. I shall not punish you for your offense. Your husband cannot tell you, so I shall. You must let each of us kiss you. Such is the nature of the test. To fight us will only cause *you* pain. Must I put you in the neck grip to do what is necessary?"

"No. Please. I will obey."

"Good. Wisdom is knowing that when the final outcome is inevitable, the battle is without purpose."

His lips joined mine then. His tongue plunged deep inside, but it found only hollowness. In a moment, he was done.

He stared long into my eyes. "I have touched you in this testing. It is a bonding, child. We four will be your bondmates henceforth. We have pledged to protect you as long as needed. Should Shaarvan or you ever require our help, we are yours."

He turned to Tem. "Shaara of Shaarvan passes with honors," he said.

"Two Warlords have bonded you to them," Tem said. "The pain of it has brought your anger and your fear. It is Shaarvan, your husband, who desires that you take this test, not you. Why do you continue? It is simple to stop. All you need to say is, 'I yield.' Would that not be better than to continue this torture?"

"It is the will of my husband that I continue," I repeated, with my eyes lowered to the ground.

"So be it, Shaara of Shaarvan."

Shapechanger three stepped forward. He, too, held out his hand. I touched him and attempted to shut out the pain. I did not struggle when he pulled me to him, but my eyes flared when his hand touched my bottom and he pushed me close.

"Is this part of the testing?" I hissed at him.

"Did I initiate your words, Shapechanger woman?"

His voice was ice, but I felt the hardness of his maleness as he pressed against me. My fear was back.

"Good, pay attention to the difference between us," he said. His eyes pressed against my will. "I shall not take you with your husband watching, but be wary of how easily my arms could hold you still and my lance could spear the depths of you.

"This testing is only of status among women. It does not mean that any Shapechanger male could not rend your dress and ride you as he wished."

His lips were like his words. He raped my unwillingness and drove his tongue in me with the force of plunder. His arms crushed me to his chest. But there was no answering spark in me, no ache of longing.

At last, he released me. "I shall pass you on to Level Four," he said, as if he were disappointed to do so, "but I have taught you a lesson you needed."

My eyes glared after him. If I'd dared, I would have Shapechanged and ripped the male's shirt to shreds.

"Three Shapechanger Warlords have sampled your body. Should a husband demand such a sacrifice of you? Is it fair, Shaara?" Tem asked. "Should a husband require such obedience from a young wife?

Choose wisely, Shaara. The last will be the *worst*. Say 'I yield,' and stop this madness."

Worse? How could the last Shapechanger be any worse than the one who had pawed my body so offensively? Tem was right. It was not fair, and I hated it. How dared Shaarvan make me endure this?

I looked over at him. His eyes were watching me. I could not read them. He would not allow that. But I knew what he would say if he spoke. He had given me an order. He had commanded me to pass.

I sighed heavily. I begged him with my eyes to rescind his order, but there was no softening in his posture or in his eyes. I knew that I must obey.

I turned to face Tem. I brushed away a tear, but I said, "It is the will of my husband that I continue."

"You are sure?"

I did not pause again. "It is the will of my husband that I continue."

"So be it, Shaara of Shaarvan."

Shapechanger four came towards me. He did not stretch out his hand for me to take. He stood and watched me.

When the silence grew so oppressive that I looked up, he spoke. "Tenor has taught you to respect us. Thedar has told you of our bonds. Spelon has taught you to fear us. I am Stegthal. If you pass my test, you will deserve Level Four, for I shall use the patterns on you."

I gasped. I almost looked to Shaarvan for help, but I knew he had told me I could pass this test if I were obedient enough. But how could he believe I could withstand the patterns of a Shapechanger male?

Stegthal reached out and took my hand before I'd recovered from the shock of his words. I had been frightened of Spelon and his violent nature, but I was even more afraid of the potency of the patterns. Even

Tren, a non-Shapechanger, had harmed my bond with Shaarvan. How could I stand an assault from a Warlord?

"Your eyes tell me your soul," Stegthal said. "I see your fear. Do you wish to stop the test?"

I started to turn my head to look at Shaarvan.

Stegthal grabbed my chin and moved it back towards him. "No, your husband has made his decision already. I asked you."

To ask to stop would not halt the test. It would end it forever, and I would not be obeying the Primary if I did so.

"Thank you, Stegthal, for your offer, but I obey my husband's wishes. I must withstand your patterns."

"So be it, little one, so be it."

His hand reached up and began to stroke my face. I thought it would feel like Shaarvan's touch, but it was simply a hand touching my skin. There was no liquid fire, no calling from deep inside me.

I felt the web as he began to entwine me. Layer on layer, the patterns enclosed me in a bondage of obedience. I wanted to fight him, but the web held me prisoner. I couldn't move. Everywhere he touched me burned with pain, but I could no longer speak. Yet, in spite of the patterns and his Shapechanger magic, I had no urge for him. I only wanted to get away.

Stegthal did not stop at my face. He continued stroking me; his hands moved to traverse my breasts. Still, I could not move, not a hand, not even a muscle to flinch away from his invasion. My horror grew. His hands didn't stop. They traveled downwards. Shaarvan was somewhere watching. Why did he allow this? Surely, my husband would not permit Stegthal to go where he was heading. The judges, Tem and Tessa, were all in the room. Why did no one stop Stegthal?

I was ready to yield to Tem. Stop the test, even if it displeased Shaarvan. I wanted to yell out, but I could no longer speak. I could no longer halt the test.

"Shaarvan," I cried out in my mind. *"Please help me. Please don't let him do this to me!"*

If Shaarvan heard, he remained silent. No one spoke or made a sound as Stegthal's hands played my body. Then the stranger, this fourth challenger, pulled my dress up, and his hands against my naked bottom pulled me closer. His fingers touched me where he had no right to be.

My tears were the only part of me free from Stegthal's Shapechanger magic. They flowed freely down my face as he thrust his finger within my depths.

"Shaarvan! Shaarvan! Shaarvan!" my thoughts were screaming, but I guessed due to the patterns that no one could hear my pleas.

"Quiet, child. It is done," Stegthal said.

He smoothed my dress back down and held me while I fought to control my hysteria and my desolation. Gently, the male's hand caressed my hair to calm me, but I only wanted to be free of his webbing.

"Breathe deeply, little one."

I obeyed his words, fighting for control. I was ashamed, and I was angry. My anger grew stronger than my shame. When Stegthal released me, he would feel my fury, no matter the consequences.

I knew he read my thoughts, but his hand continued to stroke my hair and back, and his words continued gentle and calming.

He eased the webs enough for me to speak. My sobs had a voice then, but I had no patience with their consolation.

"Let me go," I demanded.

Stegthal laughed loudly. "Ah, Shaarvan," he said. "She is full of fire. After all that we four have tried to teach her, she is still ready for battle. I salute you, Shaarvan, for your choice."

His words taunted me. My rage had grown enormous. "Have I not passed your stupid tests? Let me go!"

"Do not force me to punish you," Stegthal warned. "Shaarvan would not interfere."

He held my chin towards him. I recognized the Power in his eyes. I knew then there would be no retaliation, not by me. Stegthal would not permit it.

"Good," he said. "You understand. I shall release you on *my* time and at *my will*.

You have almost passed Level Four, but first, I shall explain to you what has occurred, what has caused your tears of humiliation and of rage. I did what I did, little one, to bond you. The others all hold a bond, but they are bonded in a different way. Although you and I have shared no joining, you are mine now. Should Shaarvan ever need me, I would give him my life, but if he should fall and go on to a higher, different Plane, then you would belong to me. That is the bond I have made between us and why I have performed it before witnesses."

"No," I cried softly. The shocks of the day had settled in on me, robbing me of whatever the cause, it was driving. Only the web held me upright through Stegthal's speech. I was in shock, shattered by too many assaults. I couldn't fight off more of his abuse.

"The test must go on," Stegthal said. "I shall kiss you now."

His lips covered mine before I had time to argue. It was, at first, a gentle kiss, but his desire began to overwhelm him. He, too, pushed my bottom towards him and rammed me with his hardness.

I whimpered, and he laughed — a conqueror's laugh. "It is eager for you, Shaara," he said. "I would not leave you unsatisfied if ever you became *fully* mine."

Once again, his lips forced me to open, and his tongue plunged within me.

I fought him, despite the webs, but he placed the dreaded neck grip on me. Then, his mouth and tongue had free access to explore me. He did not take long to find my emptiness. He released my neck and pulled away.

"I knew you were a true bond with Shaarvan. I felt it in your soul."

His green eyes flashed and branded me. I winced at still another onset of pain.

Stegthal continued. "Listen well, Shaara. I have entitlement to you. You are branded with my claim. But until that day should arrive, or if it never does, I shall be only as a brother to you."

His eyes moved away from mine, and he spoke loudly into the hall. "Shaarvan, I have claimed your lovely Shaara, as you wished. We all hope the Stars do not see the need for my guardianship of her, but I would have you know that your little one has impressed me so greatly I would willingly take her as my wife."

"You honor me," Shaarvan said.

I gasped.

"Shaara, wife of Shaarvan, passes with my highest approval," Stegthal declared, and he moved back, breaking the webs. I collapsed in his arms, but I twisted free of him and fell to the floor in tears. It was only when I felt Shaarvan's arms around me that I gained the energy to move.

"Shaarvan," I cried and hugged him tightly, weeping uncontrollably.

I should have hated him for demanding the test of me. I should have been furious, but I needed him too much. I needed his arms around me and the familiar feel of him. I needed his love.

"Hush, my love. It is all right. You did well," he whispered to me.

"But why? I don't understand why you . . ."

Shaarvan abruptly lifted me up to a standing position. "Enough, Shaara. A Shapechanger is not required to explain everything to his woman. I will permit no more tears."

Like a shroud laid across a dead man's body, so had the coldness gathered round Shaarvan.

My eyes fell to the floor. I had done everything Shaarvan ordered me to do. I didn't understand the harshness in him now.

"Shaara," my husband said, sighing, "I did not intend to be so sharp with you." He opened his arms for me to come in. "You are very young, my lovely wife. It is suitable that your mind should be occupied with Shaarac and those pleasures appropriate to you. You do not need to hold the concerns and worries of a male. Women live more comfortably in the present. We males must bear the vision of the future."

"But I want to share your visions."

"No." His knuckles caressed my cheek, as he did when I'd pleased him. "I cherish the innocence that is still in you, Shaara. You have been loaded down with far too much stress. Savor these days, my love. Share your joy and spontaneity with me. I need them to carry in my heart."

"You won't explain?"

He placed his finger on my lips, the Shapechanger sign for silence.

Teea

Starnkor allowed me to continue my bedside visits with Tevor. I was even permitted to remain during the meetings of the lords, not because he accepted my presence there, but because he still would not allow me to be out of his sight.

I was careful not to risk dismissal again. I kept my eyes lowered and strove not to become impatient with the group's slowness to make plans. But it was more difficult than it had been before. When a Shapechanger bonds a woman through joining, a closeness forms that allows him free access to her thoughts. Many times, I felt Starnkor's eyes on me, and I knew I must think of other things.

Once, when Jaster stated that we must not resort to violence against the commoners, Starnkor's hand rode my neck. Slowly, so as not to challenge him, I raised my head and attempted to meet his eyes. A sudden gentle squeeze reminded me not to speak, but I would not have. My mouth was frozen, hearing his voice speak the words I had longed to say.

"It has come too far for that now, Jaster. Even when Thenos' rule is ended, without an intensely unpleasant demonstration of the full Power of the Shapechanger, the commoners will not withdraw. They have tasted authority — unearned and unwarranted, it is true, but they will not retreat back to what they were without a struggle."

I wanted to cheer. I am sure my eyes were shining with happiness that the truth had finally been spoken. Starnkor's hand, once more, warningly tightened. I lowered my eyes.

The males argued with Starnkor for many minutes. Sharp words flew like arrows. The evening did not end amicably, but I was certain that his words had advanced the group towards a truer vision.

When they were gone, Starnkor returned us to the room where Tevor lay. "Sit down, Teea," he ordered, and I obeyed.

Ignoring me, he spoke to Tevor. "Your wife takes a strong hand, my friend. She is head-strong and feels herself to be more intelligent than the lords present tonight."

I drew in a quick breath. Starnkor was stating reasons for heavy disciplining. Had I not tried to remain quiet and meek at his side? Surely he wouldn't be harsh enough to punish me for unbidden thoughts!

Starnkor laughed. "Tevor, you must understand. I would discipline her if I thought it would change her. I would take my hand to her soft underside, but it would not change her quick mind or disguise the fact that she *is* smarter than the lords present tonight."

Starnkor's words were close to treason. The Shapechanger, if they heard him, would surely send him to Westla for more training. Males did not say things like that!

"Come here," Starnkor ordered. Automatically, I cast a glance at Tevor, seeking assistance, but, there was none. Tevor lay as he had done for a halfPass, motionless and uncommunicative.

I obeyed my Second.

Starnkor's arms pulled me close. "We should not be afraid of the truth, Teea. Variation is a component of all existence. If we males cannot accept the possibility of superior intelligence evolving in other planets, then we have ceased to accept the challenge of climbing higher on the Somber Tree."

I met his eyes, but I didn't dare speak. I certainly didn't reject his argument, but I didn't see how he meant to use it.

He drew my chin up so he could read my eyes. "It is difficult, Teea, to see wisdom when eyes are so enchanting. No wonder we males do not wish to recognize that a pleasing appearance can hide an intellectual mind."

So saying, he kissed me. I was uneasy. We were still in the room with Tevor.

"Perhaps jealousy will waken your lord," Starnkor teased me.

"Cruelty scars the soul," I said, rather daringly.

Starnkor's eyes reacted only with amazement at my response . He stood a moment, staring down at me. Then he turned and addressed my husband once again.

"You trusted me to watch over her. That I shall do, but I shall also use my judgment, and if it differs from yours, forgive me, my friend. I shall allow Teea to fulfill what I see as her Path to the Stars. I have decided that I shall permit her to speak in our meetings."

"You would do that?"

Starnkor nodded cautiously. "If your words are the mirrors of your thoughts, Teea, I shall not only permit it, but I shall also back you before the group."

I had the strangest wish to throw my arms about Starnkor and thank him with kisses, but, of course, I did not. Undoubtedly, he was well aware of it, since he snoops in my thoughts so frequently, but I am sure he understood that it was only a spontaneous impulse from the great joy inside me at hearing that I would be given such freedom. It in no way reflected that I might be softening towards him; I'd never go willingly to his bed.

Shaara

I noticed that everyone except the Level Four Shapechanger lords had departed. Shaarvan led me towards them. They were standing, leaning up against the wall, trying not to appear as if they'd been listening to our conversation.

Shaarvan forced me closer, and then stopped, greeting each of them with a short bow of his head. I kept my eyes firmly lowered. Even if I'd been permitted to meet their eyes, I would not have been willing. My face burned with mortification.

My husband dropped my hand, leaving me between the wall and himself. Then I had nowhere to hide from my shame.

"Obey me, Shaara," Shaarvan said.

I looked up. When had I not obeyed?

"You will look at these Shapechanger lords, and you will remember them, Shaara. They are your bondmates now. They will take my place when I am not at your side. You will obey them in every way, treating them with deference and deferring to their opinion in all matters. They will be your guides, your brothers, your guardians, and your *babysitters*, as needed . . ."

I did not mean to be discourteous to Shaarvan, but he asked too much. I booted the wall with an angry kick.

"Shaara! I shall not be patient with your temper tantrums," said my *loving* husband. "My time is too short. You will listen attentively to my words, and you will be respectful."

I bowed my head, but he was being so unjust.

"Look at your bondmates, Shaara," he demanded, not the least appeased by my humble head hanging.

I complied, glaring at them. Either Shaarvan didn't notice, or he ignored it.

"When you have need of them, Shaara, you may talk freely to them," he continued with his lecture. "In spite of what Spelon said, you may initiate conversation with them."

I saw the four of them laugh and slap Spelon on the back. I rarely understand male humor, and this was another of those occasions.

Shaarvan was smiling at the males, yet he'd sat and watched them kiss me and do worse. This was the husband who had almost killed Tren because he gave me the briefest of kisses? These Shapechanger, my new *best friends,* had kissed me so deeply they'd almost hit my toes!

Shaarvan began to laugh. "Shaara, they did no more than test you," he answered, although I had not spoken.

"I preferred to choose the Level Fours from Warlords who are my friends," Shaarvan explained. "So, therefore, my wife, these are Shapechanger I can trust with you. But anyone who tested you would have done what these males did, except for Stegthal's deep bonding."

I looked down, avoiding Shaarvan's eyes. Maybe if he didn't see the anger, he would ignore my opinion. For several minutes, there was silence. I writhed with rage. I knew Shaarvan was watching me, but I couldn't help how I felt. I thought he should feel equally furious. The fact that he didn't made me even more irate.

Shaarvan was quiet for so long I knew he wouldn't drop it.

"You are right, my wife. I shall not *drop it*. You are stubbornly ignoring my words. You are shutting out what I've been planning for a sixTide. I shall not allow that."

Shaarvan's friends had almost publicly raped me, and I was supposed to invite them to be my pals? I gritted my teeth and kept my head down.

"Shaara, every one of us can read you clearly, I have told you I shall not allow your anger towards them. You will thank each of your bondmates by name, and you will kiss his cheek."

At that, my eyes no longer hugged the ground. I reared up and glowered at Shaarvan. He had gone crazy. Perhaps the testing had goaded him beyond endurance. I took a step backwards.

"No," he said. His hand caught my wrist and pulled me back beside him. "I know it is your fatigue making you question my commands, Shaara. I shall forgive the slowness of your obedience, *once*, but *you will obey me in this*."

There was no compassion in Shaarvan's eyes. It wasn't fair. Where was the reward for passing all those tests? Why was I, instead, being punished? I heard a low growl from my husband. It was only a warning, but I took a step towards Thedar — he'd been the only kind one.

"My husband orders my thanks to you . . ." I began.

"Not enough, Shaara," Shaarvan said sharply.

I sighed, but my hesitation was brief. This was not a good place to give challenge, not with five Shapechanger lords watching me, and my husband on the brink of change.

I began again. "Thank you, Thedar, for testing me."

I turned back to look at Shaarvan. He nodded. Then, the impossibility of Shaarvan's command hit me. All four Shapechanger were bigger than I was. How *could* I obey Shaarvan?

I groaned. This was so unreasonable. Shaarvan shifted his position. Did I see the faint outline of his patterned fur and whiskers?

"Thedar, could you please bend over so I can kiss your cheek?"

"A Shapechanger does not bow to a woman — even if she is Level Four," Thedar said, causing the others to laugh at my expense.

I glared at all of them, except Stegthal. I would not look at him. As quickly as they had laughed, the faces of the males became impassive again, yet I saw that Thedar and Tenor's mouths twitched with suppressed humor. None of them offered me suggestions.

I looked around for a chair to move. There was nothing but benches, and they were bolted down.

"Please, could we move over there, so I can stand on the bench?" I asked the lords.

"We do not feel like moving," Spelon said.

What a jerk. I closed my eyes briefly and prayed that Barquel would spit all over his . . .

"Shaara!"

I wished Shaarvan would stay out of my thoughts.

I turned to face my husband. "Shaarvan, I cannot do this. Please, I have tried."

"If your thoughts are pleasant, you will have no fear of our reading them, Shaara. And a good Shapechanger husband does not give an order that is impossible, nor does an obedient wife fail to find the solution."

I paused and studied his eyes. "Shaarvan, could you please give me a boost?"

"No. You have tried all but the obvious, Shaara."

I heaved a sigh. It was the only sound I could make that didn't seem to get me in trouble. I knew what Shaarvan wanted, but why?

Why must the males touch me again? Why did Shaarvan want to allow them to?

This day was worse than the times with Isandor. Then only one male had pawed my body. Yet Shaarvan demanded four males touch me. I could not go through that again. I shuddered.

"Shaara, come here."

My feet dragged, and I trembled. I did not dare to meet Shaarvan's eyes. Shaarvan had told me that the bones of a woman could not support burdens. Did he not know that his displeasure in me was far more crushing?

Shaarvan's irritation would be a wall of heat and flames that I would walk into, and then I would be punished. I knew I could not win against him, but when a stone is thrown into the sky, is its path downward not already plotted? Shaarvan asked too much of me. Spelon was right. I was not a Shapechanger lord. I was only a woman.

My husband's hand reached out and tugged me towards him. He gripped my upper arms. I was prepared for him to shake me, yell at me, and hit me . . . But there was only silence. I looked up.

The disappointment in his eyes made me cringe worse than any beating.

"Oh, Shaarvan," I cried out. "I am sorry."

His arms loosened, and he let me shelter in his arms. The feel of them wrapped around me was the strength I needed.

When he spoke, each word was a thorn. The misery in his voice made fresh tears spill down my cheeks.

"Spelon would say I should beat you now because you are disobedient. Tenor believes you are but a child who needs a father. Thedar would say that words will make you understand, and Stegthal would say a husband must be all of that and more."

Shaarvan sighed. It was a cheerless sigh, and I knew I was the cause.

"I am sorry, Shaarvan. I will not argue anymore. I will do everything you tell me, no matter how awful . . ."

"Hush, Shaara," Shaarvan said. "Your bondmates will each touch you again, Shaara, not because it pleasures me. It pains me more than you will ever know, but they will do it because it is necessary for your future. And I shall endure it because I must, and so must you, my wife.

"You say you will obey me now, but I think your stubbornness will once more rule your wisdom when you are not here in my arms. Perhaps because of Isandor, this task is more than you can bear. I shall not beat you, Shaara. I shall give you a choice. You will do as I command of your own *free will* or by my Power. But you will obey my will in this. Which is your choice?"

It was very rare for a Shapechanger to use his Power to make another do his bidding. Even a slave had the free will to choose a beating or to carry out the command his master gave. I would not welcome being a marionette. The webbing of a Shapechanger was too much entrapment for me. And Shaarvan knew it.

"I will obey you, Shaarvan, by *free will*."

He nodded. "Shaara, I trust these lords with my most valued possessions — you and Shaarac. They will *not* hurt you. You must learn the truth of that. You must learn to trust them to take care of you, and you must learn to value their judgment. Now, go. Do as I command you."

I walked back to Thedar, knowing this time there could be no retreat. "Would you please help me to obey my husband's will?" I asked him.

"Gladly, Shaara," Thedar said. His hands reached down to my waist, and he lifted me up. It surprised me there was no pain at his touch as there had been before. Quickly, I pressed my lips against his cheek, and then he put me down.

"Thank you, Thedar," I said. His gray eyes smiled.

One down, three to go. I went to Tenor next. Shaarvan had said that Tenor thought I was a child. How could he have kissed me then?

"Thank you for testing me," I said to him. I held my eyes down. I remembered too clearly that he was the one I'd kicked.

Tenor's hand lifted my chin. "You are welcome, Shaara, wife of Shaarvan."

"Will you please help me, also, to obey Shaarvan's wishes?"

"Only if you vow not to kick me again."

The others laughed, but I turned red. Again, my eyes fell to the ground. "I am very sorry. I will not kick you again."

Tenor's strong hands lifted me up, and I gave him a token kiss. But when he set me down, he didn't release me immediately. I looked up. He was smiling at me. "Well done, Shaara," he said, and then he dropped his hands.

There were still the two most difficult to get through. I went to Spelon next. He frightened me the most of the four, but I could not face Stegthal, yet. I walked slowly, praying to Barquel that Shaarvan would call out and tell me I'd obeyed sufficiently, and didn't need to continue. Shaarvan did not speak.

"I thank you for your testing of me," I told Spelon, as sincerely as I could. The words were no sooner floating in the air between us than I found I couldn't breathe. Nausea hit. I collapsed in agony.

Shaarvan was at my side instantly. "You were not thankful, Shaara. Say it."

"I was not thankful," I gasped.

"She does not understand the Shapechanger lie," Shaarvan told the others. He helped me up. His hands circled me for a moment before pushing me away.

Shaarvan whispered in my ear. "Be careful how you say it, Shaara," *my love.* His words buoyed me for the rest of my ordeal.

"Spelon, Shaarvan commands me to thank you for your testing."

I could feel Shaarvan's displeasure at my wording, but he let it slide.

Spelon said nothing. His eyes watched me, but they were not as cold or as violent as I remembered them.

"Will you also help me to obey my husband's command?"

"No *please* for me?" he demanded stiffly.

The others laughed. I sighed. I had not intended to omit the word.

"Please?"

Spelon's hands went to my waist, but he did not immediately lift me. "My words to you were rough, Woman, but you held challenge in your eyes. I told you what you needed to hear. It was the truth.

"Your body felt me hard against you, and you learned to fear me. You are right to fear me, to fear all of us. Still, I would have you know, woman, that I would never take you, because you are owned by Shaarvan, and he is my friend."

Spelon lifted me, then, and I kissed his cheek quickly. If he had meant to remove a part of my fear, he had not done so.

There was only one Shapechanger lord left. He had webbed me, and done things that only Shaarvan and Isandor had . . . It was hardest to go to him. I did not meet his eyes. I hoped he would not require it. "Thank you for testing me," I said, as quickly as I could get the words out.

"I shall see your eyes, Shaara, when you speak to me," he ordered.

I raised them, but I could not meet Stegthal's eyes. I repeated my words.

"Shaarvan's wife, you are welcome," he said.

"Please, could you . . ." My voice deserted me. I cleared my throat and tried again. "Please, could you help me to do Shaarvan's will?" I ended in a whisper, but Stegthal heard me.

"I am always Shaarvan's friend and yours, Shaara. I shall do everything I can to aid him and his family."

Stegthal lifted me, and I kissed his cheek. I sighed as he set me down, but he also did not free me immediately.

"Shaara, I shall be your friend," he told me. "Do not fear me."

My voice was gone, but I whispered, "Spelon says I must."

"Spelon confuses fear with respect."

I met Stegthal's eyes. When I did so, he would not allow me to look away. For a moment, he searched my eyes. "Good," he said. "I see your fear is lessened. None of us will hurt you, Shaara. As your husband says, we will be your guards, your brothers, and your friends. You will remember that we are Shapechanger lords, and you will respect and obey us, but you are *not* to fear us."

Stegthal let go of me. I backed away. I glanced at Shaarvan, and he nodded and flashed me the sign for *come*.

It was easier to face the eyes of the four with Shaarvan at my back, but my husband had been right in forcing me to acknowledge them. Having touched and talked with each of them, I could no longer see my bondmates as the monsters I'd thought they were. But what a difficult lesson it had been.

Shaarvan and I left the four Shapechanger lords and returned to our chamber. I wanted to go get Shaarac, but my husband would not permit it. "No, he is spending the night there. It has been arranged. Now, my wife," he said, "everyone but me has pleasured themselves on you. It is my turn."

How dare he say that. Without clear thinking, I changed into a snarling she-tiger, one so enraged, it tried to rake its claws down Shaarvan's face. He threw me to the ground and with his foot secured me there.

"Change back," he ordered.

I snarled, but I Changed.

Shaarvan dragged me back to a standing position. "Never attack a Shapechanger, Shaara, no matter what your shape."

He was annoyed with me. I supposed I'd broken some rule I didn't know about, but my irritation was beyond lucidity.

"How dare you condemn me for what you ordered me to do," I said.

Shaarvan's face was blank. He had to read me to understand.

"Stars! I forgive your assault on me, Shaara. You misunderstood. I did not mean that the touch of the others was your fault. I only meant that the torture of seeing those males touch you has taken me beyond . . ."

His lips were on me, rough and driven. I should have resented the violence, but I needed it. I wanted the hands and mouths of all those others to be chased like a demon from my soul.

Our mingling that day was not of pleasure, but of necessity. When the scent of no other male was in my mind, and the touch of hands that were not Shaarvan's were expunged from my body, we lay limp.

"Now will you explain why you wanted me tested?" I begged Shaarvan.

"Oh, Shaara, woman with a thousand questions," he said. "Do you never rest your curiosity?"

"Why did you want me to be Level Four?"

"Shapechanger sorceress!" he said, and he laughed. "There are bad times coming, Shaara. They have begun already, and they all revolve around Thenos.

"You have great Power, my little Shaara, so Tessa and Tem tell me, and I think I have long known it from the strength of your will in my training of you. Perhaps that is a part of what draws Thenos to you, that and his hatred of me . . ."

"Thenos? What does . . . ?"

"Hush, woman, or I shall tell you nothing."

I shut my mouth and waited for Shaarvan to continue.

"It was Thenos who caused the slaver to capture you," Shaarvan told me. "I discovered it on Freinana.

"You must be guarded at all times, even here on Westla. I have bonded the Shapechanger lords to you for that reason."

I forgot my vow to be silent, "But haven't those other guards done just as well?"

Shaarvan smiled. It was irritating to be read so adroitly.

"There are levels to life, Shaara, like there are levels of Power. The Warlords I bonded you to are more than guards. Should I be killed the next time Thenos attacks, Stegthal will be your husband."

I remembered Stegthal offering that when I was webbed to him, but he was very wrong if he thought **I** would accept. "No, Shaarvan,"

I said, and my eyes locked with my husband's. "If you were killed, I would die, too. I would not live without you."

Shaarvan took my hands in his and kissed them. "Thank you for your words, Shaara, but you forget Shaarac. You are his protection."

"I would take him to Teea. Then, I would die, but I would never go to Stegthal."

Shaarvan grabbed my chin. Once more his anger flowed. "You forget, wife. You are Shapechanger. You will obey."

I was still shaking my head when Shaarvan continued. "I shall beat you, if I must, until you promise to obey me in this, Shaara. I am serious. You will be Seconded to Stegthal."

"Why, Shaarvan? Why?" Tears rolled down my cheeks, but I didn't attempt to stop them.

He waited until I was quiet, then he continued. "You are to marry Stegthal in a nineTide, Shaara."

"I thought I was married to you."

"Do not think like a Terran. The Shapechanger bondmates are your security. Stegthal is first. If he dies, you will be Seconded to Spelon . . ."

"No! Your fantasy is warped! I can't stand to be in the same room with Spelon."

"If Stegthal is killed, only a warrior can protect you. Spelon is second, followed by Tenor, then Thedar."

I was so angry I could have spit. "You have my whole life planned for me, don't you? Did it ever occur to you that I might not be willing to be passed from lord to lord like some . . . ?"

"Enough. You will obey," Shaarvan said and flashed Second Warning.

I was angry, but I wasn't stupid. I looked down and dried my tears. I would not let Shaarvan be killed, so this was all silliness anyway. Males and their games! I would be Shaarvan's wife forever.

"I hope so too, my wife," Shaarvan said, reading my thoughts, "but in a nineTide, you will be married to Stegthal. You have until tomorrow before I ask if you will give your obedience in this matter. If not, punishment will begin."

That night, Shaarvan turned his back to me. He'd never slept without enfolding me in his arms. He'd never lain beside me without kissing me. I realized by his actions how serious he was about it all. I slept little that night, haunted by his anger.

Shaarvan

I should have known. Why did I tell her so much? It is more suiting that I simply drag her to the wedding, and hand her over. This is why Shapechanger do not love their wives. It cripples them. It enslaves them and dilutes their Power. I shall not back down to her. She is a woman, little more than a girl, young, naive, scarcely able to Shapechange — although I have to admit her recent Saberey was excellently contrived. Still, I will not bend for her. My command will be obeyed, or I *shall* lay my hand to her bottom.

Oh, Shaara. How many times have I given you the promise, "I shall not beat you." It was a joke between us to take away those frightened eyes. And now that you no longer need the joke, I have renounced the words as easily as that. Shaara, do not force me. I cannot bear to punish you with violence. Yet, I cannot retract what has been said.

If only I could explain to Shaara . . . but that I shall not do. A Shapechanger's wife does not need explanations. She obeys her lord. So it is written.

Shaara will cry for a day, and be stubborn for a while, but she will comply. I know her. Soon, I shall see the smile on her face — it is as inevitable as the pleasure of the sun on a winter morning. Even as a slave, her joyfulness could not be suppressed.

And it is better this way. Let her wage her battles on principles. She must *not* be told of the greater whole — not now, not yet.

Above all, she must never know how much her tears pain me or how I feel — that only death could ache as much as what I must do.

Shaara

Shaarvan denied me permission to train with Tessa the next day, and he left me to sit alone in our chamber, with the guards, of course, standing just outside.

First, Tenor came and talked with me, then Thedar, and next, Spelon. To each of them, I listened, but I would not give in. I would not play this Shapechanger game. It was foolishness. Without Shaarvan, I would not choose to live.

Temina came with Tem. I wished they had not. Tem was kind. He told me I had done well the day before. I wished that I'd failed the tests, so I wouldn't have to be in this situation.

"No, Shaara," Tem said, evidently reading me as clearly as Shaarvan and the others. "The test had nothing to do with the bondings. Shaarvan would have done the bonds anyway. The testing only reassured the two of you that you could withstand a

Shapechanger who desired you. The testing refined and honed your skills, and probably made the bonding easier."

I gagged at that, but only commented about Tem's reading my mind.

"You are a projector, Shaara," he said. "You wear your thoughts for anyone with the Power to read."

"You're a fool," Temina interjected. Tem and I both turned and stared at her. She had been silent since she'd arrived, staring off into the distance. "I knew it before," she continued, "but now — you are twice a fool."

"Temina, what do you mean?" her husband asked.

"She is," the woman said. "I speak my mind. Beat me later, husband, but I speak my mind."

Tem glanced at me and shook his head. "I have never beaten you, Temina. You know that."

"You might. She will be!" Temina began to laugh.

"I think we had best go. Shaara, give in to him . . ."

Temina began to yell. "He is wrapped in his pride. She doesn't understand that. Pride of the Shapechanger, the greatest force!" She laughed again, high and loud, a cackle of desperation. Tem attempted to pull her up, but she bucked worse than a naughty landoor.

"No, husband. I have not yet told her. He will drug you, girl. Do you not know that? He will beat you each day for your disobedience, but he will drug you, anyway."

I stood up. "Is that the truth?"

Tem was holding Temina in the Shapechanger hold, but she didn't seem concerned. She was staring at me.

"Shaara, you know your husband," Tem said. "You know what he is capable of. Would he allow you to disobey him in front of his friends?"

I stared at both of them a minute, then shook my head.

"Shaara," Tem continued. "I cannot predict what Shaarvan would do. He might strip you and beat you in front of the others until you cowered and gave in. He might web you and force the Power to channel through him and command you that way. I have no way to predict, Shaarvan, but I know that if he commanded you to marry Stegthal, you will marry Stegthal."

"You fool," shouted Temina. "Twice a fool. Does he look like he is dying? He's a warrior. He has always been. He'll outlive you, strong buck like that."

Again, she began her loud raucous laughter. I glanced at Tem, but he only shrugged.

"You think no one else does this?" Temina continued. "My Second died, and my first husband is still kicking! Maybe you *are* a Terran, little girl. They were all fools there." She began to screech in loud, senseless syllables. Her arms waved up and down spasmodically.

I thought Tem would tighten his hold on her, so she could not breathe. But, instead, he pulled out a needler and quietly shot her with it. "She will sleep now," he said, as she went limp. He lifted her up and placed her over his shoulders. "Temina insisted on coming. She said she had to warn you."

I watched as Temina sagged into his arms. "She did," I said. "And I thank her for it. Tem, but what did she mean when she said her Second died?"

Tem's eyes moved to mine. "I have also been in a position of great danger. Being the Highest carries more than responsibility. There are always those who yearn for Power. The position goes to the one with the greatest force, you know, but there are other kinds of testing that must be done as well. Many do not pass those tests. Thenos, for example, was found to be unacceptable. It is almost always those found to be the most unsuitable who prove to be the greatest danger.

You have been told, I presume, that Shaarvan is in line to be the Highest of Westla, after me. That lands him in a space of dangerous meteors. Most will crash or be deflected. On some, he may need to launch an attack. Right now, his brother is the chief hazard to him. Thenos has all the Power of Shaarvan, but he has drug sickness."

"Is Thenos truly mad?"

"Yes and dangerous."

"Shaarvan didn't tell me that. He won't tell me anything."

"Perhaps I should not have."

I felt Tem probe me. I didn't protest. I needed information, and he was the only one who seemed willing to give it.

"Tessa is right," Tem said when he was finished. "You are of Priestess caliber. I shall not remove the knowledge I have given you, but you must be silent about it. It is Shaarvan's right to shelter your growth. He wishes to protect you, and that is not wrong.

"I think I would raise you differently, but knowledge changes a person. I understand perfectly why Shaarvan chooses to keep you as you are."

I started to argue, but Tem held up his hand for my silence. I did not know how dangerous it would be to argue with the Highest of Westla, even if he was my husband's uncle.

"Very dangerous," he said, chuckling as my face heated with embarrassment.

"You have no idea, my dear, how enchanting you were in your testing — brave and resilient against all odds, yet true to your husband, no matter what its penalty. But, in your testing, I came to know you better than before. You are family, child. Listen to me.

"Change is the only constant of the universe. That expression is from your own planet. It is one of the universal truths. Remember it, Shaara. Hold it to your heart. Let the understanding of it center you.

"Your path will be strewn with many changes. Tessa has told us this. These changes will help you achieve the greatness that is in you, but you must not fight each change so hard. Learn to accept the differences, to welcome them even. Discover what they have to teach you. Realize that even the Somber Tree must sway with the wind.

"Obey your husband, Shaara. He is a force like that wind — it cannot be withstood, unless you bend. You do not need to understand him or his reasons. Sway with the changes, my dear; bend to your husband's wishes."

I understood what Tem was telling me. I had heard it all on Freinana. They had called it the Wheel of Change, but the lectures had been the same. And Tem had still not explained about a Second.

He laughed and nodded at me. "You are right, the whole reason for coming to see you, and I have barely discussed it. I think Temina did it well enough."

"Others have taken a Second?"

"Most wives of the Shapechanger Warlords."

I sighed. I hated all their secrets. If anyone had told me it was a common practice, perhaps I would have been less resentful.

Tem's eyes assessed me. He was still holding back from me. I could feel it, but he *had* given me much to think on. His eyes told me he would give me no more.

"Thank you," I told him, as he left with Temina, sound asleep across his shoulder. He nodded at me and smiled briefly, but for some reason, he avoided my eyes.

I paced the rest of the day. I hated the Shapechanger. I hated Shaarvan and his stupid commands. I hated the bondmates and most of all, I hated Stegthal.

But when Shaarvan came to me later in the day, I did not wait for his question. I went down on my knees. "Please forgive my stubbornness," I begged him. "I will obey you."

His relief was great. I felt it before he shut me out. I missed the openness we'd once had. The loss of it brought tears to my eyes.

Shaarvan lifted me and hugged me fiercely. "I am glad," he said. "I did not wish to beat you."

His lips joined mine for a moment before he asked, "Who convinced you? I know it was not your bondmates. I left them in the blackest rages, drinking away their despair. They are besotted with you, Shaara, and begged me not to be overly harsh."

"Even Spelon?"

Shaarvan brushed my face with his knuckles. "Spelon gave me a lecture on how to beat a woman without harming her."

"Figures!" I said.

"Shaara." My name was a warning to be cautious.

I heaved a long sigh, then spoke. "Temina told me what no one else had. She and Tem said that many of the wives of the Warlords are given a Second. Why did you not tell me that?"

Shaarvan's knuckles caressed my face. I shivered from desire. His mouth twitched a smile at my need. "Should it be necessary to give you reasons for being obedient?"

"No," I said, before lowering my eyes.

Shaarvan lifted my chin. "I bless Temina for it. I did not know that because *everyone* did a thing, you would willingly follow. You have not done so in the past."

"I do not *willingly* do this at all, Shaarvan," I flared. "I agreed only because you ordered me to, and because Temina told me you would drug me if I didn't. Is that true?"

I thought for a moment that Shaarvan wouldn't answer, but he relented. "Yes. That is what I had decided to do."

"Yet, you would have punished me anyway?"

He nodded. "For your disobedience."

"Not even Isandor beat me every day."

"And I shall not be forced to beat you at all, my enchantress wife." He took me in his arms. I had no strength to withstand his touch or my need of him. To be the wife of a Shapechanger is to be defenseless, but there is little time for bitterness when the arms of the one you love are holding you.

Thenos

Shaarvan stays overlong in Westla. I have sent men to urge him back, but Westla has rejected their entry.

Westla refuses my messages. I am displeased. They, too, will feel my wrath. When the troublemakers on Altar have all been rounded up and dealt with, I shall wage war on Westla. No Shapechanger will discount my demands, then.

I shall be conqueror of all. It is my destiny. The Stars have foretold it. I shall seek out a reader and make him tell me the destiny of Thenos,

Emperor of the Universe — of all the Universes! I am sure he will tell me what I want to hear.

And, what of my princess? Why does Shaarvan not bring her home to me? I am tired of slave girls. I deserve better. I deserve a princess. Is that not my right?

Her throne sits empty. Her chamber lies in waiting. I have selected clothing, in white, the purest white, for she is innocent as the tales of my mother. In all those tales, princesses were dressed for their purity. But wait, princesses wear crowns. I have no crown for her. She must have one with diamonds and pearls. And in the center a large ruby will be the beacon of her position.

"Peon," I called out, and a fool came trotting towards me.

"Yes, my lord," the dirtwalker groveled.

"Lower," I demanded, wanting to see him kiss the ground with his lips. I hated his slowness, I allowed my teeth, just the tips, to grow sharp.

His head bobbed almost to the ground.

"Not low enough," I told him.

His face ate dirt. How fitting. I congratulated myself.

"Much better, Peon," I said. "I need a crown for my princess. Do you not see she wears no crown, Peon?"

The dirt worm glanced at Shaara's throne.

"Do not cast your eyes on her beauty, Peon!"

Once more, his head bobbed up and down, up and down. This time he touched the floor nicely.

"Bring me a crown suitable for my princess with diamonds, pearls, and a sparkling ruby, the size of my fist.

He rose up and began to retreat.

"Wait, you worm," I called out. "You must bring me one, too. My princess cannot wear a crown if her king has none. Did you not know that? Mine shall have emeralds, emeralds that glow in the dark. Be off now. Run."

Chapter Six

Shaara

Tides passed, but as they did, my uneasiness grew.

I dreamed I was looking down into the dark, angry waters of a turbulent sea. I was on the ship I'd dreamed of before, the one with the crack in its old, wooden bow. The ship was sinking down into the icy, cold sea. I stood with my feet anchored by a chain, making no attempt to get free. I stared into the water, watching its azure depths reach out for me. Drowning did not upset me — only the knowledge that Shaarvan was not at my side. That made me despair.

I woke up crying. Shaarvan soothed me back to sleep, but his eyes looked sad. Did he see my dream, or was it only the pain he wore now so often?

In the morning, he would not discuss it — his thoughts remained hidden behind the wall of his will.

xxxxx

As I was increasingly cut off from Shaarvan, my new bondmates became more a part of my life. I was discovering that being a Level Four had certain advantages. I no longer was required to walk with a lowered head. I was free to meet the eyes of males without being chastised. I had three friends who eagerly escorted me places whenever Shaarvan was busy.

The first time hadn't been easy. Shaarvan gave the order for them to escort me and walked away. Three sets of eyes focused on me, but I didn't know where to go. Tenor suggested an animal show. No one looked enthusiastic, but we went, and the show was out of this world — literally!

I had never laughed so hard as when the Frelion Payla flew onto Spelon's shoulder, then nibbled at his neck. The huge warrior Shapechanger, the one who had wanted *me* to be afraid, bellowed and cursed in a language I'd never heard, but from the reaction of the others, he was saying things he shouldn't. The little bird, no bigger than a Shapechanger's thumb, hopped from one shoulder to the next, back and forth as Spelon stamped his feet, swung arms about in maddened zeal, and fuzzied his muzzle with the fur of his tiger.

Then, when he finally dislodged the Frelion Payla off his shoulder, Spelon discovered the bird had left a deposit on his shirt! He spouted off again with a flow of words that caused the others to flinch and shake their heads. I thought the whole thing was the highlight of the animal show. Even when all the excitement ended, we kept laughing. And Spelon, who continued to growl a bit, finally let out a deep, gravelly grunt, then joined in.

From that day on, the three bondmates were like big brothers — in charge, protective, but fun. Thedar and Tenor were quite personable and laughed often. Spelon was still gruff most of the time, but when they all took me skiing and tried to teach me, it was Spelon who was the most gentle in his instruction. At times I wondered if he might be more bluff than bite. But then he'd look at me with his brow crinkled and his eyes darkening tigerishly, and I'd draw back in caution.

Stegthal never went anywhere with us, for which I was grateful. He and Shaarvan were always chatting with Tem. Whatever they were discussing or planning, my husband's moods grew darker. I missed him. I missed the dimples that used to flash with every smile. Shaarvan had stopped smiling.

Tessa insisted I continue with her training. I didn't see the point. Shaarvan had told me I could test no higher. But he ordered my bondmates to take me there. Perhaps my husband only cared that I was busy and not questioning him.

I worried that Shaarac would grow closer to my three bondmates than to his own father. But, when I mentioned my concern, Shaarvan laughed. "Our son knows his blood."

"But how will he remember you if he never sees you?" I asked.

My husband's eyes grew angry dark. I thought it was because I'd made him realize he had abandoned us lately. I didn't know how much my words would sting in the Passes to come, or how much truth there would be in what I'd said that day.

Tevor

They believe I cannot hear them, but I can. I heard every tear of my beloved Teea. It was an agony for me to lie on this bed and listen to her sobs, but the anguish of her weeping was far easier to bear than the moans and tender words that came so often whenever the two of them lie together.

I do not complain. No one could have been a more loving wife than my Teea, and Starnkor waited by her side patiently and adequately. I made an excellent choice, and I am pleased with it. But it is still difficult to endure their joining.

I have listened intently to the discussions held around me. It is too bad they could not tap into my mind, but the drugs I was given have depleted me. I cannot even reach my Teea, although I have attempted to do so for a halfPass.

I wanted to laugh when Starnkor introduced my wife into the circle. The Shapechanger have always been resistant to new mutations of our culture. Yet, how intelligently Teea carried herself. She shines even in a room full of indignant males. I did not think Starnkor would be able to break down their opposition, but Teea has surprised even me. She has almost won them over.

The plans they are making will not stand up to Thenos. I wish I could tell them that. Thenos is an abomination, and I believe they should have killed him, as they had once planned, but he is too strong now. He would read the mind of any assassin before the killer were close enough to shoot.

Only Shaarvan would have a chance against Thenos, and I do not wish for my son to take that gamble. Let him stay in Westla with his wife and son.

Shaarvan would be a fool to come here. Thenos would never leave them alone. In fact, I heard a rumor once that Thenos has proclaimed Shaara as his wife. How he would do that I do not know, but I fear that Thenos would kill Shaarvan to have his way.

Another meeting has ended. Again, nothing has been accomplished. My poor wife is frustrated. Her eyes are angry. Starnkor will need to soothe her again.

Why did Thenos leave me like this, mute, unmoving, and halfway to Death? My body still battles. Some of the drug has been obliterated. I can feel the lessening of the pain, but the remainder in my system keeps me prisoner.

I wish this body of mine would just end the torture. The struggle is a wasted effort, the damage too great. I do not wish to lie here forever listening to Starnkor pleasuring himself with my wife.

Shaara

The day arrived for the ceremony of my Second Husband. Shaarvan's first words that morning were to ask me if I would still obey him. Then, he took me with a special intensity that frightened me. It was as if he branded every part of me again. His lips traveled my body, marking the taste of me in his mind and in mine. Coldness entered me. I knew it was a foretelling of something horrible to come.

"Shaarvan, promise me you will not die."

"I shall not die, Shaara. No matter what our destiny, I shall be your husband, always."

My worry lessened, but the fear did not.

I dressed in what Shaarvan had chosen me, a gown in a light shade of violet. It was not Altarian, and it felt wrong.

"Shaarvan?"

He knew my question before I asked it. "You honor Stegthal in the wearing of it, my love," he said as he turned to go get our son.

"Altar," I said, although that made no sense. A thought of Shaarvan's had dribbled into my mind. I worked at it, probing.

Shaarvan was rocking Shaarac, pretending it was a normal day, but I felt his barrier quiver. It was enough to pierce inside.

"You are leaving me . . . today. You are going to Altar — *without me!*"

I flung myself at Shaarvan, half hysterical yet careful not to crush Shaarac. "But you promised never to leave me, Shaarvan!"

I dropped a kiss on our little boy, tickled his tummy so he laughed, but all the while my mind was screaming, No! No! No!

"Shaara, oh, Shaara, my wife. I did not want you to know, not until after." His knuckles brushed my cheekbones gently, lovingly, then took a moment to blow razzberries across his son's fat, little arm.

"You must understand. I have no choice. I have to go. Stegthal and your bondmates will watch over you and take care of you. You and Shaarac will be safe. You must obey your bondmates, not argue, Shaara. Stegthal will treat you well, but he is not used to one so rebellious. Behave and make me proud."

Shaarac was on the floor, crawling like a speed monster. We watched a moment, then embraced. I leaned against Shaarvan's chest and listened to the sound of the steady beat of his heart. I focused on it, memorizing the sound, the smell of him, the way it felt to be held.

"Why can't I go with you? I promise not to pry into your secrets. I'll behave and do whatever you want me to do!"

"Good. It pleases me to hear you say that. What I want you to do is to stay here with Stegthal and the others."

"You have tired of me then?"

Shaarvan's arms tightened. I could scarcely breathe, but I didn't want him to loosen them. I didn't want him to ever let me go.

"How can you ask me that, Shaara? You are my soul. You know that, Shaara. I would take you with me if I could — but I cannot. Altar is not safe for you or for Shaarac. Trust me in this. I *must* go back, and you *cannot* come with me."

"You can't leave me!"

"Obey the Primary. It is my command."

Shaarac was pounding on my feet. I bent down and picked him up. He had started to fuss, wanting his breakfast.

Shaarvan watched, his eyes one moment filled with love for his son, and the next with ferocity and a stern finger a hand span from my face. "You are never to be away from the presence of your bondmates, Shaara, promise me."

I nodded, bouncing Shaarac up and down so he wouldn't explode with rage at our ignoring his wishes.

"I promise," I said. It was only a whisper, but it was all that my voice would permit.

"Good. Time to eat, my son tells me."

Shaarac's appetite was good, but neither Shaarvan nor I did more than pretend to munch on the slab of baked bread.

Tem stopped by to pick up Shaarac and take him to the nursery. I sat in my chair, trying not to cry as Shaarvan kissed his son goodbye. If I had not been attempting to memorize the moment, I couldn't have watched. As it was, the tears I'd struggled against obstructed my sight.

And then it was time. As we passed through our door, my hand reflexively gripped the wood.

"Must I drug you, Shaara? I would rather not."

I let go of the door but clutched at his arm. "If you love me, how can you give me to another?"

"*Because* I love you."

Shapechanger males do not speak of love. It was the first time Shaarvan had ever said that. I wanted to stop and savor it, to talk of how much it meant to me to hear it, but his lips ended any words.

When he pulled away, he looked down at me with angry eyes. "I lend you to another for a time, Shaara, but remember — I hold your heart, your soul, and your mind. *You belong to me, always.*"

The ceremony had many people in attendance, but my eyes were only for Shaarvan. He looked so handsome in his dress whites. His eyes were locked in the private torment he had carried for more than a twelveTide, but his dimples smiled at me when he caught me staring. A wave of love swept over me.

Just before the ceremony was about to begin, Spelon and Shaarvan began to argue. They spoke in an alien tongue, so I couldn't understand their words nor break through the heavy blocks of their minds, but I knew that Spelon's anger was a black wave of rage. Tenor and Thedar tried to distract me. They didn't look happy about the argument going on, but they refused to discuss it.

The ceremony was brief. Shaarvan stood before the standing audience of acquaintances and called Stegthal his best and closest friend. Then, with a formal declaration, Shaarvan transferred my governance to Stegthal. My husband passed my hand to his Second. Shaarvan told the watchers that I was to be Stegthal's possession if he, Shaarvan of Altar (and a long list of names which was Shaarvan's lineage), should meet an early death. Shaarvan spoke words in a language I couldn't follow. The eyes of all my bondmates shifted to me, and I heard their names and Stegthal's.

Next, it was Stegthal's turn to talk. He gave his promises, then repeated how he would give his life for Shaarvan and for Shaarvan's family.

Stegthal raised his hand and touched Shaarvan's. They closed their fingers into a joined fist as Stegthal formally accepted me as his honored wife. Under Shaarvan's watchful eyes, I could only bow my head, but inside I was saying, *no, no, no*. The clasped hands of Shaarvan and Stegthal moved to touch my head. They rested them there as they spoke more gibberish. Finally, the hands separated, and both males placed their palm on each of my shoulders.

Together, they turned me to face the assembled watchers. Stegthal spoke some more in the alien tongue, and then everyone went their separate ways, and by that, I knew the ceremony was over.

Strangely, I had not been asked to say a single word, nor at any time had my presence seemed necessary.

There were no flowers, no cake, no photographer. It had been a boring ceremony, to tell the truth — so much of it incomprehensible — at least to me. And when the Shapechanger ambled off in silence, it seemed more funeral than marriage. I was thankful that, at least, no one felt the need to congratulate me.

The bondmates, Shaarvan, and I began walking. I realized by our direction that we were heading to Shaarvan's ship. I knew I should be brave for Shaarvan. I tried not to cry, but tears have a will of their own.

At the ship's entrance, Shaarvan kissed me deeply. His Shapechanger magic coiled around me, lapping at my skin. It was a kiss that satisfied yet brought no hunger. I felt temporarily fulfilled. Yet, if that kiss was supposed to hold me until he came back, why did my arms ache from emptiness the moment he pulled them away from his neck?

"When will you return?" I asked, but he didn't answer, only passed my hand to Stegthal.

"She does not know. I could not tell her," Shaarvan said.

What hadn't he told me?

"Obey all your bondmates, Shaara," Shaarvan said, then turned and walked up the ramp.

Without thought, I leaped forward, ready to sprint onto the ramp. "Shaarvan! Take me with you, please. I love you!"

He didn't pause or look back.

Stegthal grabbed me and half-lifting me, returned me to his side. I twirled about and kicked him in the shins. I would have struck other areas if he hadn't twisted me about and slammed me up against his body. His arms tightened, feeling like the chains in my dream. I bent over and bit. Too bad I was too wild in my grief to Change.

The ship's ramp wrinkled up and collapsed inward. The heavy clank of the door lock echoed in my mind. I wailed as Stegthal dragged me backward, retreating us to a safer spot. And even though it was too late to reach Shaarvan, I fought like a crazy woman.

I jerked and yanked, pried, and pinched until the moment when the ship lifted. Then, stunned by Shaarvan's desertion, I watched as the ship shot up through the eye.

The moment the Saberey's eye closed, my breath expelled. All forces of life drained from my body, and I collapsed. I wasn't allowed to fall, although I wouldn't have cared. I was a child's discarded rag doll. All meaning, all reason to live, had just been stolen.

Stegthal carried me through the spaceport paths. I think I must have been in shock, too lifeless even to cry. I wasn't aware of the bondmates or of being held. My eyes were closed, and I kept seeing the moment Shaarvan's ship passed through the great Shapechanger eye to disappear into blackness. Like a movie reel stuck on one scene, the vision looped without pause.

The space harbor of Westla, although enclosed within its metallic globe of a planet, was an enormous place. Ship after ship sat in singular silence. My eyes scarcely saw them until a mushroom vessel's engines revved up. That drew my eyes.

"No!" I cried out. I knew it wasn't Shaarvan's ship. My sanity had not completely departed, but the ship's noise and the smell of its engine exhaust was the catalyst for my awakening.

I sobbed then, not as I had before, but as a subjugated wife, struggling to accept what the Shapechanger had done to me once again. My tears at that moment were the anguish of a grieving widow — the desolation, the wretchedness, the loss. And once started, I couldn't stop. Words flowed with my tears, words as useless and without purpose as my struggles against a Warlord.

I grieved, and then I ranted again — over Shaarvan's unfairness, Stegthal's cruelty, being forced to leave my Landoor, and then for the loss of Tren and Crimson Black. "Shaarvan promised he would never let me out of his sight . . . that wherever he went, I would go . . . He said we would never be parted . . . that he loved me . . . that we were one heart, one mind, one soul . . . How could he leave me . . . ?"

My throat grew scratchy, my voice gave way, and I clung to my carrier's shirt as if it were a child's comfort blanket. My tears had already saturated its fabric.

My eyes stung. They felt red and swollen. I didn't care. Pain was good. But my tears were temporarily gone. I was left with only an occasional sob and hiccoughs that refused to stop. I'd been carried through a series of tunnels and out into the common area before I even realized whose shirt I was clinging to. The realization nauseated me.

"Put me down. I don't want you to carry me. I don't want you to *ever* touch me!"

I suppose I was lucky the Shapechanger understood my hysteria. He didn't discipline me in any way. He simply placed me down and allowed me to walk, but his hand rested on my neck, and I was rational enough by then to know the implications.

I scarcely remember passing through the corridors. I only recall that I walked at the side of the male I hated most. But most embarrassing of all was the fact that I couldn't let go of the shirt I'd cried on. Like a toddler, my hand held it fast. Nor did Stegthal make any attempt to pry it free.

The silence as we walked was gloomy. The others didn't speak, and only my hiccoughs punctured the quiet.

Mostly, I just plodded along, but somehow, I saw that we were passing Shaarvan's residence.

I pulled hard on Stegthal's shirt and stopped. "We need to go right," I told them.

I was looking at my other bondmates, but none of them would meet my eyes. For the first time since Stegthal was named Second, I looked up at him. "The dwelling is over there," I said.

"Your home is with me now, Shaara," Stegthal said. "Come along."

It had been a rough day, and I hadn't had time to think things over. Would I have been better prepared had I known Stegthal better? Or would I still have begun a war with him I had no chance of winning?

No, it had not been a merely rough day, but a hideously despicable day — a day only comparable to the time I'd been paraded in front of a room full of men and sold. Today was even worse than the day Isandor raped me and beat me, and I attempted to take my life. This day just kept going on and on, each moment progressively more horrible,

Perhaps beginnings are supposed to be like that. Doesn't every story immediately plunge into problems and then get worse before anything gets better? More often than endings, anyway. Endings are static, no place to go. They finish in tragedy or happiness, whatever the writer chooses, but endings don't continue. It's just over, and the characters dissolve back into dust, and the reader knows there's nothing more.

Funny, isn't it, because life's not like that, clear and finite. One day slips into another within a flow of Tides and Passes that are seemingly unceasing, and it's only with your diary or in your thoughts that you can go back and attempt to sort it out. Then, you can draw the blue line for the beginning and the red line for the ending. Only when you look back, can you decide where the start was and where the ending's resolution commenced. But, while you're caught up in living it, that division is completely unclear.

The day that Shaarvan left me was like that. My imaginary red and blue pencils couldn't predict. I thought this was all temporary. Temporary was bad enough. A sevenTide, a close my eyes and this torture would be all over, and then I'd be back to good times. That's what I thought, what I hoped.

Because I had no clarity, except that I knew I didn't want this.

I definitely didn't know then about life divisions, or that moments like this were actually where the red and blue pencils were warning me about Change. If I'd known about beginnings and endings back then, my horror would have been even greater.

To read more about Shaara:

Book Five of the Shaarvan Series

Shaara: Beginnings and Endings

www.ingramcontent.com/pod-product-compliance
Lightning Source LLC
Chambersburg PA
CBHW071314250626
47159CB00004B/1416

* 9 7 8 1 9 1 7 7 3 6 2 5 1 *